AT LAST

AT LAST

LEE WHEELER

A Chapin's House Book

Published by Chapin's House LLC

PO Box 264

Mendenhall, PA 19357

This is a work of fiction. Names, characters, places and incidents either are the product of the author's imagination or are used fictitiously, and any resemblance to an actual person, living or dead, business establishments, events or locales is entirely coincidental.

Copyright © 2020 by Lee Wheeler

All rights reserved.

No part of this book may be reproduced in any form or by any electronic or mechanical means, including information storage and retrieval systems, without written permission from the author, except for the use of brief quotations in a book review.

*Dedicated to all the dogs
in shelters waiting for people
to give them forever homes.*

Adopt Love.

CONTENTS

Chapter 1	1
Chapter 2	15
Chapter 3	23
Chapter 4	35
Chapter 5	41
Chapter 6	46
Chapter 7	54
Chapter 8	68
Chapter 9	77
Chapter 10	88
Chapter 11	115
Chapter 12	136
Chapter 13	141
Chapter 14	158
Chapter 15	161
Chapter 16	174
Chapter 17	180
Chapter 18	183
Chapter 19	188
Chapter 20	202
Chapter 21	211
Chapter 22	225
Chapter 23	236
Chapter 24	239
Chapter 25	243
Chapter 26	248
Chapter 27	254
Acknowledgments	263
About the Author	265

CHAPTER ONE

"Hey, you girls better be careful in there. Any nutjob walking up on the High Line can see into those rooms." The Uber driver turned around in his seat as they got out of the car into the heavy summer evening.

Henley laughed and handed him a tip. "No worries. We can handle it. I promise."

"What was he talking about?" Quinn asked as the three women walked toward the hotel.

"People walking on the High Line can see into some of the hotel guest rooms." Henley pointed to the elevated urban park that ran for over a mile along the abandoned overhead freight rails.

"Yeah." Claudia grinned. "And the photos are on the Internet."

"You mean photos of people in their hotel rooms?" Quinn asked.

"Oh, yeah, naked photos."

"Don't they close the drapes?" Quinn asked.

"Close the drapes? They open them. Hotel management put up signs to warn guests people can see into their rooms from the High Line, but the signs just caused people to do more and more outrageous things. Outrageous naked things," Claudia said. "The hotel can't figure out how *not* to encourage even more crazy stuff."

"Maybe they could board up the windows," Henley said. "There's a video of a woman wearing a robot mask standing buck naked in front of a window."

"She's apparently doing the Macarena," Claudia said. "It's on YouTube. Totally ridiculous, but also totally captivating. Like a car wreck."

Quinn laughed. "Only in New York."

"Robot girl was from Des Moines," Claudia said.

"Claudia, what's the deal here?" Henley nodded to the crowd standing outside the hotel. "That line to get in is at least three blocks long."

Young women in swingy short skirts or long sleeveless dresses with slits way up the sides waited anxious to get inside to party. Young men surveyed the women, taking quick glances and feigning indifference while calculating their chances. Everyone posed and primped hoping to get a nod from the bouncer and gain access to the dance club on the top floor of the hotel.

"We waltz up to the front, give them our names, and walk right in the door." Claudia made a swooping *before me* motion with her arm, her head held aristocratically high.

"We're just going to cut in front of all of these people?" Henley asked. "This makes me uncomfortable."

"I saved this hotel so much money on a tax thing, consider this a perk of my extremely boring job."

"We're walking right into the hottest club in the city." Quinn shook her head of wild island curls, her voice as smooth and seductive as Angostura rum. "It's like we're celebrities. Which of course we are."

"Not." Claudia smiled at Henley.

Vibration from the music grew stronger as the elevator rose to the top floor of the hotel. By the time the doors opened, music pulsed in their blood, and they gyrated out ready to dance.

Bodies squirmed on the dance floor jockeying for space and attention. The water in a large amoeba-shaped pool sloshed in time with the beat as throbbing neon lights slashed through the water and pulsed in opalescent shades of blue, green, red and purple. Henley squeezed a path through the crowd of people until she found a small open spot to the left of the pool where the three friends could dance together.

Henley synchronized her every movement to the music. Precisely. Her body was lithe and graceful but contained, always contained. An innate sense of spatial boundaries allowed her to avoid the crowd of sweating humans. Tonight she felt an unusual joy, a heady optimism was bubbling in her—that was new. And she liked it. Her job...her friends...the man in her life. Things were so great she had to resist going through her days knocking on every wood surface she saw.

She couldn't help but sigh contently. She was grateful. For every single bit of it. Especially for these two women. The women of her heart.

Claudia's tiny body jerked with frantic determination to some music she heard in her head, music definitely not in the room. Her arms flew out at angles striking anyone who got close, and her long, gleaming black hair flew haphazardly in all directions as she flung her head back and forth. She looked ridiculous. But she did ridiculous with a definite flair. Claudia was twenty-nine but looked sixteen. Henley smiled at her, the kind of smile that comes from a best friend who knows everything and loves you without question.

Quinn's eyes were closed, her head thrown back, curls bobbing, body swaying. She never opened her eyes, and yet no one came within even a few inches of touching her. Henley always imagined there was a magnetic field surrounding Quinn. A field Quinn could use to pull people in or keep them away as she desired.

Tears swelled in Henley's eyes, and her heart thumped.

Hunter, the gorgeous man she was dating, was going to meet her later. They'd been together for almost six months, and she thought maybe tonight was the night he would take dating to a more serious level. A couple of weeks ago he had held her with such gentleness and whispered sweet words during a lovemaking session. She thought he'd said, "I love you," but when she looked at him dazedly, and maybe a little jubilantly, he quickly repeated, "I have you." Thankfully, she hadn't reciprocated and her embarrassment was internal. She still thought he was getting close to saying those three words. And she thought tonight just might be the night.

———

SOMETIME LATER WHEN the dance floor was even more crowded, and she felt sweat bead on her back, Henley tapped each of her friends on the shoulder and pointed to a small couch by windows that looked out over the city.

"I like this place," Henley said as they crowded together on the velvet cushions. "But who thought putting a pool in the middle of a dance club was a good idea?"

"It gets a lot of press," Claudia said. "Tons of photos on Instagram, some of them pretty glamorous. It's a place to be seen."

"I'm glad my firm didn't design this hotel. Imagine being in a room under the pool when the ceiling bursts open and floods it with chlorinated water," Henley said.

"That could certainly spoil an evening's activities." Quinn winked at Henley.

"Look at those women in the pool." Claudia scowled in the direction of the pulsing pool. "Why would someone come to a dance club to go swimming?"

"Notice there aren't any guys are in the pool," Henley said.

"I can't figure out what they're thinking." Claudia continued scowling at the women. "They get all dressed up—make-up, hair, clothes—come to a popular club, and what? They see a pool and can't resist jumping in and ruining the special look they spent hours on. I don't get it."

"They don't even hang up their clothes." Quinn threw her arm in the air. "Thousands of dollars of clothes just flung on the backs of chairs. That white dress on the floor looks like Stella McCartney's Mirabell dress. A four-thousand-dollar dress is on the floor sopping up pool water. I should rescue it. That's criminal."

"Of course you're worried about the clothes." Henley laughed. "Maybe you could conduct a citizen's arrest, confiscate the clothes for their own safety. Maybe that, what was it, Mirabell dress, could go into witness protection."

"And they're almost naked. Those bikinis barely qualify as bikinis. They have no tops and the bottoms are more like strands of thread. Why are they naked in a dance club? In public? With strangers?" Claudia chopped the air with her hand as she spoke. "Do they think people can't tell they're naked because they're in the water? Don't they realize we can see *through* the water?"

"They want people to see them," Henley said. "They're proud of what they've got. The pool gives them an excuse to strut around and show off their amazing bodies."

"I disagree. I don't think they're proud. I think they're desperate for attention," Claudia said. "Did you see the swimsuits in the vending machine outside the door?"

"Seriously?" Henley said. "A vending machine with swimsuits?"

"I think they have size 0 and size 2," Claudia said.

"Leaves me out." Henley laughed.

"Me too," Quinn said. "Hey Claudia, you can swim."

"If I swim, you swim. Suit or not."

To change the subject, Henley flung her arm out with a flourish to Quinn. "That's quite a dress. Who designed it?"

"Who designed it?" Quinn cocked her head and widened her eyes in an expression of mock incredulity. "It's fabulous, isn't it? Who do you think designed it?"

Claudia tipped her head toward Quinn and said to Henley, "I could be wrong, but I'm guessing she designed it."

Henley laughed. "I think that's a good guess."

"You win. It's an original Q by Quinn Design." Quinn stood and took her time turning around so her friends could inspect all the little details of the dress.

From the front it looked like a simple black dress, but a Q by Quinn Design was anything but simple. The dress molded to Quinn's body, but the fabric allowed it to slide along her skin rather than stick to it like a pressure bandage. The back of the dress was open, open all the way down past the hollow in the small of Quinn's back where small strips of fabric in different vibrant colors criss-crossed drawing the eye to the curve of her hips and her perfect ass. Her friend looked stunning, Henley thought, but then again, Quinn would be stunning in a bath towel. *Especially* in a bath towel, she realized with a laugh.

"I didn't design the shoes though." Quinn lifted her foot for their inspection. "They're Jimmy Choos."

"It's lace." Claudia touched the shoe with the tip of her finger.

"Those shoes are so gorgeous, I don't think I could ever wear them. I'd put them in a case and hang them on a wall like art," Henley said.

"They're exquisite, aren't they?" Quinn said. "Lace makes men think of negligees."

"They're hot," Claudia agreed. "Men are going to drool over you in those shoes."

"She doesn't need Choos for that to happen." Henley laughed.

"Hmmmmm..." Quinn purred. "If you want to talk about exquisite, take a look at him."

Henley turned around to follow Quinn's gaze.

"That suit's Italian, maybe Zegna, but maybe bespoke. The waist is nipped in just a little to show me his very well-sculpted body. He tried to dress it down with that divine little T-shirt, but there's no way to dress down that suit or that body."

"Nice." Henley nodded. "European?" she asked, knowing Quinn's preferences in men.

"Oh, yes." Quinn moaned. "I know just what I'd like to do to him."

Claudia turned around to look at the man and bolted from the couch, knocking into a small table. She beamed a smile that said schoolgirl innocence, comfortable sophisticate, consummate professional and mud pit wrestler all in one flash. Henley had seen that smile many times yet always enjoyed watching the confusion it caused. Only her closest friends knew Claudia's secrets. To everyone else she was indecipherable.

"Mr. Comtois, thank you so much for inviting us. Your club is extraordinary. We're thrilled to be here." Claudia extended her hand.

"Show him the shoes," Henley whispered to Quinn.

"I'm glad you were able to come tonight." He took Claudia's hand and kissed it. "Claudia, just Pierre, please." He set the three glasses on the table and poured the champagne. Henley caught Quinn's eye and side-glanced his smooth, soft hands, his perfect manicure and his bare ring finger. Quinn nodded.

Pierre's gaze slid over Henley with an appreciative smile but quickly moved to Quinn where it lingered.

Of course, Henley thought. When was there ever a man who wasn't instantly entranced by Quinn? She watched as Quinn walked her gaze down his body an inch at a time, caught her bottom lip between her teeth and brought her eyes back up his body where she met and held his gaze. He squirmed.

Classic Quinn. She loved doing that. It was her trademark. Well, one of her trademarks. And a few other things. Things that made Henley blush. Henley smiled knowing Mr. Pierre Comtois was way outmatched.

"Pierre, these are my friends, Henley Rana and Quinn Gayle," Claudia said.

Henley and Quinn stood and shook his hand. Quinn turned to the side ever so slightly so he could appreciate the back of her dress.

"Henley and Quinn." He gave a slight bow. "It's my pleasure."

"This is an impressive place," Henley said. "Putting a pool in the middle of a dance floor is an interesting idea."

"Because of the pool the club gets a lot of publicity, and that helps the hotel. My favorite thing, though, is the garden on the roof. New York is much like my Paris with all its energy and vitality, but sometimes I long for peace. The parks here are nice but often noisy, so I tried to create a place of solitude on the roof. We have a small bar up there so people can have a drink and hear themselves when they talk to each other."

"Do you offer yoga in your rooftop sanctuary?" Quinn smiled at him and gave him the sleepy eyes that no man ever resisted.

"If you plan on attending, I'll arrange for classes immediately." His dazzling smile would have made a lesser woman fall at his feet.

"I'm working on a project with a roof garden," Henley said. "I'd love to see how your garden is constructed if that would be possible."

"At your convenience. Claudia has my cell. Give me a call." Pierre turned to Quinn. "Of course you are all welcome."

"You should have a casual dress code because of the pool and a garden," Quinn said. "People dress in high fashion to come here because it's a hot club, but they toss their expensive clothes on chairs."

"If we had a casual dress code, I wouldn't have seen you in that dress tonight." He reached for Quinn's hand and kissed it.

Henley saw the expression of naked desire on his face and grinned at Claudia, who was stifling a laugh. They'd seen it many times and knew what was coming next. Quinn smiled at him. Her famous, or was it infamous, smile that said, "Oh, yeah? Think you can handle me? Bring it on then. Show me what you've got."

He looked away. She didn't. One drop of sweat appeared on his forehead as he took a step back. "I would love to talk longer, but some other commitments demand my time."

To Claudia he said, "I'm looking forward to seeing you on Monday."

The women watched him weave his way through the crowd with aplomb.

"Pierre!" Henley fake swooned on the couch. "Oh my God, Claudia, you forgot to mention him."

"Mr. Comtois? I'm going to call him Mr. Come Here." Quinn took a drink of Cristal managing to make even that look sensual. "Or maybe Mr. Come With Me."

"My job may be boring," Claudia said, "but he's not bad to look at."

"Not bad? He's delicious." Quinn took another sip of champagne. "Did you see that suit? It fit him perfectly. Every square inch of him."

"Were you only looking at his clothes?" Henley asked. "He was gorgeous. I wanted to run my fingers through that wavy hair."

"I can assure you I was looking at the whole man."

"I love his manners," Claudia said. "They're elegant. So European."

"Impeccable manners, but he's got hungry eyes," Quinn said. "Claudia, are you interested in him?"

"No. Nooooo. He's a client. But Quinn, I work with him. If you're interested, that's cool, but don't take him out to the deep end and let him drown. Okay?"

"What? Would I do that?" Quinn held her hands out, palms up.

"Ha." Claudia snorted, almost choking on her champagne.

"Yeah, not Quinn. She'd never do that." Henley laughed, shaking her head with such exaggeration her entire body shook. "No, not Quinn. She doesn't even like the deep end."

"You really wanted to see the garden? That wasn't an excuse to see him, was it?" Quinn asked.

Henley shook her head. "Green light to go for him, Quinn. Glass water for smooth sailing. I do want to see the roof. I might get some ideas for a project I'm working on."

"Is that the building for the Calder Prize?" Claudia asked.

"Yep." Henley nodded. "Maybe if I win, they'll finally make me a partner at my firm. They promised me last year that this year would be my year, but you know they said that the year before."

"Hey, how you fine ladies doing tonight?"

Henley's first glance took in the guy's hair slicked back with so much gel it looked like strands of fettuccine. With a longer look she saw his soul patch, a gold earring and black jeans painted on his knobby-kneed skinny legs. She smiled, shook her head no and turned back to her friends.

"Be nice. I just want to talk to you pretty girls. You can talk to me. I won't bite. Unless of course you want me to." He pulled back his lips to show his teeth.

"She told you no. Take a hike," Claudia said.

"Come on. Don't be like that." He gave them a look that was supposed to be casual cool but wasn't even close.

Claudia stood and glowered at the man who, despite the fact that she was only five-foot-nothing, turned tail and left. She stood for another minute to ensure he didn't make a return visit. Claudia was so petite all of her clothing was custom-made. Most of it, despite Quinn's best efforts, was navy or black like the little black dress she wore that night. She did have on a pair of silver sandals. Flats.

Henley and Quinn smiled at each other.

"Our girl in action," Quinn said.

"Thanks for protecting us, Mouse." Henley grinned.

"Henley, I thought you were designing an art museum for children," Quinn said. "What's up with a roof garden?"

"I'm trying to incorporate nature into the museum. The idea of a roof garden popped into my mind. It'll be a kick-ass muse for the kids. They can come to the roof, soak in nature, open their senses and creativity, find inspiration and then go back into the museum and make their own art."

"How's your submission coming?" Claudia asked.

"I'm still in the brainstorming stage. After I'm done with the drawings, I'm going to build a model," Henley said.

"Have you done one of those since you finished school?" Quinn asked.

"The contest doesn't require it. I could submit a CAD drawing I made on the computer, but I think it will give me an advantage."

"That's a lot of work," Quinn said. "I remember you in grad school sweating over those models, glue in your hair."

"Bits of moss stuck to your face," Claudia said. "You spent so many hours bent over carving those little pieces, I'm surprised you don't have a hunch back."

"You want to pull out all your tools, carve that wood, bend that wire, don't you?" Quinn teased.

"A little, I guess. I'm sorta looking forward to it. Moss hanging in my hair is so seductive."

"Super sexy," Quinn cooed.

"Yeah, right." Henley laughed. "Because that look got me *all those guys* in grad school. Oh, I forgot to tell you Hunter might stop by tonight."

Claudia and Quinn moaned in unison.

"I don't get what you see in him, Hen," Claudia said.

"You've met him." Henley shrugged. "He's hot. You have to admit."

"Yeah." Claudia dragged out the word. Henley looked at her quizzically so Claudia went on. "He is hot, I guess. But he's so self-absorbed. If the conversation isn't about him, he has no interest in it. It kind of makes him unattractive."

"We have a good time. He's taken me to some great places."

"All those fancy limos going to all those fancy restaurants with the best seats." Claudia's lip curled as she talked. "That's nice, but is that really what you want? It doesn't seem like you."

"I got to see Lady Gaga backstage at Madison Square Garden."

"I'm sorry to say it, but he doesn't do all that stuff for you," Quinn said. "He's just trying to show off what an important person he is."

"I think I'm lucky he's interested in me." Henley dipped her head. "I've never been sure why he wants to go out with me."

"Stop it." The words exploded from Claudia. "Don't you ever say anything like that ever again. He's a rich, superficial ass, and you're beautiful and talented and most of all you're pure goodness."

For a second Henley imagined smoke billowing from Claudia's ears. She looked to Quinn.

"What she said." Quinn pointed to Claudia. "Does he pay attention to anything that's important to you?"

"He wants me to help him create a foundation to help the homeless. I'm interested in that." Henley looked hopefully from one friend to the other.

Claudia responded by rolling her eyes. "Oh yeah." Her voice dripped with lazy sarcasm. "I forgot. He wants to help the homeless. You believe that?"

"I'm sure he told you some story about how he didn't need any more stuff. How he wants to do good with his money—not like all the other dripping-money-rich hedge fund guys he works with who collect stuff like cars and houses and ostrich skin jackets," Quinn said.

"He probably even called the money 'dirty money' or something like that. And you fell for it," Claudia said. "He read your body odor and knew just what to say to you, and you gobbled it up."

"Read my body odor? I smell? Like what? Desperation? Or I smell gullible?"

"Of course not," Claudia said. "You smell like goodness. I don't know what that smells like. Maybe chocolate chip cookies."

"French onion soup slow cooked with butter and red wine." Quinn moaned. "With lots of Gruyere melted into little brown bubbles on the top and stringing from the spoon."

"French onion soup?" Henley said. "Really?"

"That's goodness to me."

"I'm not chocolate chip cookies or French onion soup. And I didn't fall for some line."

"I probably should have said that he read your body language. Something told him to appeal to your goodness. I'm sorry, Hen, I don't want to hurt your feelings, but he's an ass," Claudia said. "You're always kissing frogs hoping for a prince, but I promise you Hunter is no prince."

"He's a wolf," Quinn said.

"Wrong fairy tale," Claudia said.

"He's still a wolf."

"There he is." She stood and waved. "Could you please be nice to him for tonight?"

Quinn rolled her eyes, and Claudia made a gagging sound.

Henley watched Hunter saunter across the dance floor. The crowd parted for him. The suit he wore revealed his broad chest and shoulder muscles. He walked with his shoulders back. Head up. A slight knowing smile. His visage said power, money and confidence. He invited stares, expected them, and he got them from many women whose blatant stares begged for his attention. Henley flushed with pride and desire. They all wanted him, but he wanted her. A memory of the night he woke her in the early morning by dragging one finger down her spine made her body tingle in anticipation of what waited for her later that evening in his arms.

His pace slowed, and he stopped in front of a blonde who had pulled herself out of the pool. She was wearing only a red thong and struck a pose in front of him. *She's a beauty*, Henley thought. There was no way to deny that. Even dripping wet it was obvious. How much of that body was hers and how much was paid for didn't matter, because it was perfect.

The woman looped her dripping arms around his neck, her head tilted back, red lips open and inviting. Hunter put his hands under her almost naked ass lifting her as she wrapped her legs around his waist, dark water spots appearing on his suit. He kissed the wet woman the same way he kissed Henley—deeply and passionately. Henley stared at them for several long heartbeats. She sensed Claudia and Quinn standing next to her, heard their sharp intake of breath, heard someone, probably Claudia, say, "Rat bastard." Henley blinked several times, unable to make the pieces fit together. The frozen smile on her face fell at the same time her chest constricted and her stomach turned.

They were still lip-locked when Henley stumbled through the crowd, Quinn and Claudia close behind. Shrugging off the arm Quinn tried to put around her shoulders, Henley smacked the elevator button hard enough to make her palm sting.

"Please stay." Henley backed away from them. "I'm leaving, but there's no reason for you to go."

"Come on back, Hen," Claudia said. "Let's face him down. Don't let him chase you away. We'll stand together. We've got you."

"I'm not you, Mouse. I can't do that." Henley turned and faced the elevator.

"We'll go too," Quinn said.

"I need to be alone to deal with this myself. I love both of you."

Henley stepped on the elevator and glanced up at her friends. Quinn's face was clouded with sadness, Claudia's twisted into fury, her dark brown eyes flashing black under the unrelenting strobe lights. The last thing Henley saw as the elevator doors closed was Claudia marching back to the bar, her long black hair streaming behind her streaked with neon. She looked like a high priestess full of power and magic. Her friend was going to battle. Henley wanted to crumple into a ball and disappear.

CHAPTER TWO

HENLEY PRESSED her head against the elevator wall and felt it vibrate with the beat of the music. The percussion reverberated through her body. It pounded, *Fool. Fool. Fool.* How could she be such an idiot? What was that thing about the definition of insanity? Doing the same thing over and over and expecting a different outcome? That was her. The same thing over and over. Would she ever learn?

When the elevator doors opened, she staggered into the night where heavy air hung over the street. The city in August was always sticky and stinky. The noise of the street beat its own musical cadence continuing the *fool, fool, fool* chorus already pulsing in her head.

Henley walked to the beat of the city noise, head down, hands in her pockets, block after block. Her heart synchronized with her steps as she pounded forward. If she walked until her body ached, maybe she would learn never to be man-stupid again. Pain would sear the lesson in her muscle memory. Tears ran down Henley's face. Tears of anger. Tears of embarrassment. Just tears. Stupid damn tears. He wasn't worth it, hadn't been worth it, but she had defended him to Quinn and Claudia. And now she was a fool. Again.

With every step an image of a different man she had dated flashed into her mind's eye. Henley thought in images, full-blown pictures of her every thought. She didn't realize until college that not everyone thought in images. Now the men she'd dated paraded through her mind in technicolor and made the whole awful situation even worse. Eric, who stood her up for prom, was first. Next to make an appearance in the mind movie that was romping at full speed through her psyche was Samuel, of course. He was laughing—with her, or at her, she wasn't sure. She shook her head to move that memory away. Blake and Julian appeared. Julian was smiling his special *who me* smile that was so infuriating. And Vance. And now Hunter. The movie always ended back where it began with her sitting alone on a lumpy paisley couch at the boarding school stood up for prom by a pimply-faced boy she barely knew. She had to make this movie stop playing.

It did come to an abrupt stop with her sudden realization that no one she had ever dated—*no one*—had ever really cared about her. The thought almost brought her to her knees. Not a single man? She mentally shuffled through them. No. Not a single one. She wanted to slump down onto the sidewalk—maybe just stay there until morning. She might have just done that if she hadn't noticed a blue glow coming from a storefront in the middle of a side street. She couldn't figure out why there was a flickering blue light. The other stores on the block were all dark. Seconds later she was down the street peering into the glowing window at an enormous canvas propped up against the wall. A man dipped a brush into a mason jar half full of paint and released a swath of blue that streamed across the canvas dancing and sparkling like phosphorescence in the ocean. She wondered whether the canvas was really undulating or it was just her head throbbing from the walk.

After a few minutes her eyes moved to the man. He was a piece of art. Black curls fell from his ponytail and spilled over a face full of angles and angst. His jeans rode low on his hipbones and paint splattered his bare chest. The mason jar that dangled from his fingers sloshed paint on the floor.

He was transfixed by the canvas, seemingly oblivious to anything and anyone. He stepped forward, to the side and back, forward, to the side and back. One, two, three...one, two, three. He reached his brush to the canvas and withdrew. It was like he was waltzing with the creative muse, pleading and demanding attention. He did it again. And again. The struggle was written in the creases of his face furrowed in concentration.

Henley half expected to feel the recoil from the frustration rolling off his body in waves so dense they were almost visible. She felt like a voyeur eavesdropping on an intimate conversation between lovers. As she pulled herself away from this invasion of privacy, she tripped over an empty cardboard box. When she glanced back to the window, the artist was staring at her—intensely staring at her, like he was cataloguing her. Her parts. The pieces that together made her, assessing them with his artist's eye. She felt exposed. Naked.

He didn't smile. Didn't look away from her. She watched him absorb her face and her body into his consciousness. He seemed to draw her lines and curves and patterns and set them into his memory like he was filing her away in a database for future use. A cool breeze drifted down the street. Without a sweater to tug around her body, she smoothed her flippy skirt and crossed her arms over her chest, clasping her bare skin now covered with goose pimples. She wanted to run, but the message from her brain to her feet went awry.

He opened the door and stood without saying a word.

The box she tripped over sat dented and cockeyed on its side. She heard rustling from garbage bags dumped on the cracked concrete sidewalk for morning pick-up and knew the rats were on the hunt. An odor floated from the ruffled bags and spread like oil on the humid air. The city still beat its ceaseless cadence.

She walked through the open door.

The spiky heels of her sandals caught on the layers of paint on the floor, crusted and peeling. She felt like she'd walked through a magic wardrobe into Narnia—an artsy Narnia or maybe a sketchy Narnia—but certainly some place where everything was different. Pushed up against the wall in the back was a futon messy with crumpled sheets dangling on the floor. A flimsy curtain hung from a makeshift cord in front of the futon. In the corner a microwave with a coffee maker perched on top balanced precariously on a small table. Brown bags leaned against the wall, some with groceries poking out of the tops, others trash. There was a bare blue bulb in a rickety floor lamp leaning lopsided in the corner. What stopped her just inside the doorway wasn't what she saw, it was what she smelled—turpentine and oil paint floated around the room like ghostly vapors. Memories threatened to form but flew away when he turned and looked at her.

She met his stare and noticed his long black eyelashes and the dark circles under his eyes. In that stare she found intensity and deep sorrow so familiar that her breath caught for a moment. She inexplicably wanted to reach for him, to comfort him, but her eyes flicked to his bare paint-splattered chest, and she backed away.

"You like to watch." His tone implied a statement not a question.

"It's beautiful," she stammered, nodding at the canvas. "I've never seen anything like it. I was...sort of hypnotized by it. How do you create that sparkle and sense of movement with paint?"

"What are you doing here?" His eyes never left her.

She studied the scaly paint on the floor. "I...um...I was walking home and saw the blue light from the corner. I was curious."

"Do you always look inside people's homes and watch what they're doing?"

"This isn't exactly a home now is it?" Henley took a few steps to the door and struggled to channel Claudia putting some steel in her voice. Her fingers stroked the hard, smooth facets of the amethyst in her necklace.

"It's my home."

"A storefront is an invitation to look inside. That's the point of having a storefront with big windows. Besides, if you don't want attention, why do you have a blue light bulb in the lamp? It's unusual, so people notice it." She waved her arm at the window. "And you don't have drapes."

"If that's what you thought, why did you try to run?"

Henley glanced at her high-heeled strappy sandals. No wonder she felt unbalanced. It wasn't him—it was the shoes and the lumpy floor. It certainly wasn't those black curls falling over his face or his intense eyes or that chest. Certainly not that chest.

He interrupted her thoughts and nodded to the canvas. "You think it's good, yes?"

His mood seemed to lighten, and there was a hopeful chord in his voice.

"I do. The blue light made me curious, but when I saw the painting I couldn't leave. The paint is alive on the canvas."

"What's your name?" he asked.

"Henley."

"Henley? Is that your given name?"

She nodded.

"Where does that name come from?"

She shook her head. "I don't know."

"You're quite beautiful. Your hair is the fire of Ireland, and your blue eyes are Irish too. But your coloring says Mediterranean. I could paint you."

"That's an original line. Do you have a lot of success with that one?" She laughed, but he didn't.

"And what does Henley do professionally?"

"I'm an architect."

"Ah, you design houses. Perhaps that's why you're curious about what goes on inside them?"

"I design buildings, not houses. I try to understand how buildings work, how people use them. It helps me in my work. Do you live in this studio?"

He nodded. "I do. You don't approve?" His gaze was steady. Penetrating. Unperturbed.

"No, it's not that. I was…I was curious."

"Ah, curious again. That could get you in trouble, you know. I bet you live in a lovely brownstone or at the top of a fancy skyscraper."

Henley stared at him. Was it a compliment or an accusation? She couldn't read the expression on his face. She was once again moved by the depth of sorrow in his eyes and wanted to ask about his pain, but the images of Hunter kissing the wet girl flashed in her mind, and she remembered her vow.

"I should be going. Thank you for letting me see the painting."

She tried to run to the corner to hail a cab, but her sore feet just couldn't manage the effort. Almost to the corner, she noticed a man leaning against a streetlight and veered to the other side of the street. The strappy sandals came off the second she slammed the cab door shut. She knew the images of the blue painting and the man with the paint-splattered chest and the haunted eyes would remain in her memory album for a very long time.

―――

AS SHE STRUGGLED with her keys, Henley heard the landline ringing inside her brownstone. Bella barked joyously, impatiently scratching the door. The moment she got the door open, Bella jumped into her arms. She flung her purse on the chair and grabbed the phone.

"Hen? Is that you? Hen?" Quinn's voice came blaring through the receiver before Henley could get it to her ear. "Are you there? Are you okay?"

"Quinn, I'm fine. I'm okay."

"Oh, thank God. Claudia and I have been calling your cell all night."

"Sorry, I shut it off in case Hunter tried to call. I should have realized you'd be calling." Henley tilted her head back in an effort to avoid the dog tongue bath. Bella settled for licking her neck.

"Hen, you left before the good part."

"What could have possibly been the good part?"

"She pushed them in."

Henley flopped on the couch and sunk into the overstuffed cushions, Bella in her arms. Bella immediately rolled over and offered her belly to be rubbed.

"Who pushed who? Where?"

"Claudia pushed the skanky wet girl and Hunter."

"I don't get it. She pushed them?"

"Into the pool."

"*What?* No. She didn't."

"Yes. She. Did."

"Oh, my God. What happened then?"

"She's so cool. She stares at them for like a minute. She just stands there all calm and cool. She didn't push them and run. She didn't try to hide. She owned it. She pushed them and stayed to watch. They're all sputtering, flailing arms and legs all over the place. The wet skank was caught under him so she's freaking out, coughing and spitting water. He tried to get off her, but his clothes got all tangled and pulled him down. The skank was pissed."

Henley swirled her finger around Bella's belly in soft circles as she listened to Quinn.

"I burst out laughing. I laughed my ass off. Hunter saw me and was furious. I swear his face was lava red, like his head was ready to burst open and spew. I wish I'd thought to get my iPhone out. That was a YouTube moment. But Claudia, she says, 'Oops. Sorry.' And she flips her hand like 'you're nothing' or 'you're a gnat.' She turns and strolls out. No rush. Like, just take me on. It was classic."

"Mouse roars. Underestimate her at your own peril." Henley sighed. When she stopped rubbing Bella's tummy, Bella nudged her hand to ask for more.

"Damn straight on that one. Nothing Mouse won't do for someone she loves. She's ferocious."

"I met an artist tonight."

Henley's voice was soft, so soft Quinn didn't hear what she said.

"You did what?"

CHAPTER THREE

Henley's hand moved with confidence across the drawing on the drafting table adding shadows and texture to give the sketch substance. She absently pushed her hair behind her ears only to have it fall again. When her phone rang, "Hunter" flashed on the screen, she paused, pencil in hand, and stared at the phone. Moments later, she hit decline and continued to work. She glanced up to find Brett leaning against her door frame surveying her office, his gaze lingering on the carved wood pieces that covered one wall. He was so polished she could practically see herself in his shine.

"You look gorgeous with the sun coming in the windows and hitting your hair. There are shades of tangerine, strawberry and honey. Enough to make me hungry." He laughed and walked into her office.

"Who painted those?" He pointed to a row of bright abstracts on the wall. "A niece or nephew? You don't have some mystery kid, do you?"

"No." Henley closed her eyes for a second and sighed. She wasn't going to explain to him how much those paintings meant to her. He could never understand. "Can I help you with something?"

"Just going to the meeting. Want to walk with me?"

"Thanks. I need to finish something. I'll be there in a few minutes."

"Okay. See you there."

She watched his retreating figure and shook her head.

She waited several minutes to let him get a good head start and walked out of her office. As she rounded the corner, she saw a group of men down the hallway surrounding Wesley Kahn, the managing partner of the firm. Brett was telling a story with an abundance of enthusiasm. Wesley's hand was clasped on Brett's shoulder as Wesley threw his head back in laughter. Henley beelined around them and into the conference room, where she sat in the front row next to one of the two other women in the firm. Finally, Wesley strode into the room, his long arms dangling at his sides, the ever-present cockeyed grin on his face, trailed by his entourage.

"Glad to see everyone today. This is a great Tuesday. Tuesdays are always great, don't you think? My favorite day of the week."

Everyone in the room smiled and nodded to him. They all knew every day was his favorite day, every client was his favorite client and everyone in the room was his favorite person. The thing that made it charming was that it was true; his ebullience was irrepressible, and they all loved him for it.

After an hour split between work and cheerleading during which every person in the room was given a round of applause Wesley said, "I'm sure all of you know the submission guidelines for the Calder Prize were announced two weeks ago. This year they're asking for a design for a children's museum. I know some of you are considering entering. This firm has a storied history with that contest. Five of our architects have won in the past. I'm hoping one of you will make it six. I'm sure I don't have to mention that winning the Calder would be impressive to the committee considering partnership. If you need any information about the submission guidelines, you can ask my secretary."

Brett was loitering outside the door when Henley walked out.

"So are you entering the Calder this year?" he asked.

She nodded. "I am. You?"

"Don't know. Thinking about it. Maybe we could talk about it? Bat some ideas back and forth? Maybe over a drink tonight?"

"Thanks. I can't though. I have to work."

"Fair enough. Another time. Something to look forward too." He winked at her.

BELLA SNORED in her bed next to Henley's feet. The pendant light cast such a bright light on her work it could have been midday under a blazing sun rather than shortly after dusk. Perched on her Sikes stool hunched over the drafting table in her study, Henley rolled her favorite pencil back and forth between her fingers as she stared at the white paper covering the table. She treasured her Staedtler Mars pencils partly because they were perfection but mostly because her Aunt Izzy had given them to her. Izzy didn't make it back from the Sudan for graduation because of a plane delay, but the pencils and an antique printer's case were exquisite gifts.

Henley always sketched her designs by hand before putting them in the computer. The moment she placed the first black pencil line on blank white paper always felt magical to her. It felt like the beginning of a new relationship when all the hopes and dreams seem possible and made her tingle with anticipation. Fortunately, her designs didn't end up the way her relationships did. Fighting for inspiration, she closed her eyes and conjured images of the imaginary worlds she'd discovered in the books of her youth: Narnia, Middle Earth, Oz, Fantasia and of course all the places the Starship Enterprise visited.

Under her hand the garden sprang to life. Around the edges of the roof she drew a ten-foot-tall steel fence. It was a necessary safety feature, but she planned to use it as the backdrop for her imaginary world. She added a wire grid system so vining plants could cover the fencing creating walls of green surrounding and enveloping the space. She planned to also hang wooly pockets from the grid and fill them with otherworldly looking epiphytic air plants. Next, she sketched a walking path around the perimeter and drew some support beams for a roofing system she was considering. She sketched in a clear plexiglass roof that would make the garden seem to be open to the sky. There was a plexiglass roof in her office building, and she loved working in the rooms on the top floor where she felt limitless. And since her goal was to engage all the senses in this imaginary world, she penciled in an area for a garden with fragrant rosemary, mint and basil. Light would be important, but she didn't have a plan for it yet. This was a start.

Bella startled in her bed when the iPhone vibrated to the ringtone "Lyin' Eyes." She cocked her head at Henley as if to say, "What ya gonna do with that fool?" Hunter's name disappeared from her screen when Henley hit decline for what seemed like the hundredth time. She carefully laid the pencil on the iron pencil ledge built into the vintage table.

"He won't leave us alone will he, Bella, baby?" Sensing an opportunity, Bella rolled over onto her back and waved her stubby little legs in the air. "Who could resist that belly?" Henley cooed, bending over to stroke Bella's smooth pink skin. "Hot tea sounds good. Do you want a treat?"

Defying her many years, Bella rolled over, jumped out of bed and scrambled to the kitchen.

Settling back down at her drafting table with a mug of hot tea warming her hands, Henley paused to look at the photos of her favorite buildings that covered one wall of her study, all in identical charcoal frames with white matting. Her eye stopped at the Dancing House in Prague. The lyricism and joy flowing from those two buildings caught in what she always thought of as a tango made her heart skip. A little skip of joy. Smiling and nodding at each of the photos she stopped at Falling Water. Then and now, the house seemed to defy the laws of physics. She didn't know her mother was sick when they'd visited the magnificent home. Within about a year, she was gone, and Henley's life went upside down.

Henley rubbed the cuts and dings in the spalted maple wood of her drafting table to try to rev up some mojo. She'd rescued the table from an architectural salvage yard, restored the rusted and grimy iron Dietzgen base and refinished the wood top, cleaning and polishing the wood but leaving all of the grooves and nicks. It wasn't that she believed ghosts of long dead architects who had used this table would reach their boney fingers from their ancient graves to grasp her hand and move it along the drawing or anything, but she did believe touching the wood allowed her mind to calm and open so ideas could set their seed and root. Rubbing the grooves in the table was sort of a tactile yoga for her. Her fingertip traced the thin black lines of fungus mottling the wood and giving it character and distinctiveness. This table was her touchstone, reminding her beauty is found in many places.

After licking her container of frozen yogurt sparkling clean, Bella fell sound asleep snoring little burbles.

Henley lost herself in imaginary worlds.

HOURS LATER, when her joints groaned from hunching over the drafting table, she stood and stretched into the mountain pose, reaching her arms to the sky for several minutes, breathing deeply and exhaling with mindfulness before dropping to the ground. Palms flat on the floor, she walked her feet back and held the plank for several minutes. She shook it out with a deep, cleansing breath.

"There's so much work to do on this, but I don't think I can do more tonight." She stroked Bella's sleek fur before sharpening each of her pencils with a small piece of fine sandpaper and wrapping them in the Yasutomo Niji pencil roll Izzy had also given her. Sharpening her pencils was habit. It always felt professional and ordered. She used the iron crank to lower the angle of the table so it was flat. "I'm ready for a hot bath and a cool glass of wine, but first I think you and I have some business to do, don't we, Bella?"

Henley slipped on her sneakers and snapped Bella's leash onto a collar that was embroidered with red and pink hearts. When "Lyin' Eyes" sang on her iPhone again, she stuck it into her pocket and went out the door. Bella was sniffing her way down the block when Henley noticed Hunter marching toward them. She wouldn't be able to pick up Bella, walk home, unlock the door and get inside before he reached her, so she grabbed Bella and sprinted toward the crowds of people on Seventh Avenue, hoping she could get to Simon's bar two blocks south.

"Henley, stop. I've called you a billion times. I need to explain." Hunter yelled at her from half a block away. He was gaining on her.

With Bella safely snuggled in her arms, she lengthened her stride and darted through the light just as it was changing, racing to Ah Bar in the middle of the next block. She didn't want to talk to him. And she looked messy.

"You need to hear what I have to say. Stop. Do you hear me? I told you to stop, now stop," Hunter shouted to her from the intersection where he waited on the light.

She kept walking. Holding Bella tightly to her chest. Moving fast. Head down. A growl rumbled deep in Bella's throat.

"It was nothing. That girl doesn't mean anything to me. I only met her the night before, and she was excited to see me. She didn't tell me she was going to be there that night. Hey, Hen."

Henley cringed. Only her friends called her Hen.

She stopped in front of Ah Bar, turned to glance at Hunter, who was within about twenty steps of catching her, shook her head no and went inside.

Four Simonettes graced the bar, three blonde beauties and a raven one. They turned to stare at Henley when she walked in the door. All dressed in skinny jeans and revealing tops, they looked Henley up and down and quite obviously concluded she was no threat. A huge smile burst onto Simon's face when he glanced up from the drink he was making. The women twisted in their seats to watch him bolt from behind the bar and throw his arms around Henley. Tiny little disapproval lines tried to form between their eyebrows but were successfully thwarted by Botox.

Bella stuck her head out from under Henley's arm and kissed him on the chin.

"Bella! Hen, I don't think dogs can come inside the bar."

Simon kissed Bella on the top of her head and said, "Sweet baby, I'm sorry I called you a dog. I know you're a baby, Bella baby, but you still can't be here."

"I'm sorry, Simon. I didn't know what else to do. Hunter followed us as I was walking Bella. We ducked in here to get away from him. I'm not ready to deal with him. I wish he'd just go away."

"Hen, you need to tell him it's over. His ego won't let him believe he's been dumped. You gotta lay it out."

"I will. I'm just not comfortable with it. I need to figure out how to say it." Actually, she was still hoping he would just go away, and she could just pretend the whole embarrassing thing never happened. She didn't owe him any kind of *it's over* conversation after what he did.

"Here, give me your phone."

Simon quickly typed in a text and hit send.

"Simon, what'd you do?"

"Just told him thanks for the memories, but there won't be any more. Nice and clean. Now he's not going to bother you anymore."

"Well." Henley huffed out a breath. "Okay. Yeah. I could have done that. I should have done that."

"I'll get Jordan to cover the bar, so I can walk you home. Just a sec." The Simonettes turned in their seats to follow Simon's walk. Quinn nicknamed the ubiquitous beauties who frequented Ah Bar in hopes they would catch the eye of the extremely desirable bartender the Simonettes, and the name had stuck. Henley mentally sent them a "good luck with that" wish.

"You don't need to walk me home. I have Bella to protect me." Henley kissed Simon on the cheek when he came back.

"I'm not sure what Bella could protect you from. She's talented at attacking treats, but I think everything else is probably safe." Simon's rolling laugh filled the bar, and the Simonettes sighed a collective sigh. "Come on. I'm walking you home."

The women watched them leave. Henley thought about saying, "Don't worry, he'll be right back," but decided against false hope because, she knew with certainty that Simon wasn't going home with any of them.

BELLA TURNED around three times and precisely three times, scratched the bathmat into a pile, curled up in the middle of it and licked her frozen peanut butter and banana treat. Henley put a towel in the warmer Claudia had given her. It was one of those indulgences she would never have purchased for herself but now couldn't imagine living without. A hot towel after a bath was even better than hot sheets just from the dryer. She poured lavender bath oil into the clawfoot tub and stepped into the hot water with a moan. With her head resting on the bath pillow, wine glass in easy reach, the lavender transported her away.

The thought of Hunter made her want to slide under the water. Her friends were right about him. She could see all their objections so clearly now. It was like when sawdust was washed off the windows in a new building, and the outside came into focus. She needed to figure out a way to never let it happen again. Her sore legs reminded her of the punishing walk she took from the club to the art studio, which led her to thoughts of the artist. What was the right word to describe him? *Intense?* Yes, he certainly was that. *Gorgeous?* Yes, in a very, um, earthy way. *Talented?* Definitely. *Unnerving?* Yep, he was unnerving. *Dangerous?* Hmm. No, she didn't think so.

Images flashed through her mind—blue paint splattered on his chest, the sensual strokes of paint flowing across the canvas propped against the wall, the muscles tensing and releasing along his back as he forced the paint on the canvas, into the place and shape he wanted, bent it to his will. His eyes studying her. Her face. Her body. She ran her soapy hands up the inside of her thigh.

Bella had fallen asleep in the lulling steam.

HOURS AFTER THE SATISFYING BATH, the brownstone was quiet and Bella was snoring when Henley woke with a start, heart pounding, palms clammy, a scream caught in her throat. She instantly felt for Bella, who was curled next to her. Where was she? Her room. Her bed. Her eyes darted around the room. *Inhale. Hold. Exhale. Repeat. Repeat. Repeat.* She stared at the model of the Guggenheim Museum in Bilbao, Spain, sitting on her dresser. *Breathe in. Breathe out.* The building helped distract her mind and allow her nerves to calm. It was her talisman. Her love affair with that building compelled her to study architecture.

It had been during a senior trip to Spain. She'd been talking to Quinn and Claudia about something of profound teenage significance, motioning with her hands to emphasize the importance of her words, when the bus turned down Uribitarte Pasealekua Street and the museum came into view. Henley had stopped talking, her hands frozen midair in some incomplete gesture. The sun was glinting off the rolling walls and roof of the museum. The world fell away, and all she saw was that building. That building, with its undulating surfaces, sunlight and shadow playing together to create a sense of movement across the sleek surface, was like no building she had ever seen. In that moment she knew she would design buildings that would move people the way the museum had moved her. Even though she hadn't yet, she knew she would. Her time was coming. She smiled, rolled over, cocooned around Bella and snuggled into her pillow.

The image of the canvas with the vibrating blue paint slipped into her mind followed closely by the artist whose eyes were filled with sorrow. Ten minutes later she gave up trying to sleep and got up.

After bundling her hair into a messy bun, Henley pulled on yoga pants and a long-sleeve T-shirt and roamed back and forth in her kitchen, opening and closing the refrigerator door, pouring a glass of wine and putting it down without taking a drink. Bella moved to her dog bed by the couch. Henley straightened the room, repositioned the throw pillows, and dusted the furniture. With a jar of diluted milk in one hand and a soft cloth in the other, she stood on the couch trying to dust the giant stag horn fern mounted on the wall. Wobbly-legged, she see-sawed back and forth on the cushion as she tried to find a spot to balance in order to polish the fronds to a high shine with the milk.

Suddenly she set the milk down, kissed Bella's head and said, "I'll be back in a little while, Bella. Love you, baby." She grabbed the bottle of wine and walked to Seventh Avenue where she knew there would be a cab regardless of the hour. It was New York City after all.

———

TWENTY MINUTES later she was at the studio window and the artist was stroking the canvas with his brush. Her breath whooshed out and didn't return quickly, leaving her woozy. The painting wasn't finished, but the progress was astonishing. Stunning, really. Long sweeping strokes covered swaths of space. Now he was filling in other areas with small strokes, decisive and urgent scattered around the canvas. His efforts didn't seem frantic as much as maybe possessed. Without taking his eyes off the canvas, he reached behind him and opened the door.

Henley stared at the open door and quietly stepped inside.

"Couldn't sleep?" he asked.

"No."

"Had a hot bath?"

She nodded.

"And a glass of wine?"

She nodded again and held up the bottle.

He found some mismatched plastic glasses and set them on top of the microwave. One glass had a crack running about an inch down from the rim. Careful not to reach the crack, Henley poured the wine, which looked black under the blue light shimmering through the room. Once again, a memory tugged at the edges of her mind as the scent of paint and turpentine teased her nose. It seemed sweet, and she wanted it to linger, but the memory floated away.

They sat on the messy futon where he sprawled back against the wall, and she delicately balanced on the edge.

"Explain your Irish red hair and blue eyes with your olive coloring." His eyes scrutinized her face.

She hesitated. It wasn't that she didn't want to answer him. She didn't know the answers.

"I can't. I don't know. My mom was Spanish with dark eyes and black hair. I don't remember my dad. He died when I was young. So...that's it. I just don't know." She paused not wanting to say more. "Where are you from?"

"Italy."

"Are both of your parents Italian?"

"Yes."

"You haven't told me your name."

"It's G."

"G? Just G? As in the letter?"

"Yes. G."

"You're a man of few words."

"I'm a man of many words, but they're in my head. I don't say them out loud often. After you were here last time, I got the feeling you might understand what I'm thinking, yes?"

"I...don't know. I'm not sure." The thought made her uneasy, so she changed the subject. "How many years have you been here?"

It took a while before he answered. He may have been hurt by her reaction to his question. "I came from Italy six years ago."

"Have you ever had a show of your paintings at a gallery?"

"Not yet. Friends of mine own galleries and have offered me a showing, but it's not time yet. The art will tell me when it's the right time."

"Has the art given you any hint when it might be ready?"

"I haven't asked, and she hasn't said. She's spent some time ignoring me, but I'm hopeful we're on speaking terms now."

"Your art is a she?"

"Yeah. Like a hurricane, full of fury and awe. She takes me over."

Henley studied his eyes as he spoke. Where she had seen sorrow before, she now found wisps of hope. They escaped and circled her heart. She resisted the urge to reach out to him and rub her hand along his back. To tell him she understood.

"Where can I see your work?" he asked. "Are one of those big skyscrapers yours?"

"Ha. No. You can't see my work anywhere yet. I'm still early in my career. Normally someone with my years of experience, especially a woman, would be assisting an older architect, but I've won a few contests so that's given me some better opportunities. I hope you'll be able to see my work soon."

"I have the sense that you're very talented. I think that's because you care."

Sometime later he tipped his glass back, allowing the last drop of red wine to roll down the side of the cracked glass and into his mouth. As she stood to leave, he wrapped his left arm around her waist, pulling her to him. The kiss was delicate and full of longing, yet tentative, and he pulled away quickly and went to the canvas.

"I need to finish this piece." Standing in front of the painting, his back to her, he said, "Will you be here on Saturday?"

He didn't need to see her nod.

CHAPTER FOUR

Henley leaned against the stone doorway to the shower while Quinn and Claudia finished dressing for spin class. The room was completely tiled in black—walls, ceilings, floor—and inlaid with lighting. Henley always felt like she wasn't sophisticated enough to work out there.

"I need some more details about this," Quinn said.

"Me too," Claudia added. "You mean after you left the nightclub you met an artist?"

"The night Hunter took the plunge?" Quinn patted Claudia on the back.

"Yeah." Claudia laughed. "That night, the night Hunter went for a swim, you met an artist? How'd that happen?"

"There was a blue light coming from a storefront, so I walked down the street to look at it. I could see a blue aura surrounding a man as he worked on a painting. Watching his creation take form, it just, well it...sorta knocked me out, so I stood there for a while. He noticed me watching him and asked me in."

"Wait a minute." Quinn pulled on tiny lime green shorts that matched a lime green sports bra top. "It was one in the morning, and you followed a blue light into some guy's place? I know the situation with Hunter upset you, but are you crazy?"

"Yeah, Hen, are you crazy?" Claudia added.

Both women glared at her. The ferocious love in those stares caused Henley to smile which just made them all the more upset with her.

"Hen, this isn't funny. You know that's not safe. What were you thinking?" Claudia's voice rose in octaves as she spoke. "You went inside some rando guy's place? Was the blue light some kind of tractor beam?"

"I wasn't thinking." Henley shrugged. "It just happened."

"Well, who is he? If he's an artist, have you looked him up?" Quinn asked. "Is he on Instagram?"

"I didn't think of doing that." Henley adjusted her bike shoes, avoiding eye contact.

"I'll do it." Claudia pulled out her phone. "What's his name?"

It took a while, but Henley finally said, "G."

"G?" The muscles in Claudia's arms quivered.

"What does that mean? Just the letter?" Quinn said.

"Or is it Gee? As in Gee Whiz, or Golly Gee?" Claudia snarked.

"Or maybe G spot," Quinn added.

"Don't even go there. My head will explode," Claudia warned Quinn. "What's his last name?"

"I think it's just G. I don't know, maybe it's a marketing thing."

"I'll google that, but I don't expect anything good," Claudia said. "At least Beyoncé, Madonna and Cher all had full words as names."

"What else do you know about him?" Quinn asked.

Henley followed her friends from the dressing room and couldn't help smiling at the contrast. Claudia, covered from neck to toes in black spandex, walked next to Quinn in two slashes of lime green.

They took their places on three bikes next to each other in the back of the room. Seven enormous screens filled the front of the room.

"He's talented, and his work is moving. At a first glance, it looks simple, but it's actually quite complex with hidden nuances, and it's immensely elegant."

"Ugh. Stop it with all that art crap." Claudia glowered at Henley over her phone screen. "I don't find anything about an artist named G on Google."

"What else do you know about him?" Quinn asked again. "You know like...where's he from? Who's his family? Where'd he go to school? Where does he live? Little stuff like that."

"He's from Italy. I don't know about his family. I don't know where he went to school. He lives in his studio." Henley ticked off the answers.

"Oh, lovely. This just keeps getting better." Quinn shook her head.

"He lives in the studio? Do you mean in an apartment above the studio?" Claudia asked.

"Um, no, he lives in the back of the studio. He lives with his art. It's probably his way of putting himself into the work."

"I'll bet he has a junky futon and a hot plate in the back." Quinn moaned as she threaded her fingers through her corkscrew curls and fluffed them, a habit that attached itself to her at a stressful time during her childhood.

Henley stared at her feet again, refusing to look at either of them. They leaned over their bikes pushing into her space, so she couldn't avoid them.

"Does he?" Claudia pressed Henley.

"He has a microwave, not a hot plate," Henley said on a long breath out, her head down.

"Are you kidding me? No, Henley, you can't ever go back there. I don't care how much his art"—Quinn put her hands out palms up and shimmied them—"*moves you.* You understand? That one time was it. You cannot go back there."

"I went back last night." Henley's voice was quiet, and she still wouldn't look at them.

"What?" Claudia slid off her bike and stood in front of Henley. "That's not true. Hen, tell me that's not true. You did not do that."

"Okay? Everyone ready to ride?" The young woman in the front of the class stepped onto her bike. The screens all flashed images of a mountain trail. "Let's do it."

"We're not finished," Claudia said to Henley.

Music blared over the loudspeaker as the instructor shouted "saddle up" and proceeded to work them hard for the next forty-five minutes.

"Hey Quinn?" the instructor said. "You need some water?"

"No, I'm good."

"Yeah. Maybe next time you should push it," the instructor said. "You're supposed to sweat so you need water."

Quinn rolled her eyes at Henley. "I'm not sure this is fun."

"It's not supposed to be fun." Henley panted.

"Then why do we do it?" Quinn tossed her curls.

Henley leaned back so Quinn could see past her to Claudia, who was pedaling frantically, sweat-soaked hair falling from her ponytail across her face which was frozen in concentration. They both grinned.

Later, toweling off after a shower, Quinn said, "Henley, from the time we first met in boarding school I knew you had a massive heart crammed into your skinny little chest. You were so sad and so lost after your mom died. You would have done anything to be loved again."

"You flitted around like some sad little fairy trying to spread goodness when it was obvious your heart was shattered," Claudia agreed. "You were trying so hard to get people to like you, it was heartbreaking."

Henley pursed her lips. She'd heard this before. "It was a terrible time after Mom died, and Aunt Izzy sent me away to boarding school, but I don't understand your point."

"Your judgment about men is messed up," Claudia said. "Maybe because you were so hurt. I don't know. But you constantly choose bad guys."

"And this sounds like another one." Quinn laid her hand on Henley's back. "We love you and are just trying to protect you from another mistake."

"We know you really want the happily ever after, but you can't get it like this." Claudia laid her hand next to Quinn's.

"Look, I understand your concern. He's talented, and we had a connection, some kind of a connection. I'm not sure what it was, but I'd like to help with the art."

"Your compassion is one of the things that's terrific about you, but you have to be careful. People will take advantage of you," Quinn said. "I wonder if you're trying to be Izzy."

"Izzy doesn't have anything to do with this." Henley struggled to keep her voice from rising. She knew all this came from a place of love, but it was still frustrating.

"She flies all over the world helping kids," Quinn said. "Maybe that's why you're always trying to help everyone, including this starving artist."

"He's not starving. I promise I wasn't thinking of Izzy when I was at his studio."

"Ugh," Claudia groaned. "Don't go there. I don't want to know what you were thinking about."

"I'd like to help him get his work into a gallery, and then I'll back away. Is that a deal?" Henley said.

"Um. No." Quinn shook her head. "You can't go back there."

"Maybe I could come with you?" Claudia dropped her navy blue shift dress over her head and stepped into matching kitten heels.

"What? Like a nanny? You're *not* coming with me."

"Will you at least promise not to go there at night?" Quinn asked.

"I'll promise not to go at night." Henley sighed. "I'll agree to that. Okay?"

"Pierre has some contacts at galleries because his hotels have art in the lobbies. I can ask him to help," Claudia said.

"Oh, now it's Pierre. It used to be Mr. Comtois. Claudia, you're holding out on us," Quinn said. "How *is* that *gorgeous* Frenchman? I've been having some pretty delicious dreams about Pierre Comtois."

"I told you. It's not like that at all. We work together. He's my client. Nothing else," Claudia said. "Also, I get the impression he's a serious player. The most magnificent women hang all over him. They fly in to stay at the hotel just to see him. Women send him flowers and gifts. One woman sent him her underwear like he's some kind of rock star. He might be able to help get him an art show at a gallery. You want me to ask him?"

"Thanks. Please do ask Pierre, that gorgeous Frenchman who you are definitely, absolutely, positively not interested in, if he can help." Henley smirked.

"And if I give you a lead, you can give it to him, and that will be it. You will have done your good deed and you'll be finished, right?" Claudia said.

"And you'll be done with him. Right?" Quinn added.

Both women stared at Henley.

"You guys are relentless." Henley sighed. "I'll give him the leads and that will be it. Satisfied?"

"Not really," Claudia said.

CHAPTER FIVE

"THE BEST INTEL I can get on this is that they hired BB&R to design a new jewelry store and something blew up, so they're looking for new architects." Wesley Kahn paced around the conference room table. "All this has happened really quickly. I got the call yesterday morning and met the founder of the company—that's Andrea Scavo— for lunch. He's not saying what went wrong with BB&R, just that they want new blood on the project."

"This is *the* Scavos from Scavo Industries in Italy?" Brett asked.

Wesley nodded sharply.

Brett whistled. "Why a jewelry store? They're never been in the jewelry business, have they?"

"It's the same people, but I don't think this store is part of Scavo Industries. I think it's a new venture." Wesley was still pacing the room, running his hand along the backs of the chairs as he walked, his head bobbing like he was listening to Led Zeppelin.

"Are we looking at this project as an opportunity to get some Scavo Industries work?" Henley asked.

"Definitely." Wesley nodded emphatically. "We should all have our eyes open for new opportunities. Oh, Henley, you should know they asked for you specifically to be assigned to this project."

Henley jerked her head to Wesley just as there was a knock at the door and two men walked in.

"Mr. Scavo." Wesley extended his hand. "I'm happy to see you again. I'd like you to meet Brett Kaufmann and Henley Rana. The two people who will be working on your project."

"This is my son Stephano," Mr. Scavo said, quickly pivoting to Henley. "I'm looking forward to working with you, Ms. Rana."

"Thank you, Mr. Scavo. We appreciate this opportunity. I'm excited to hear about your new project."

Brett stepped into the conversation, nudging his body slightly in front of Henley. "I'm a big fan of many of the Scavo Industries buildings. They're very progressive."

"Thank you. I appreciate that." Andrea nodded and turned back to Henley, who was subtly trying to take in his details so she could describe him to Quinn later.

His charcoal-colored cashmere jacket over the crisp white linen shirt and black wool pants was the picture of elegance. He was every woman's dream Italian man, Henley thought.

When the introductions were over, everyone settled at the long table. Stephano sat too close to Henley, forcing her to lean away from him. Andrea sat directly across the table from her, his blue-gray eyes fixed on her face. She didn't think she'd seen that color of blue anywhere except maybe in a Picasso painting. They were mesmerizing but so intent she wasn't sure where to look. She picked up a pen and prepared to take notes, her eyes cast down on the paper.

"Could you tell us about the store?" Wesley asked. "I know we discussed it in depth yesterday, but I'd like Brett and Henley to hear it from you."

"Of course. Our jewelry is the quality of a Tiffany's or a Van Cleef & Arpels, but we allow the stones to remain in a raw state so each piece is truly unique." Mr. Scavo spoke with his hands. "They are one-of-a-kind pieces. The raw stones convey an energy, a sort of fire. They retain their connection to the earth. We're looking for a building that is as unique as our jewelry."

"You don't want a classic formal store like Tiffany which is pretty...grand?" Henley was making notes as she talked. "You're looking for a design that conveys luxury but without a, um...would you say...pretentious atmosphere?" Henley raised her eyebrows in a question.

Andrea nodded. "Exactly. You've got it right off. I think we've made a good choice to come here." He glanced at Stephano, who glared back at him. "The store certainly needs to be viewed as a top level store, but I don't want the staid old-school look. Our last architects just couldn't get away from the very formal idea of a luxury jewelry store."

Henley had assessed Stephano the instant she met him. His attitude was evident in the way he carried himself. He thought he was quite an example of maleness and was not happy about being there. His gray suit was shiny, and his mustache was too close to Salvador Dali. She wasn't sure what was up between the two men—father and son—but knew she needed to pay close attention to the dynamic.

"Sounds like a fascinating challenge," Wesley said. "This is the type of design we excel at. We have buildings around the world that are innovative. I think it's fair to say that it's our specialty. After we spoke, I put together a portfolio of our designs that I thought would interest you. Henley, would you mind handing these out?"

When she handed a bound portfolio to Stephano, he grasped her hand and wouldn't let go until she looked at him. He laughed and released her hand only after he had kissed it. Once she sat back down, she wiped her hand on her skirt.

The meeting was winding down when Wesley said, "Thank you for your confidence. This is my favorite project of the year. It's going to be exciting, and I can assure you we will do an excellent job for you. Your new store will be extraordinary. We'll have a number of our people working on the project, but Brett will be in the lead with Henley as his second. Whenever you need anything you can contact either of them. And obviously I am available at any time."

Mr. Scavo stood and walked around the room, his head lowered and his arms behind his back, fingers intertwined. "Brett, I mean no offense by what I'm going to say. I have no doubt of your capabilities, but I've read about Henley's work. I'm aware of the contests she's won and think her work shows great creativity. I think her work on the Alvarez building in Cleveland and the Simpson building in Memphis show that her instincts and aesthetic are what we're looking for here. I'd like her to lead the team."

Henley held her breath, afraid if she let it go, she'd discover he didn't really say what she heard.

"I'd like her to be the lead architect." Mr. Scavo turned to face the people seated at the table. Henley let her breath go.

"I don't think we should question their staffing choices. They know their people better than we do," Stephano said. "We don't have experience with any of these people. You just decided to jettison our old firm and move here at the last minute. Let Mr. Kahn manage his people."

Andrea shot a warning glance to his son, who shook his shoulders in umbrage.

"I realize I may be overstepping," Andrea said. "But you know what they say about the client." He shrugged. "Either I'm always right, or I always get what I want. One of those things works here. I would appreciate it if you would put Henley in the lead spot."

"Um. Well...well...of course," Wesley stammered. "Of course. You're right about the client. We try to be responsive to your wishes. Henley did do excellent work on this projects, but she wasn't lead on them. Well...of course...I have every confidence that she'll be great. If you need anything though, please feel free to contact Brett or me at any time."

As she listened to Wesley, Henley was trying to comprehend what had just happened and to stop the excessive blinking that must make her look like a fool. If they saw how surprised she was, they'd probably change their minds. She needed to rouse herself from the stunned stupor and pull herself out of the chair to offer all the expected platitudes as they left.

She couldn't wait to tell her aunt about it at dinner that night. She was lead architect on a high profile project. She wasn't Wesley's first choice but that wasn't surprising. It still stung though.

CHAPTER SIX

"How'd you find this restaurant?" Izzy dangled a small pale orange bun from her fork. "And what is this again?"

"Roasted carrot buns. They're like little dinner rolls but made with roasted carrots," Henley said. "This is one of the hardest reservations to get in Manhattan."

"And it's only vegetables? They don't have anything else?"

"That's why it's called Dirt Candy. Get it? Candy from the dirt. You'll love it. It's super creative and everything is delicious."

"Last week I was offered a stew of something that smelled really awful. I managed to discreetly throw it away. I get offered all kinds of stuff, local culinary delicacies." Izzy cringed, putting on her ick face and shaking her head. "You know me, I've never had much interest in food. It's always seemed to me like too much hassle. Plan it. Shop for it. Pay for it. Prep it. Cook it. Clean up after it. And what do you have when it's over? Poop. That's it. Poop." Izzy sliced the air with her hand. "And in this country we don't even turn poop into compost. It's the best fertilizer, but we flush it away."

"Thanks for that, Izzy." Henley glanced around at the other tables. A few heads turned to gawk at the striking woman, tall with steel gray hair pulled into a French twist, who held herself with not only perfect posture but also with perfect poise and absolute confidence. She was wearing black wool trousers and a white cashmere sweater, and of course, her spectacular ever-present square diamond earrings. Those earrings were the only jewelry Izzy ever wore. Their extravagance always caught Henley by surprise, even though she'd seen them for as long as she could remember.

"So how's work?" Izzy took a drink of her cosmo.

"I'm project manager on a new project to design an unusual jewelry store."

"You're project manager on a project." Izzy clapped her hands. "Congratulations. I'm so proud of you. They finally got some sense at that firm of yours."

"I know. It's...good." Henley hesitated as she spoke.

"But?"

"Well, my boss didn't choose me. He got pushed into it by the client, who insisted on me, so I feel a little, don't know, fraudulent."

"Nope. Don't do that. Show them you were the right choice. Show off your fabulous skills. They were fools not to choose you first. Who did they want? That bootlicker, Brett?"

Henley nodded.

Izzy grimaced. "Look at it like this, it's even better that the client chose you. The word is out that you're great. Maybe that will help the management see how talented you are."

"I'm not sure how he knew my work. My projects so far haven't been large. He even knew about the contests I won."

Izzy clapped her hands again. "Of course he did. I'm so proud."

Henley couldn't help smiling at the pride and confidence that circled Izzy like a halo, and she offered thanks to the universe for her aunt.

"The client's interesting," Henley said. "He's Italian, very sophisticated. He kept staring at me during the meeting. Every time I looked up from my notepad his eyes were on me."

"I'm sure that's because he was dazzled by your brilliance and beauty." Izzy smiled. "But if he tries anything inappropriate you know where his weak spot is, right?"

"Take the palm of my hand and smash it into the base of his nose." Henley demonstrated the move by pushing her palm in the air in a jabbing movement. "That's what they said in the self-defense class you made me go to."

Izzy shook her head. "Nooooo. That wouldn't be the spot to smash." Izzy popped an olive in her mouth. "What'd they say these fried olives are stuffed with? These things are pretty good."

"Feta and garlic." Henley's voice dropped to almost a whisper. "You know Mom would have turned sixty next week."

Izzy watched the cadre of chefs behind the counter, all wearing bandanas on their heads and moving with practiced synchronicity.

"Heard," rumbled from the kitchen as people jumped to fill the chef's orders.

"She's been on my mind too. I miss my sister."

"I miss my mom. I've been thinking a lot about our life recently. One thing I never understood is why she gave up dancing. She never wanted to talk about that time in her life."

"She just didn't want to anymore. It looks like such a glamorous life to be on stage under the lights dressed in beautiful costumes with elaborate sets in front of crowds of cheering and clapping people. It's the dream of every little girl who puts on a pair of toe shoes. But the reality of that life is much different. Those dancers are almost always in pain. They peel those toe shoes off after a performance to find a bloody mess of hamburger toes. It takes hours of work to break in a new pair of shoes so they can wear them at all. Dancers soak and stretch their shoes and stuff them with cotton, but even with all that effort the shoes still hurt. They dance with sprained ankles and hurt hips and shoulders. The audience never sees that part of a dancer's life. Your mom was in constant pain."

A waiter in black pants, a white shirt and black apron appeared with two bowls. "Excuse me. I have roasted potato soup decorated with crispy vinegar potatoes and tomato pearls. The potatoes are roasted to dehydrate them, so when the broth is added the desiccated potatoes suck it in creating a full flavor experience." He set one of the bowls in front of Izzy. "And this is portobello mousse served with truffle toast and sautéed pear and cherry compote. Enjoy." He set the mousse in front of Henley.

"I thought she loved dancing." Henley cut into the creamy mousse and broke off a piece of crispy toast.

"She did. She loved it. She lived for it. But it was a love hate thing. No one would endure that kind of pain unless they truly loved to dance. It's such a sweet and salty combination of pleasure and pain. The schedule was grueling with all the rehearsals and then the performances. She had to be away from you a lot, and she hated that."

"What was it like to watch her dance?"

Izzy leaned back in her chair and stared at the ceiling. The emotion that passed over her face was bittersweet too, the essence of melancholy.

"My sister was magnificent." Izzy sighed, still staring at the ceiling. "It was heart-stopping to watch her. She could effortlessly leap so high it seemed she must be on a wire. People thought it was a stunt, because no human could fly like that. Probably the most striking thing about Dori though was her elegance of movement. Consummate grace. Watching her was to see poetry in motion. She was in a class by herself."

"And she gave it all up."

Izzy shook her head. "It's...I...Henley, I'm not sure what I can tell you. She changed. Change is an essential process for all existence."

"Is that *Star Trek*? Are you quoting *Star Trek* to me again?"

"Of course," Izzy laughed. "Spock."

After the waiter cleared the dishes from the table, he produced a wooden crumber from under his sleeve with the flair of a magician extracting a rabbit from a hat and precisely removed the single miscreant speck of food from the tablecloth. They sat in silence as he laid fine silver forks with walnut handles on their silver rest with an equal flourish.

A second waiter set a large, squat bowl in front of Henley. "This is our Asparagus Paella. The vegetables are tossed with a mixture of olive oil, lemon zest, salt and garlic. We lay them delicately on a grill. When they have just the tiniest bit of wilt, we place them on top of exquisitely herbed rice and tomatoes."

He set a plate in front of Izzy. "And for you, our world-famous Cauliflower and Waffles. We smoke the cauliflower with chunks of maple and serve it over crispy waffles. It's finished with a drizzle of freshly chopped horseradish and heavy cream." The women smiled and nodded their thanks.

"You know there weren't any photos of her on stage around the house," Henley said. "Once I asked her to see photos, but she said didn't keep them. I can't remember seeing her dance."

"You did see her dance. Once. It was an amazing night. She danced the role of Princess Odette in *Swan Lake*. Of course you were way too young to understand that the Princess and Siegfried decide to drown themselves in the end. Disney's got nothing on those Russians when it comes to child-scaring tragedy. You wore a darling red taffeta dress and precious little red sequined shoes. I was in New York and sat next to you."

Izzy ran her fork back and forth through her fingers like a baton majorette.

"No one has ever told me that story." Tears brimmed Henley's eyes. "But the odd thing is...I already knew it."

"Really? Didn't you just say you'd never heard it before?" Now Izzy absently turned one of her earrings.

"I don't remember ever hearing it, but I've dreamed it many times. I dreamed exactly that outfit, the red dress and those red sequined shoes. I just didn't think it was real."

"Oh, Hen. That dream was a gift. It was real, honey. I'm surprised you have any memory of it at all since you were only four. What a beautiful night." Izzy sighed. "The next time you have that dream, cherish it. Try to grab it and hold it close. Your mom loved you so much."

She was still turning those earrings.

———

AFTER THEIR ENTREES were cleared the waiter appeared again. "Tonight for dessert we have red pepper velvet cake with peanut brittle and peanut ice cream or zucchini ginger cake with zucchini cream and zucchini candy."

"Red pepper velvet cake? Is that different from plain old red velvet cake?" Izzy asked.

"It's similar, but our cake is made with juiced and pulped red peppers. The red peppers make it lighter and more delicate than other red velvet cakes."

"I'll have another glass of wine, please," Izzy said.

"I'd like the red pepper cake, please," Henley said to the waiter.

"You should try it. It's really good. I think I'll make one and take it to work," Henley said to Izzy, who choked on her wine.

"Honey, you can't cook any more than I can. You inherited that from me."

"I can cook."

"No, you really can't. Just ask your friends. They razz you behind your back."

"No, they don't. They do it right in front of me." Henley laughed. "Mom was always working on those little houses in her studio, so there wasn't time to teach me to cook."

"Your mom was famous for those little houses. Many of them are in museums now, you know. She was talented in so many ways, but she couldn't have taught you to cook because she didn't know how either. We made a vow when we were little that we would never cook or clean when we grew up. I've never done either. And never regretted it for a single second." Izzy laughed. "How are Quinn and Claudia?"

"Quinn is Quinn. Incomparable. She picks up life and swings it about by the throat. Right now she's waiting to hear if her spring line will be picked up by Nordstrom. And Claudia landed a big new account and is hoping for a promotion from it. The client on the account is French. He's gorgeous and elegant, perfect hair, perfect suits, perfect manners."

"I know the type. You have to worry how many women are enjoying his perfection."

"I'm sure Claudia can handle him, but she says she's not interested."

"She seems like a precious fragile sculpture."

"A sculpture made from solid steel," Henley said.

"She might be so successful because people underestimate her."

"People who mess with Claudia, or the people she loves, are very sorry."

"And is there any special Frenchman in your life?"

Henley paused. "I did meet an Italian artist."

"Now we're talking. Details, please."

"Claudia and Quinn think he's sketchy, and they want me to forget about him."

"They're smart girls, and they love you, but you have to make your own decisions. Why don't they like him?"

"He lives in his studio, so they think he's a bum."

"Is he?"

"No. He's an artist, not a bum. They think I have really bad judgment about men. I do have a pretty bad dating history. But I can't get this guy out of my mind. There was some kind of a connection that I can't explain. I'm going to his studio to give him some information Claudia gave me about art galleries. Maybe that'll be it, or maybe it won't. I don't know."

"You're a smart girl, Henley. I trust your choices. Mistakes are the quickest way to learn a lesson. They're how we learn to live life. Mistakes are life lessons."

"Is that *Star Trek* again?"

Izzy smiled. "Nope. That's your Aunt Izzy."

"How long are you going to be in town this time?"

"Three weeks." Izzy stared out the window.

"Really? Three weeks is a long time for you to be in one place. Is there a man who's keeping you here?"

"Not at the moment, but there's one waiting in London."

"And one in Paris? One in Prague. And another in Johannesburg. If I know my Aunt Izzy." Henley teased her aunt, who kept staring out the window at the take-out Thai restaurant and the grimy graffiti decorating the vacant buildings across the street.

"You know me—there's always someone waiting somewhere, but never at home. My advice is to take a chance on your artist." Izzy looked back at her niece. "Regret is a terrible thing to live with."

CHAPTER SEVEN

Henley cupped her hands around her eyes to peer inside the studio. There was no sign of life. She knocked on the door again.

Several minutes later she heard shuffling and banging. The lock turned. G rubbed his eyes and blankly blinked at Henley in the piercing bright sun. His sweatpants were stained, T-shirt ripped, feet bare, toes long and thin.

"You said Saturday," she said.

"Saturday?" he muttered. "What are you talking about?"

"You said to come on Saturday." She paused but he didn't say anything. "Could I come in for a minute? I have something to give you."

He stood to the side. Henley walked in, glancing sideways at him.

"One of my best friends, Claudia, she's tiny, but she has a huge spirit. She's powerful. We've known each other since high school. Claudia and Quinn are my best friends. We were roommates at the boarding school I went to after my mom died."

Henley kept her eyes on the paint-stained floor. When she paused for a breath, she glanced up at G, who was scrubbing his face with his hands.

"Sorry. I didn't mean to say all that." Her eyes darted around the studio. Crumpled sheets hung off the futon on the floor. A plate piled with food scraps teetered precariously on top of the microwave and empty tea bottles littered the floor like debris washed in and abandoned by the tide. Trash spilled from the burgeoning bags propped along the wall. A whiff of turpentine floated over many other odors.

"Um. Anyway. Claudia's an accountant, and one of her big clients owns hotels that display art in their lobbies."

G continued to stare at her, his body languidly propped against the wall like he would drop bonelessly to the floor without it.

"Ohhhh." Henley's breath escaped in a long sigh when she noticed the painting. "It's finished. It's extraordinary."

She whirled back around, jubilant. He didn't move. Expressionless.

"Your piece is done. It's...it's...finished...isn't it? It is, right?" she stammered. "It's wonderful."

He continued to stare at her.

"Oh. Well, umm, Claudia's client, Pierre, called a couple of gallery owners who said they would be willing to see your work. This is the list." Henley held out a piece of paper.

A muscle in G's face twitched. Henley took a step back.

"Why do you think I need your help? Did I ever ask you for help?"

He glowered at her. Dirt embedded in the paint on the floor flaked up in scaly patches like psoriasis.

"No," she whispered as she reached behind her, feeling for the door.

"Why do you keep coming here? You were standing outside my window watching me. Then you came back uninvited. Now you show up again offering help I don't need and don't want."

Henley grabbed the doorknob, and yanked the door open so hard it banged against the wall. The doorknob came off in her hand, and she flung it down on the ground where it skipped several times.

Screw those damn life lessons.

"YOU WERE SO RIGHT about the artist guy." Henley and Claudia sat on stools at Ah Bar watching Simon entertain his crowd of regulars.

"Sorry to say I'm not surprised," Claudia said. "What'd he do?"

The door opened and Quinn entered. The claret sweater in fine cashmere fit her like it had been poured onto her wet and dried against her skin. The skirt fluttered around her legs swaying when she moved. Quinn had sewn thin strips of fabric in a jumble of colors on a wide waistband, each strip slightly overlapping the other so they opened and closed when she walked, showing hints of skin and a promise of more. On her feet were sandals made from tiny gold chains. Heads around the bar turned, mouths gaped and conversation stalled. Henley blinked a few times in case it was a mirage. This was a lot even for Quinn.

Quinn kissed Henley and Claudia on the cheek and sat down. "Oh, Drink Boy," she singsonged to Simon, whose face lit up the room when he saw her.

"I made something special for the three of you." He set a martini glass of shimmering gold in front of each of them.

Henley took a tiny sip. Then a bigger sip.

"Simon, this is incredible." Henley slapped her hands on the bar and tilted her head to the heavens. "*Wow*."

"It's outrageous, isn't it?" Simon raised his arms in triumph. "Drinks are my superpower." The Simonettes clapped.

"Who needs invisibility when you can make drinks like this?" Henley laughed. "In college when those books talked about the nectar of the gods, I'm pretty sure you found the recipe."

"I'm so excited about it. It took me hours in the chemistry lab to concoct it. Just wait until my next one. I think I'm going to put absinthe in it." Simon's laugh filled the busy bar as he grabbed bottles and poured drinks. "Or maybe helium. Imagine if I could put helium in a drink and everyone would talk like Donald Duck. Wouldn't that be a blast?"

"Can you do that?" Henley asked.

"Nah, helium is only in liquid form at -269 degrees C. Wouldn't it be cool if I could? It's fun to even think about it. That would be super stupendously outrageous."

"He's so good at this. He must be the yummiest bartender in the City," Quinn said. "Every time he swivels his hips half the customers in this bar have an orgasm."

"I gotta agree with you on that," Claudia said. "To hell with that Harvard degree in particle physics. He's totally adorkable."

"Is he dating anyone?" Quinn asked.

Simon danced behind the bar tossing bottles, laughing, sliding drinks to customers. Women pushed closer to the bar to watch him move.

"I see a lot of girls trying to get his attention but no one succeeding. See those women with business cards in their hands? He told me once that he gets over a hundred numbers on a weekend night," Henley said. "He puts them in the recycle bin not even looking at them. He's never gotten over that girl...Jo."

"The one at Brown?" Quinn asked. "It's been years now."

"She crushed him," Claudia said. "I remember you stayed with him for weeks, Henley. The breakup destroyed him."

"I had to tell him when to get up, when to brush his teeth, when to eat, when to go to class. He could only follow instructions."

"And yet he still aced every class," Claudia said.

"That's Simon."

"He's one of a kind." Quinn tipped her glass to him and gave him the Quinn smile. He gave her his *Who me* smile in return.

"Those five years he spent at Harvard getting his doctorate didn't give him enough time to get over her?" Claudia asked.

"It did give him time, I guess," Henley said. "But Harvard was still school, it was serious work. I think this stint as a bartender lets him cut loose, to be happy with no pressure for a little while," Henley said. "That particle physics thing will still be there in a year if that's what he wants. He loves what he's doing now. And he's a natural at it."

"He does seem to be having a blast," Claudia said.

"And bringing joy to everyone," Quinn purred.

"Did I tell you Simon walked me home the other night? He's such a sweetheart. Hunter followed me so I came in here," Henley said.

"Hunter was following you?" Claudia asked.

"I took Bella for a walk, and he saw me. He shouted stuff like how he wanted me back, junk like that. I just kept walking."

"Did you tell Mr. I Like Skanky Wet Blondes to shut up and go away?" Claudia asked.

"I came in here with Bella. Simon was so sweet about it."

"You need to face Hunter and tell him to go away," Claudia said.

"I agree with Claudia," Quinn said. "Hunter's the type who's not going to take no easily. You hurt his massive ego."

"Already done."

"Really?" Claudia said. "You talked to him?"

"Kinda. Simon texted him. Told him it was over."

"What?"

"From my phone. It's over. Simon sent a pretty blunt text, so I don't think I'll hear from Hunter again."

"Well okay, that's one way to do it," Claudia said. "You said something happened with the artist? Did you give him the gallery contacts I got from Pierre?"

"Did you see him?" Quinn asked. "Did you go to that crappy studio?"

"Hold your objections." Henley threw up her hands. "First, yes, I did go to his studio. It was in the daytime like I promised. I obviously woke him up because he could barely utter two words. Now that I think about it, I'm not sure he's ever uttered more than a few words to me. That is until I tried to give him the contacts from Pierre. Then he exploded."

"He *exploded*?" Claudia jolted up so quickly her long, sleek hair whipped around her face. "What's his address? Where's that stupid studio?"

"Sit down, bruiser." Quinn patted Claudia's arm. "You can see she's fine."

"He asked why I thought he needed my help. And why I kept coming back there. Embarrassing stuff like that."

"You know he does have a bit of a point," Quinn said.

"I know. I'm sufficiently horrified about it. I'm swearing off men."

"Good luck with that," Quinn laughed.

"You don't need to be done with men," Claudia said. "You can still look for your prince if that's what you want, you just need to make better choices."

"You're looking for a prince?" Simon asked. "That's a tough get."

"No, I'm not looking for a prince. You know me better than that. They're making fun of me because they say I kiss frogs."

"Yeah." Simon shook his head thoughtfully. "Kissing frogs is not a good idea."

"You know they don't really mean frogs, right?" Henley smiled at him. "I'm not looking for a prince, but I do want a family. It's ok to want a family. To hope for a family." She looked at each of her friends waiting for agreement.

"Were you listening to our conversation, Drink Boy?" Quinn asked.

"Always." Simon laughed as he slid two drinks down the bar. "Quinn, I will listen to you. Anytime. Anywhere."

He grabbed a pint glass and tossed it back and forth between his hands.

"You're a big talker, Simon." Quinn's laughter joined his in perfect harmony. "What you doing with that glass?"

"The glass? I'm so glad you asked." Simon leaned over the bar and whispered to the women, "I'm going to make magic. You want to make some magic, Quinn?"

"Are you making me an offer, Big Talking Drink Boy?" Quinn

winked at him. "Better be sure you can handle the answer before you make the offer. What kind of magic do you have in mind?"

"Witness. First, I will pour beer into the glass." Simon stuck the glass under the tap.

"And then drink it? Amazing." Claudia laughed. "I always knew you were brilliant."

"Claudia, I'm hurt by your low expectations." Simon grabbed his chest with his hand and feigned distress, sucked in a breath and released it with a long, overly dramatic shudder.

Henley's heart swelled watching him show off. His inherent goodness infused every silly thing he did with irresistible charm.

"Now watch." He poured nuts into the glass.

"You dumped nuts into a glass of beer? Simon, are you okay?" Henley asked.

"Watch and be astounded." His face glowed with happiness.

"Look, the nuts are floating to the top," Claudia said. "And then falling to the bottom."

"And rising again." Henley stared at the glass. "Like the Walking Dead."

"It's a lava lamp!" Simon spread his arms in an excited big ta da.

The Simonettes clapped and laughed enthusiastically.

"The surface of the nuts is uneven so the bubbles from the beer catch under them and float them to the top. The bubbles break when they get to the top and boom—the nuts fall. Then the whole thing happens again."

"You're a pretty cool guy, Simon," Quinn said.

"Aw shucks, just a drink boy I think you said, Quinn." He put on a lazy Southern drawl that dripped with honey, and his infectious laugh rang out in the bar once again. All the women turned to look at him and a collective satisfied sigh floated over the music.

"A drink boy and a chick magnet." Claudia nodded to the women crowded around the bar.

"They're all hoping he'll look at them," Quinn said.

"And go home with them," Claudia added.

"Who could resist him? Not only is he darling with those shaggy blond curls and beautiful topaz-colored eyes, but his personality cannot be contained. He's like a sparkler of happiness. He's a magnet for everyone," Henley said. "Not only women. Children, grandmas, dogs, everyone. Bella would abandon me for him in a split second. Even Izzy is madly in love with him."

"A doctorate and he's making lava lamps with beer and nuts." Claudia didn't take her eyes off him.

"He's such a people person. Look at him dancing and playing around. He knows all the eyes are on him, and he loves it. He can't work in an office, because he can't sit still. He'd shrivel up or break out or go crazy," Henley said.

"What's he going to do with a degree in physics if he can't be in a room with computers, books, telescopes, stuff like that?" Quinn asked.

"I don't know, but he's happy that's what's important," Henley said. "He'll figure it out when he's ready."

"And the drinks are mighty terrific." Claudia finally turned back to her friends and tipped her glass to them. "So no more sullen artist guy, Hen?"

"Nope. I'm done. I'm saying it again. I'm not getting involved anymore. Write it down. I'll sign it."

"You mean you're not getting involved until the next time, sweetheart." Simon leaned over the bar and kissed her forehead.

"He knows you pretty well." Quinn laughed. "Maybe you should consider him?" She nudged Henley and tipped her head to Simon.

"Nooooo. We're friends. Brother-sister kind of thing."

"I don't know." Quinn made a low purr in her voice. "Maybe time to rethink that?"

———

HER FRIENDS OBJECTED, but Henley insisted on walking home from Ah Bar alone. Maybe walking would help her sort out the tangle of jumbled feelings. Compared to her friends, who were so strong and sophisticated, she felt pathetic. Why did they love a doofus like her? She tried to muster the energy to be angry with herself for constantly making poor decisions, but discovered she was just too tired to beat herself up...again. Lost in thought, she walked up the steps to the door of her brownstone, keys in her hand.

"So I was right. You do live in a beautiful brownstone. I figured someone as classy as you would live someplace like this." Henley swung around, her heart beating faster, hand going to her pocket for her phone. G was sitting on the stone steps in front of her home.

"What are you doing here?" She tried to steady the chatter of her teeth and straightened her back. "Answer me. What are you doing here?"

"I'm here to say I'm sorry." His eyes were cast on the ground and his hands locked behind his head.

Henley waited. Conversations in the distance floated by as horns honked and sirens caterwauled through the streets. Henley shifted her body so she could run towards the voices.

"I was rude. I was just awful."

"How do you know where I live?" Henley kept her eyes on him, her hand on the phone, her body tensed to run.

"You told me you lived at Seventy-Sixth around Columbus, so I walked by all of these buildings. I told a neighbor I was delivering some work for you." He finally lifted his head and gazed at her.

"I heard you loud and clear this morning." She tried to keep the tremor from her voice, but she didn't quite succeed. "You told me to get out. Don't worry. I won't bother you again."

"I was an idiot. I'd been looking forward to seeing you that evening and was surprised to see you at my door in the morning. You were the last person I expected."

"And that explains what you said to me? That justifies how you treated me?"

"It doesn't. No. I was an idiot."

"Yeah, so you said. Wait here. Bella's going crazy inside. She needs to go for a walk."

"Who's Bella?"

Henley walked out of her house with Bella in her arms and set her on the sidewalk.

"Bella, I assume? A dachshund? She's got a lot of white in the hair around her face. How old is she?"

"I'm not sure. I rescued her from a shelter. Probably about twelve," Henley said. "Would you please explain to me again what happened this morning? You were so angry."

G bent down and petted Bella, cooing in her ear. "Aren't you a precious beauty?" Straightening, he faced Henley. "There are no excuses, but I'll tell you the facts. I didn't sleep the night before because the painting was whispering to me like an insatiable mistress. I couldn't stop painting."

"The painting is truly magnificent," Henley said.

"Thank you. I had a massive surge of energy…a kind of crazy, consuming, electric energy that circuited through my body and possessed me. I was painting and painting and couldn't put the brush down. I was exhausted. It was like a vampire had sucked all the blood out of me. I went to bed sometime after seven in the morning."

"What do you think caused that energy?" Henley asked.

"You."

"Me?"

"You. I'm certain. When you came into the studio the first time, I felt your energy. I was struggling. There was an idea hiding somewhere in the muck of my heart or brain or soul or wherever the hell creativity lives. It was taunting me, but I couldn't reach it. It would show itself in flashes, but I couldn't see the whole image, and the pieces I could see wouldn't fit together. After you left it burst into my mind fully formed. I envisioned the entire painting. It laid itself out on the canvas in front of me. *You* caused that to happen."

"I'd like that to be true, but I doubt it."

They meandered down Seventy-Sixth Street towards Central

Park as Bella investigated every tree, patch of dirt, trashcan and piddle mark left by other dogs who passed by that day.

"When you showed up in the morning, I don't think I was even awake. I was sort of sleepwalking. I needed to clean up the studio. I planned to cover the painting, so I could reveal it for you."

"And I screwed that up by coming early."

"I know it's silly. I wanted to share it with you and watch you experience it, and the place was such a mess."

"It's not the neatest of places to begin with." Her shrug said, *Sorry but you know it's true.*

"I suppose it's a mess, but I don't see it. Where I live doesn't enter my mind. I guess I've been sort of lost."

Bella stopped walking and jumped up, putting her front paws on his leg. When he picked her up, she snuggled into his arm.

"I guess she's had enough walking. She usually doesn't like new people."

"Dogs know when someone loves them."

"*Tesoro*," he whispered into Bella's ear as he stroked her head.

"*Tesoro?*"

"Treasure. She's a treasure, aren't you, precious?" He kissed Bella on the top of her head.

"*Tesoro*, that's lovely," Henley sighed. "She is a treasure. She was dearly loved by an older woman who lived on the Upper East Side. When Bella's person passed away, no one in the family would care for Bella. They dumped her in a high-kill shelter. When I found her, she was in the back corner of a concrete cage shaking. She didn't understand what had happened. She desperately wanted her person back and didn't know why she was left in such a scary place. It's sad for all the animals in shelters but especially for the older dogs who come from families who loved them. All of the dogs in shelters are scared and sad, but those older dogs are devastated."

When they stopped at a stoplight, Henley reached over and gently stroked Bella and kissed her head.

"Most shelters only keep dogs they think are adoptable. A dog who's cowering in the back of a cage won't be considered a good candidate. The dog doesn't realize that its life depends on it being happy and outgoing. It's hard to be happy when you're terrified. When I got Bella out of that cage, she molded her body into mine like she was trying to sink into me."

"The world can be a sad and lonely place." G stared off toward the ornate carved stonework and elaborate wrought iron railings of one of the beautiful brownstones. "I don't know why you thought I needed help to find a gallery." He hesitated. "I told you when I was ready, I knew people. Your offer of help seemed like you thought I couldn't do it on my own. It seemed like pity. I snapped. I'm sorry."

Henley nodded. "I can see that now. You did tell me you had connections. I just wanted to help."

"When my brain finally woke from the dead, I understood your offer was made in kindness, not pity. I felt like …" G gestured with his hands. "*A culo.*"

She raised an eyebrow and tilted her head in a question.

"An ass."

"So maybe we can start over?" Henley said.

"Yes. *Grazie.*"

"Hi, I'm Henley. Pleased to meet you." She held out her hand.

"Ciao, I'm G." He placed her hand next to his heart, just above where Bella was snuggled. "I would like to know you better, *cara.*"

Another raised eyebrow.

"It means…something like…dear. But it can mean different things depending."

One more raised eyebrow.

He shrugged.

"Would you like to sit on the steps? I can take Bella."

"I think she's happy in my arms."

"I imagine she is."

"What are you working on now?" He lowered himself onto the step so as not to bother Bella.

Henley sat beside him close enough for their legs to touch.

"I'm designing a space for a new jewelry store in the Upper West Side. The jewelry is very organic and earthly, but super elegant. Simple lines and reliance on color and contrast make it unique."

She felt his eyes on her face as she talked and wanted to touch him. She wanted to stroke his face. She wanted him to reach out and draw her to him—and more, she realized. Much more.

"The challenge is to create a store that is the right vessel for this unique jewelry. The store needs to have the same organic feel as the jewelry. This isn't New Mexico turquoise. No offense to the New Mexico artisans—their work is beautiful—but it's not this jewelry. The building needs to be a conduit for the product, not a warehouse. The best buildings reflect their purpose." She was saying words, but her body had a conversation of its very own going on, and she was having trouble sorting the two out.

Bella was curled in the crook of G's bent left arm. He laid his right hand palm up on Henley's lap. She slid her hand into his and warmth tracked through her body. The sight of Bella gently cradled on his lap, slowly closing her eyes, his long fingers curled around her plump bottom holding her securely to his chest, touched Henley. When she lifted her eyes to his, an emotion she couldn't read flickered on his face.

"It's similar with art. The medium an artist chooses for the work affects how the piece is interpreted. Oil paint on wood creates a much different impression than pastel on vellum. A figure drawn with charcoal feels different than one created with acrylic paint. Every artist considers which medium will best speak to people and make their point most effectively."

They stared at each other for several long minutes before Henley said, "I think many people underestimate the effect that art can have on both a person and on society. It's powerful. It can influence opinion and thought."

"I think about Picasso's painting *Guernica* often. Do you know the painting? The horror and atrocity of war practically peels off the canvas. It's like an odor that sinks into your cells. You're forever changed by having seen it. Some things are so shattering they seem to alter your genetic code, and you become someone different. Someone you don't recognize."

"*Guernica* did that to you?"

He seemed to sag, his body diminishing. "In a way. It did. And other things." His cadence slowed, and that sorrow flicked in his eyes again. "I don't know how anything I do could ever make an impact like that painting. Sometimes I think I'm wasting time painting pieces that will never make a difference, but I keep painting anyway. People are so distracted these days it's hard to get anyone to pay attention. If I screamed into a canyon, the only voice I'd hear in response would be the echo. Sometimes I'm not sure what I'm doing."

"Your work touched me. I'm sure it will touch others too."

"I didn't mean to get off on my existential angst. Will you give me your number? So I can text you rather than sit on your steps for three hours."

"You sat here for three hours?"

He carefully settled a sleeping Bella into Henley's arms and swept a fingertip across her cheek and down her neck. His face just inches from hers, he kissed her. There was nothing tentative about the kiss. She leaned in, hungry for more, but he pulled back.

"I have a favor to ask."

She nodded.

"I need your help."

CHAPTER EIGHT

Henley dropped a stack of folders on her desk and sorted through a pile of papers.

"Will you be joining us?" Andrea Scavo's warm smile filled the room.

"Mr. Scavo, it's so good to see you again." Henley jumped up extending her hand. He drew her in for a brief hug, kissed her on both cheeks and placed his big warm left hand over their clasped hands.

"Please, Henley. Call me Andrea. You hurt my feelings when you call me Mr. Scavo. It makes me feel old and unwanted."

His handsome face, distinguished salt-and-pepper hair and manicured short beard were certain to elicit sighs from women everywhere, but to Henley, it was his zest for life that radiated from him that was most endearing.

"Andrea." She paused to smile at him. They had only been working together for a few weeks but had developed an appreciation for each other.

"*Grazie, infinite.*" Nodding a gallant thank-you, he put his hand on his chest.

"You're early," Henley said.

"We started about thirty minutes ago. We waited, but Brett said we should go ahead. I decided to come look for you."

"What? Brett said what? The meeting was to start at ten."

"Stephano said the time was changed to nine."

She quickly turned her back to him on the pretense of picking up her laptop so he wouldn't see the anger rise in her face. Brett. His games never stopped.

"I'm sorry. I didn't know about the change, but I have all the work right here." She tucked the laptop under her arm and quickly touched the amethyst stone hanging from her neck.

When Andrea and Henley walked into the conference room, Brett immediately walked to her. "Henley, I'm so glad to see you. I was worried. We only just got started. I tried to wait for you."

"Henley, so kind of you to join us." Stephano waved some papers and rose halfway in his seat.

"Nice to see you, Stephano."

"Brett's been taking us through the design." He put the papers down on the table.

"Really?" Henley whirled to Brett, who quickly looked away. "You showed them the design?" Fury crept in around the edges of her voice. She had a quick vision of slamming her palm just where Izzy had recommended.

"Don't worry, Henley. Calm down." Brett put up his hands. "We just got started. I didn't do the big"—he made air quotes—"*reveal*. Mr. Scavo asked for a break to try to find you. He was very insistent." He motioned to the image on the smart technology wall. "It's all yours. Take it away."

Henley took a deep breath and let it out slowly, forcing the fury to recede. "Thank you. I'm excited to show you the plans for your new store."

The door opened and Wesley bounded into the room. He leaned into Henley and whispered, "I'm glad you're here. I heard there was a problem."

"No problem," she answered quietly.

"Mr. Scavo, I'm so pleased to see you again." He grasped Mr. Scavo's hand and pumped it vigorously. "Would it be okay if I joined the meeting for a few minutes? Henley showed me the designs for your new jewelry store earlier this week, and I found them absolutely thrilling—thrilling, I tell you. I was stunned into silence, and that doesn't happen to me very often." He laughed and clapped his hands. "I told her I wanted to come to this meeting so I could see your reaction."

Whatever response Andrea made was drowned out by Wesley. "Another example of why she's already won three major architecture prizes. Go ahead, Henley. Dazzle them." He laughed again and leaned against a wall.

"Thank you, sir. I hope I live up to that billing." She noticed Andrea watching her intently. He seemed...proud of her. "As we've discussed before, your jewelry needs to be displayed in a way that celebrates its uniqueness. The boring glass cases and sterile formal setting found in other jewelry stores won't work here. The design I'm going to show you is unusual, so please take a few minutes to let it settle in, and let me explain before you react."

She clicked a button on her iPhone, and an artist's rendering of the inside of the store flashed on the smart wall. Andrea's head jerked back, and his eyes widened, but within seconds a smile spread across his face. He was clearly intrigued by what he saw. Stephano, however, drummed his fingers on the table.

"Your reaction is what I hoped for, Andrea. This is unusual, but after the initial surprise, I got your attention and curiosity and excitement took over."

"You got my attention, all right." Andrea jumped up and walked closer to the image, excitement evident in his body language. "It looks like a cave."

"It is a cave," Henley said.

"It's really a...a...*cave?*" Stephano muttered, shaking his head. He looked to Brett, who rolled his eyes, as if in commiseration.

Effing traitor, Henley thought.

"A cave is the perfect location for your primal jewelry. A cave suggests that the pieces themselves were birthed in the same violent collision of tectonic plates that created the gemstones." Henley pointed to the drawing with a laser. "The walls will be made from a textured material that will resemble the rough surface of a cave. We'll weave chokes of metal ore through the textured material when it's wet, so the walls will glisten under strategically placed lighting. The floors will be polished cement, so they will look like stone with the same chokes of metal ore. The cave will evoke the earth at its most elemental. For safety reasons we did away with the stalactites and stalagmites. But since they're so cool, we might include a few around the periphery where the customers can't walk."

She paused. "Are there any questions or should I go on?"

"Are you planning on giving people a pickaxe and a pith helmet too?" Stephano stared at Henley. "This is supposed to be a high-class store, not a Disney experience. It's not a playground for children, it's for adults. How's this for a question? Where's the *jewelry*? Did you forget this is a store to sell *jewelry*?"

"Great question, Stephano." Henley smiled at him. He wasn't going to rattle her. She was on a roll, and it felt good. "I have some drawings to illustrate how the jewelry will be displayed."

She flashed another drawing on the smart wall next to the first one.

"Each piece of jewelry will be placed in a crevice carved into the wall of the cave. Studies have shown that people today don't want to just buy things, they want an experience. This store will give them that. The customer will go on a great quest to hunt for jewels hidden in the crevices of the cave. In a way it is a playground, Stephano, but this one is for adults. Adults with exquisite taste and the desire for a unique experience."

The door opened slightly and a young woman slipped into the room and whispered to Wesley, who nodded. He gave Henley a *well done* salute as he slipped out the door. As the woman followed him out, Henley noticed both Stephano and Brett lean over in their seats to watch her walk away. They straightened at the same time, and realizing the other man had also been looking at her very shapely derriere, knocked fists and nodded sharply without missing a beat. Brett caught Henley's eye and gave her what was probably supposed to be a "the things we have to do for business" face scrunch and eye roll. She didn't believe that for a moment.

"What about security?" Stephano stood, stuffed his hands in his pants pockets and paced around the conference room. "Those boring cases as you call them are used for a reason. This jewelry is expensive. You want to stick it in…in…holes in the walls. This is ridiculous."

"Security an important point, Stephano." Brett turned in his chair and nodded reassuringly at Stephano. "We don't want people walking away with that beautiful jewelry. Henley has a great plan for that."

"Security is critically important." Henley glanced at Stephano trying not to be dismissive. "Each of the crevices will be protected by invisible infrared beams controlled by a security employee. If any piece is removed from its crevice before the beam is turned off, an alert will be sent to the iPhones of the employees, and the front door will lock discreetly."

Henley stole a glance at Andrea, who was leaning back in his chair, his hand stroking his beard, his eyes dancing. "What's your plan for lighting the jewelry?" His voice was deep and comforting, almost encouraging. She liked him more every time she worked with him.

"The lighting is one of my favorite parts. I think you'll love it." She put up another drawing. "Each crevice will have its own lighting tailored just for that single piece of jewelry. Different colors of light will amplify each type of gem. Perhaps a slight pink glow for accentuating rubies, while topaz will have gold undertones. The lighting will be controlled by an app on the iPhone so it can be customized with a tap."

Andrea was still stroking his beard. "That will emphasize and enhance the specific assets of each piece."

"Exactly." Henley nodded. "I want the customer to think of shopping at Scavo Jewelry as an experience. We want to lure people in and entice them to discover the jewelry. The nuanced lighting is one more way to pique their curiosity and create that experience customers want these days."

"When people are spending the kind of money this jewelry costs, they want to examine it under a bright light so they can scrutinize it." Stephano was still marching around the conference room. "How do you plan for that to happen with your lighting scheme?"

"She's got that covered too, Stephano. She's thought of everything." Brett smiled and flourished his hand at Henley like a ringmaster.

Henley shot a glance at Brett, not sure whether to be offended or grateful.

"Even though I am intrigued by this, Stephano does have a point. People will want to examine the piece of jewelry carefully before buying it," Andrea said.

"Yes, of course. When a customer chooses something, an associate will remove it from the crevice and display it at a table in an adjoining room." Henley flashed a drawing of the adjoining room on the wall. "This room will have the same low lighting so it doesn't startle people. There will be a long table polished to a glorious shrine made from an ancient tree that has fallen and been recovered. Industrial grade lighting on flexible cables mounted will be under the table. The associate will simply pull the light over the table and allow the customer to view the piece under the light. The light will be intense but narrow so it will only focus on that piece. When they are finished, the light will be returned to a slot under the table."

"See, told you," Brett said. "She's thought of everything."

Andrea walked around the room studying the drawings projected on the wall. "I like it." There was a bright energy in his bearing. "I like the mix of technology with the fundamental geological elements of the earth. It's an intriguing contrast. I'm very pleased with what you've done."

"I'm thrilled you like it," Henley said. "It will be the most extraordinary jewelry store in the city. The proper home for your jewelry."

When the meeting was over, Stephano and Brett left the room together. Henley overheard a bit of a conversation about a restaurant she'd been to with Hunter. It was a pretentious place she had to admit. Andrea lingered at the door of the conference room and put his hand on Henley's arm.

"Thank you for your work. This project is important to me. It's going to be a tribute, so it needs to be very special. I also want to thank you for handling Stephano so gracefully. His response to your designs was unacceptable. I'll have a talk with him."

"He did seem to have a negative attitude. I'm not sure I could have said anything he would have approved of."

"He's good friends with the man at the firm who originally worked on this project. He was angry about it being taken away from them and argued quite forcefully to keep it there. If you fail, then he can say he was right, and I was wrong," Andrea said. "Second sons always have a lot to prove, especially in Italian families. He never felt he was as important as his older brother."

"That's a lot of pressure on me." Henley smiled and patted Andrea's arm.

"Nothing that you can't handle from what I saw today. You're very talented."

"This project is the most interesting of my career," Henley said. "Thank you for your confidence in me. I'm honored you choose me to work on it. Really, it means so much to me that you liked my work and trusted me with this project. I can't thank you enough."

"When this project is over, you will come to Italy and stay with my wife and me. She will cook for you, and we'll relax and laugh. Yes?"

"Thank you. I'd love to visit you and your wife." Henley's heart felt tight in her chest as she thought of his wife and family and imagined what it would be like to have a family like that.

"Perhaps I'll introduce you to a nice Italian man. Unless you already have a boyfriend? You could bring him along. He would be welcome too."

He winked at her.

"WHAT WAS THAT? What in the hell happened in there?" Henley turned on Brett the second the door to her office closed.

"Henley, I don't know what you're talking about. They loved the idea. The meeting was great. We had a great tag team approach going. You got the old guy rocking along with the design. He was eating out of your hand. And I got his kid under control. Together we were unstoppable." He put out his fist. She turned her back to him.

"Did you change the meeting time?"

"No. Hell, no. I got a phone message that the time changed. I assumed you got the same call. It didn't even dawn on me that you didn't."

"Who called you?" Henley faced him, eyes blazing, fists on hips.

"I don't know. I didn't pay attention to who left the message."

"And you just went ahead with the meeting without me?"

"What did you want me to do? Cancel it after they were already here? I slow walked it to give you a chance to get there."

She glared at him. "Where did you get the presentation?"

"Your laptop, of course."

"You took it off my laptop?"

"Yeah. So what? What's the big deal? Everyone at the firm has access to everyone's work. I don't understand why you're so upset."

"Did you change anything?"

"Of course not. I just uploaded it to my laptop so I could present it."

"Okay. I guess it all turned out okay." Henley's posture relaxed.

"Okay? It was great. You should be pumped. We work so well together. We were like pistons in an engine firing on command. It was like...uh...I don't know...I don't mean to embarrass you, but it was like great sex. Don't you think?"

She had to admit that it had gone really well. And yeah, they were good together. With a bit of a smile, she said, "I certainly won't go that far, but it did go well."

"Henley, I'm sorry about what happened. Is there some way I can make it up to you?"

CHAPTER NINE

THE SECOND HENLEY walked through the door Bella made a leap for her. Henley caught her midair and snuggled her squirmy body.

"Bella baby. My sweet baby," Henley murmured, gently kissing her little light-bulb-shaped head. "My love. I'm so glad to be home."

She carried Bella up the steps to her bedroom and set her on the rug where she watched as Henley changed into blue jeans with embroidered flowers up the sides and tugged on her boots.

"Today was sort of a crappy day, Bella, but we're going to do something fun tonight. Should we go for a walk? Do you want to go see Quinn and Claudia? It's going to be a celebration."

Bella wagged her tail with so much enthusiasm her little feet almost lifted off the floor.

"First, let's put on the new sweater Auntie Quinn bought for you."

Bella squirmed and wiggled as Henley pulled the sweater over her head. Just as Henley successfully got one foot through the armhole in the sweater, and moved to the next, Bella pulled the first foot back out. Finally, after several failed attempts, Henley smoothed the sweater down Bella's long body.

"Bella, you are gorgeous. You could be a model. Imagine a dog sweater in cashmere. Only your Auntie Quinn would think of that. Maybe she will put you in one of her runway shows. Shall we go show her how adorable you are?"

Bella rolled onto her back for a belly rub.

———

BELLA SPOTTED Quinn and Claudia halfway down the block and took off running, pulling the leash from Henley's hands. Quinn crouched down holding her arms out, and Bella dove into her.

"Bella, you're a beautiful girl." Quinn kissed Bella's head as Bella tried to cover her with kisses. "You look amazing. Who gave you such a gorgeous sweater? Somebody who loves you. Such pretty pink cashmere for such a pretty girl. I saw this on my last trip to Italy and knew it would be perfect for you."

Turning to Henley, who had run down the street after Bella, she said, "I think she likes me better than you. Is it okay if I take her home with me?"

"Anything I have is yours, *except* her." Henley laughed, gathering Bella from Quinn.

The air was crisp, but they were cozy next to the restaurant's outdoor patio heaters. Bella sat on Henley's lap, draping her long body over the crook of Henley's arm and putting her little feet on the table so she could be part of the discussion, even cocking her head to Quinn and to Claudia in order to follow their conversation.

"You look frazzled. Everything okay?" Claudia asked.

"It wasn't a good day. I had an important meeting today and everything went to hell. The time got changed, but I didn't get the message, and they started without me," Henley said. "One of the clients hates me, but the top guy—who happens to be his father—seems to really like me. He acts like we've known each other for a long time, which feels a little odd."

"Maybe he's looking for a *lovah*." Quinn used her special lover voice.

"Nah. He invited me to come to Italy to meet his wife."

"Oh, kinky. Even I wouldn't do that."

"Stop. That's not what he meant. I don't want to talk about it tonight. We have some celebrating to do."

The waiter hustled over with menus. He set a dog biscuit and a small bowl of water by Bella.

"You're so kind." Henley smiled at him and then at Bella. "Bella, look what he brought you."

"Would you like me to pour the champagne now?" The waiter set up an ice bucket.

Claudia nodded to him.

"It's a celebration." Quinn lifted her arms to the stars, threw her head back and shouted, "Thank you, universe."

"I'm so proud of you, Quinn," Henley said.

"Tell us how it happened," Claudia said.

"Give us all the details. Every little thing," Henley added. "Who called? What'd they say? Did you scream? Did you cry? Everything. Spill."

"I was in the shower when one of the Nordstrom buyers called. I jumped out and almost broke my neck on the wet floor as I grabbed a towel with one hand and the phone with the other. She said they'd take every single piece from the spring line. She was blasé about it, sort of disinterested and robotic. It was nothing to her but everything to me. I wanted to scream, but I managed to remain calm until she got off the phone. Then I danced. I danced all over the loft like we used to do in Jamaica when I was a kid, delirious manic dancing. At some point the towel got lost, but I continued to dance. I don't know if anyone saw in my windows, but if they did, I hope they smiled at the joy." She lifted her arms to the sky again. "*Woo-woooo.*"

"If anyone was watching, there's no question they smiled at you dancing naked." Henley laughed.

"Your loft has floor-to-ceiling windows, with no curtains. I'm sure you had an audience in seconds. Have you checked YouTube?" Claudia asked. "I'll bet it was uploaded in minutes. You probably have a million hits by now. You should monetize it."

Henley looked at Quinn, pointed to Claudia and nodded her head in emphatic agreement. "What she said."

"Just imagine walking into that gorgeous new Nordstrom in Columbus Circle and riding the elevator up to the floor with the fancy women's clothing." Henley's hushed tone was full of dramatic anticipation. "The escalator moves slowly up and up and up. As it reaches the top the clothes come into view. There's a sign. 'Q by Quinn Design,'"

"Racks stuffed full of clothes with your label," Claudia said.

"You're going to be a star," Henley squealed. Bella tilted her head and gave Henley little kisses on her chin.

"I am a star. I will be a superstar," Quinn corrected.

"I can see customers fighting over the Q by Quinn Design." Claudia laughed. "With fistfights over the last red dress."

"To Quinn, my brilliant, talented, naked dancing friend who has always been destined to greatness." Henley touched her glass to the other two glasses with a tiny resonating clink.

Holding out her glass, Claudia said, "To my friend who will give us astounding discounts and get us into the fashion shows with the best seats next to celebrities."

"Thank you, my dearest friends who make my life so wonderful. It means so much more to me to be able to share this with you." Quinn took a drink of her champagne.

"Love you both." Henley swiped at tears running down her face.

"Stop it. This is joyful," Quinn said.

"These are happy tears." Henley stroked Bella's head as Bella tried to lick her face. "Q still makes me laugh though, Quinn. It makes me think of James Bond."

"Will secret agent things be sewn into the clothes?" Claudia asked.

"There will be some surprises." Quinn tipped the last of the champagne from her glass into her mouth and nodded to the waiter. "Another one of these." She threw her arms up in the air again. People turned and smiled at the women.

"To add another little bit of joy, I saw the rooftop garden with..." Henley waggled her eyebrows at Quinn. "Mr. Pierre Comtois. Fantastic."

"The garden was fantastic?"

"Pierre is fantastic." Henley stretched the word out like taffy. "And he had a million questions about you."

"I'm sure you told him I am fantastic."

"Of course."

TWO HOURS and two bottles of champagne later, the waiter cleared the plates and dropped off the bill.

"Quinn, I have a favor to ask," Henley said.

"Of course, anything for you."

"Could you keep Bella this weekend? I'm going to Montauk."

"Montauk? It's after Labor Day. Why are you going to Montauk?" Quinn asked.

"We always go to the Hamptons together," Claudia said. "And why are you going all the way to Montauk? There's nothing going on out there this time of the year."

Henley stroked Bella's long back as she snuggled into the crook of her left arm.

"Henley?" Claudia said.

"I'm going with G," Henley murmured.

"You're what?" Claudia pushed her chair back, scrapping it against the cement.

"It's okay, Claudia. Sit down. She didn't say that. Did you, Henley? We just both misunderstood. Say it again," Quinn zinged her. "Go ahead. We're listening."

"Stop." Henley held up her hand. "He's a good guy. You don't know him."

"No. Say that again," Quinn scoffed. "I want you to hear what it sounds like. Just listen to yourself. Say it again, slowly and clearly."

"Maybe you will hear how ridiculous you sound," Claudia added.

"I'm going with him. He's a good man. I can feel it."

"A good man?" Claudia scoffed. "I've heard that before. You have terrible taste in men. Always have."

"Stop it, Mouse. You're being mean," Henley said.

"We'd rather be mean than have you dead with body parts strewn all over a Montauk beach. I'm serious, Hen. This is no joke." Quinn voice rose in degrees as she spoke. "What do you even know this about guy? You said you weren't going to talk to him again."

People at other tables stopped talking and leaned in to listen. A few grabbed their phones to have them at the ready.

"Quinn, I love you. I'm touched by how much you love me, but he's not going to kill me. You're being dramatic."

"He may or may not kill you. He probably won't, but it's a ridiculous risk to take with this guy you don't even know. If he doesn't kill you, what about breaking your heart?" Claudia asked. "Your track record with men is in the toilet."

"Thanks for that image. I'm very aware of my track record. I manage to beat myself up about it often. The other night at dinner Izzy said mistakes are the quickest way to learn a lesson. It's possible I've learned from my mistakes, and I won't make them again." Henley offered a small hopeful beseeching smile first to one friend and then to the other.

"If you had learned from your mistakes, you wouldn't be going off to a beach with a man you don't know but who you believe is a good man." Claudia hit the word *believe* with a full punch of sarcasm, slashing her hand through the air as she spoke.

"Ditch Plains," Quinn said. "That's the name of one of the big beaches out there."

"Great!" Claudia practically shouted. "The perfect place for him to ditch your body parts. Ditch Plains. Can't make that stuff up."

"The thing I can't understand is why you would go with him. You hardly know him. You're not a couple. Are you going to stay in the same room with him?" Quinn asked.

"I'm going because I'm his energy."

"What?" Claudia sputtered. "His energy? What the eff does that mean?"

"You're his energy?" Quinn said. "He's going to suck the life force from your body like in some bloody science fiction movie?"

"More like some freaking *Criminal Minds* TV show." Claudia smacked her hands on the table. "You're going away to a deserted beach with a guy you barely know—who we haven't even met, I will add—because he wants your energy?"

"I'm afraid not. You're not going." Quinn's eyes burrowed into Henley. "I'm going to lock you in your room."

"It's an art thing," Henley said with forced calmness. "When I first met G, he was working on a massive painting. The canvas stretched twenty feet long and ten feet high. It was impressive, but there was something missing. He told me my presence that night gave him the energy to see it, to envision what it would become. The next time I was there, it was magical."

"It was magical," Claudia mocked. "G....what a pretentious shit. G, he's so important he only needs an initial. Poser."

"Stop it with the art stuff. This is about a man, not art. You don't know this guy. You...don't...know...this...guy." Quinn slowly and clearly enunciated each word.

"I'm going," Henley said. "He asked me for help with his art, and I want to help. I'm honored he asked for my help. He's an artist." She looked from one friend's stony face to the other. "I want to be involved."

Both women stared at her in silence.

"Quinn, I would appreciate it if you would keep Bella for the weekend."

"I could sew some pepper spray into the collar of a Q Design shirt for you." Quinn heaved a long and loud sigh.

"I love you." Henley put her hand on Quinn's arm. "I'll be careful. Don't worry."

"We're not done talking about this," Claudia said. "I could rent the beach house next door."

SIMON PLOPPED down on a bar stool next to Henley, who was twirling the ice in her drink. Only two Simonettes adorned the bar. They both swiveled in their chairs to study the situation that was unfolding with their favorite bartender.

"Where's the rest of the thrilling trio?" he asked.

"They're not talking to me." Henley sighed dramatically and twirled more ice.

"The universe must be out of alignment," Simon said. "The sun is going to rise in the west tomorrow."

"I'm going away for the weekend with the artist I told you about," Henley blurted out without looking at him.

Simon scowled at her. "Why would you do that?"

"You too?" Henley heaved an even louder sigh.

"Hen, what do you know about him?"

"I got all that and more from Claudia and Quinn. It's about the painting."

"What about the painting? Are you posing for him?"

"You're going to laugh."

"Probably."

"I'm his energy for painting. It's like being a muse."

"And Claudia and Quinn gave you crap for being his muse?"

"They did." Henley's voice rose in indignation. She tilted her head toward Simon, a small hopeful smile tipping the corners of her mouth.

"Hen."

Her smile faded.

"Come on. Doesn't that sound like a pretty impressive pickup line? I may become a painter so I can use that line."

"You're going to use a pickup line?" She scrutinized him and instantly wished she hadn't said it. It was an unfair question.

"This isn't about me," he whispered.

She saw the hurt in his eyes and draped her arm around his shoulders.

"Of course it's not. I'm sorry. I don't know how to explain it. There's something about his painting that moves me. I want to be part of it."

"Hen, listen to yourself. The painting emotes? Really? Way over the top."

"I don't understand what's happening, but I can't let it go. I can't let him go without trying…I don't know…to understand him."

"This isn't safe. Maybe I could go with you? Where are you staying? I could get a room next to yours."

An expression of shock flushed up his face as a thought obviously bloomed in his mind.

"Wait a minute. Are you staying in a hotel? Are you staying in the same room? You're not a couple, are you? Henley, I just don't get this."

His shoulders bunched, and he walked around the bar where he slammed glasses down on the brush scrubbers. Henley quickly got up and went to him. She laid her hand gently on his arm, afraid the glasses might crack. He turned those topaz eyes to her, and she melted. He could always do that to her. The depth of his love and compassion filled her with warmth.

"It's okay, Simon. I promise, it's okay. I understand your concern. I'm not sleeping with him. He rented a house. I'll have my own bed. We're not a couple, but we might become one. I don't know. He isn't going to hurt me, at least not physically. If I get my heart broken again, it's a chance I'm willing to take. It's not like it would be the first time. Prior experience confirms I will live through it."

"What if you can't live through it this time?"

His expression was so sorrowful, she instantly wrapped her arms around him and whispered, "I can live through it. We all can live through a broken heart. Hearts mend. Hearts are stronger after they've been broken." She nodded to him. "They are, Simon. I promise."

They stood together behind the bar, her arms around him, his hand still on a glass.

"Can I change the subject? I need to talk to you about something else." It took several long moments before she released him.

He set the glass back on the side of the sink. "Anything for you. You know that."

"Yesterday I had an important meeting about that jewelry store project I told you about. First, I was late for the meeting, and when I got there a guy I'm working with—Brett—was giving my presentation."

"You're always early. How'd that happen?"

"I'm not sure, but I suspect the client's son changed the time. His name's Stephano. He wanted another firm to handle the project, so he wants to make me look bad. Brett says he doesn't remember who called him about the time change. He says he figured they also called me."

"That's plausible." Simon nodded his head, deep in thought.

"Yeah, but it's also plausible that Brett and Stephano are working together to make me look bad. Or I'm paranoid."

"What's your gut say?"

"My gut doesn't know. Brett always acts like he's a team player, but I'm not sure if I'm on his team. The other thing that worries me is he took the presentation from my firm laptop. The children's museum project for the Calder Prize is on that laptop—all my design notes and drawings and my research. So he could have seen that stuff when he took the presentation. I don't know if he opened the files. Can you figure out if he looked at them? I can't believe I'm even asking you this. But the whole thing doesn't make sense. He probably didn't look at them, but I don't want to take chances."

"How'd he get into your laptop? Does he have your password?"

"It's a business laptop. We all share a password. My boss thinks it will boost creativity and get us to work together and exchange ideas—that kind of thing. We're encouraged to look at other designs in progress and offer comments or criticisms. In reality no one does it."

"So you don't keep your personal stuff on it? None of those nude shots I took of you?"

"Ha. You wish."

"Oh, did I dream that?" At last the smile was back on that face Henley adored.

"I shouldn't have put my stuff for the Calder Prize on it, but I never thought of anyone actually looking at it."

"Leave your laptop with me, and I'll figure it out by the time you get back from Montauk. I'll be able to tell you if he opened those files and if he copied them. About the artist guy, we're all just worried. So give me all the details. Are you taking the jitney?"

"Yeah."

"Then give me the jitney times, the place you're staying, the artist's phone number, when you're leaving and when you're coming back." Simon grabbed an order pad from behind the bar and dropped it on the bar next to Henley with a pen.

"Okay, fine. I'll text you." Henley pushed the order pad away. "I have to send the details to Claudia and Quinn anyway."

"Promise to text me a few times a day, and I'll keep track of you. If there's a problem, I'll come out there and beat him to death with his paintbrushes."

CHAPTER TEN

"This is a quite a bus," G said as they made their way down the wide aisle and lifted their bags into the rack above the seats. "I don't understand why it's called a jitney though. It looks like a bus to me. What does the word *jitney* mean?"

"I'm not sure. Since it's going to the Hamptons, maybe they thought *bus* sounded too plebeian." Henley sunk down into the soft plush seats next to him.

"Have you been on the jitney before?"

"Many times. Claudia, Quinn and I rented a house in Southampton for several summers. We always took the jitney out because driving's such a pain. We didn't usually go all the way out to Montauk though."

"I've heard about the crazy parties at the summer houses. Did you throw bashes at the house you rented?"

"Absolutely. It was a blast. We invited friends to come out, and they invited friends who invited friends. Most of the time we didn't even know most of the people who showed up. I probably had the most fun when it was the three of us and our friend Simon. The last year we rented a house in Southampton we tried to keep it small, but somehow the word kept getting out. At the last party we threw someone got sick in the pool. Oh, and someone else got high and thought it would be funny to break lamps. People were sleeping all over the place, on the floor, on couches and they weren't very, um... modest, let's say. I guess it just got old. That's when we stopped renting a house."

The jitney tottered as it maneuvered its way through twelve lanes of traffic on the Brooklyn-Queens Expressway. This part of the trip made Henley's stomach queasy. For some reason the jitney always took the outside lane of the overpasses that were stacked on top of each other and crisscrossed the expressway in Queens. The swaying made her feel like the jitney would fall over the railing onto the road below. Her stomach settled as soon as they reached the flat road running across Long Island to the very end that was Montauk.

As G stared out the window, Henley studied him. He was wearing a black long-sleeve pullover with the sleeves pushed up to his elbows. She knew from her many shopping trips with Quinn it was made from a top-quality pima cotton. It fit him precisely as it should have. She recognized the little skull patch on his faded black jeans because Simon had a pair like them. Quinn got Simon a deal on them because they were insanely expensive. She resisted the temptation to run her hand along his leg. His profile was a little scruffy. The kind of scruffiness that takes a lot of effort to appear effortless. She leaned her head back, closed her eyes and within minutes was lost in a daydream in which she felt that scruffy beard rough against her bare skin.

THE COTTAGE WAS TINY, but there was a wonderful big porch. There was no yard, one step off the porch was into sand. Henley set her bag on the blue-and-white-striped couch in the front room. She could see into the closet of a kitchen containing a small white refrigerator and a two-burner white stove. G opened the door to the single bedroom where two double beds were covered with simple patchwork quilts. Henley suppressed competing emotions of relief and disappointment. This wasn't anything like the fancy party houses she had rented with Quinn and Claudia. It was lovely in its simplicity.

She decided to leave her bag on the couch and walked straight out to the ocean's edge. The wind tousled her hair, blowing it first into her eyes then straight back. It seemed to blow from every direction. She was standing on a tip of land surrounded on three sides by ocean. For a moment the ground felt shaky, and she had the light-headed feeling of falling. A few deep breaths helped her equilibrium return, and she felt silly for having vertigo while on solid ground.

Standing a few steps to her side with his hands in his pockets, G peered down the beach.

"It goes on for miles," he said. "I can't even see the end of it."

"I think it's something like 110 miles of beach. We're at the end of the earth, sorta."

"I wanted to come because it's remote. I think it will be inspiring."

"When we staying in Southampton, we would usually come out here for the day. There were always wall-to-wall people and bumper-to-bumper cars. After Labor Day the crowds are gone."

"I was hoping it would be deserted so nothing distracts me from my work. Let's get groceries. I'll cook for you."

"What's on the menu for tonight?" Henley asked.

"You'll like it."

"I will? How do you know?"

"I just know. I know you."

Henley started to object, started to tell him it was presumptuous to say he knew her when they had just met, but shut her mouth when she realized she had told to her friends that exact thing.

Instead she said, "You apparently know how to cook."

"I just might surprise you."

HENLEY LICKED one side of her fork and then the other, not caring if he found her manners atrocious. At least she successfully fought the urge to lick the bowl, pushing it out of reach on the small wooden table they'd moved from the dining room to the porch. Chaise lounges turned the long way beside the table served as their chairs. A chill breeze coming in off the ocean caused Henley to wrap her sweater tighter.

G drew the ocean air into his lungs and released it in a low mournful whistle.

"That's bad luck," Henley said.

"Whistling?"

"At night. Whistling at night draws evil spirits. That's what Quinn says. There's a Wordsworth poem about it too. 'He the seven birds hath seen, that never part. Seen the Seven Whistlers in their nightly rounds.'"

"What's that mean?"

"It means death is coming when the seven birds put a person in their sights."

"You know that poem by heart?" G turned to look at her.

"Poetry's a thing in my family. For Quinn it's a British thing that whistling at night foretells death. We used to tease her about it at boarding school."

"Is she British?"

"Jamaican. So sorta."

Moonlight shimmered on the waves rolling up on the beach towards the cottage. Seabirds talked in the distance.

"You were right." Henley sighed.

"Yes?"

"That was the best pasta I have ever tasted. Delicate but yet full of distinct flavors. I could have been influenced by the setting, eating out here on the porch with the ocean whooshing just feet away, the moon, the cool breeze. All that."

"It would have been good anywhere. My mother is an extraordinary cook. She taught me well."

"Not lacking in confidence, huh?" Henley teased.

"I'm confident about the things I'm confident about. I'll tell you the secret to pasta. It doesn't have to be fresh, but it has to be excellent quality if it's dried. Boil the pasta until it's just al dente then sauté it in the red wine."

"I've never heard of that. Your mom taught you that? Tell me about her."

"Maybe some time, but now there's dessert."

"Noooo," Henley moaned. "I can't eat another bite. I'm not sure I can get up from this chair after that big bowl of pasta."

"The pasta satisfies, but dessert will bring you joy. I promise, *cara*."

AFTER DESSERT, they turned the lounge chairs to face the ocean and sat together in silence. The stars slowly dotted the darkening sky then exploded filling the darkness with sparks of light.

"There are many more stars here than in Manhattan. When my mom died, my aunt told me she was in the stars watching over me. The nighttime sky gives me a sense of something bigger than me."

"No lights here to drown out the stars," G whispered.

"I think we should organize a lights-out project for the city. If everyone shut off every light for fifteen minutes or maybe even an hour, the stars could come back. Children would be in awe."

"I would be in awe," G murmured.

"Hmmm. We should figure out how to do that. Look...there's Jupiter." Henley pointed to a spot in the southern sky. "And there's Mars. They're in conjunction."

"Is the moon in the seventh house?"

"No," Henley answered before she realized he was joking. "You know that old song? If you're not careful, I'll sing 'Aquarius' for you, and you'll be sorry."

"I'd like that."

"You would not. You'd bury your head in the sand and scream to block out the racket. That is one thing I can say with absolute certainty. Dogs howl when I sing. I can't believe I'm going to say this since I'm stuffed, but that chocolate thing is so delicious I need one more bite. There's something about it that's going to make me crave it even in my dreams."

"The drizzle makes it unforgettable. I whipped a bit of balsamic vinegar into Amarena sour cherries. Here, give me your plate."

He returned with a sliver of chocolate torte on the small plate, sat next to her on the lounge chair, cut a forkful of the dessert and offered it to her. Her eyes on his, she leaned forward and took the offered bite. The chocolate was dense and smooth on her tongue. G placed his left hand on the lounge chair just behind her back so she leaned against his arm. He bent forward. His lips touched hers.

Henley felt the calm she knew from yoga class when life slowed to a stop and tranquility streamed through her body. She stroked her hand up his back.

"That was delicious." He smiled at her as he got up from the chair. "*Cara*, we must go to sleep now. I have a lot of work to do in the morning."

She could hear dishes clanking in the sink. The refrigerator door opened and closed. The facet turned on and off. She should clean up since he cooked, but she didn't.

She retreated to the bedroom, the bedroom with two beds, and sat on the edge of one of them. Her bed, she thought. In spite of all the things she said to Claudia and Quinn about this being for the art, she had to admit feeling disappointed.

She texted Quinn and Claudia, "No worries. Separate beds. Only art. LU."

Rummaging in her bag, she bypassed the deep rose colored silk chemise tucked into the side pocket and pulled out a long white nightgown.

"How very proper," she muttered under her breath.

A CHUBBY PENCIL dangled from his fingers as he watched the birds dance on the wet sand. He'd been up for hours. He could tell himself he'd gotten up because he wanted to catch the moment when the sun crested the horizon and bathed everything in gold and shades of purple and pink, but the truth was he couldn't stay in the same room with her any longer. This trip was a mistake. He'd known it was a dangerous temptation, but he'd taken the risk anyway. She'd opened something in him that allowed him to paint again. The way he used to in Italy. He'd buried himself for the last six years pretending to paint but painting only crap. Painting crap but not able to stop. Hoping with every blank canvas to find himself again.

Then she appeared at his window in the middle of the night like she'd been transported to him—delivered to him from some god. She not only woke the creative spirit, but other feelings too. Feelings he couldn't face. Feelings he had buried and wanted to keep buried. Lying in the bed next to hers, he'd watched her sleep with her right hand tucked under her chin, her hair messy across the pillow, her lips slightly open. The outline of her body was distinct under the sheet, causing sparks to circuit through his body like pinpricks in his limbs as if they were trying to awaken from a long sleep. When she cried out in the night, he had jumped to comfort her only to realize she was still asleep. He couldn't stay in the room so close to her and not reach for her, so he came outside to sketch. He sketched the golden dawn and the ocean, the sand and the birds, but mostly he sketched her face. From the memory etched in his mind.

He was finishing another sketch, one of her eating pasta the night before, delight filling her face when the cottage door banged open, and she walked to the ocean's edge. She planted her feet in the sand and stretched her arms to the sun.

He watched for a few minutes, then shouted, "Hungry for lunch?"

She turned, her hands shielding her eyes, searching for him

before finally finding him at a table on the side of the house. "Lunch?" The birds out chattered her words, so she walked closer. "What about breakfast?"

The sun caught golden glints in her hair. He was irrevocably undone by the prim white nightgown covering her from neck to ankle. Backlit by the sun, the gauzy cotton allowed him to see the curves of her body through the whispery fabric. An ache started in his belly and burst through his body like a gasoline trail struck with a match. He needed to smother that fire. He had to keep her at a distance. He could not have her. Maybe they should leave. He could make up some excuse. She was looking at him, waiting for him to answer. What was the question again? He couldn't remember what she had asked.

She tilted her head. "What about breakfast?" She was still shielding her eyes from the sun.

Oh. Yes. That's what she'd asked. He needed to answer, but he had no words. It was minutes before his brain and tongue connected. "Breakfast at one o'clock?"

"It's one? I haven't slept that late since, well since, I don't know. Maybe never. How about breakfast for lunch? I'll cook for you."

As she walked into the house, he watched the wind blow her hair straight up and caress the fabric around her legs and her waist. Her face was still lined with sleep. He imagined his hands sliding over her body, across her hips, up to her breasts and so much more and tightly closed his eyes to stop the dream. The nuances drove him to corral his tools into a box and walk to the water's edge. If she had seen the expression on his face, she would have known exactly what he was thinking. He couldn't allow that to happen.

———

AFTER HENLEY PUT eggs into a pan of water and set it to boil, she went into the bedroom and slipped into a beautiful cerulean sundress. The front of the dress was square across her chest—pretty and discreet. But the back...well the back, that was sex, pure unadulterated sex. It was bare all the way down to her tailbone showing her curves with triangle cut-ins at the sides to further emphasize her waist. It was made from long strips of silk gathered at the waist, each strip of fabric was about four inches wide with a one-inch strip of lace in between. The lace was sheer enough to allow the hint of a body underneath but narrow enough to ensure only a hint. Quinn called the design "subtly sexy." Quinn certainly didn't know she had brought it on this trip. The white cashmere sweater with small pearl buttons Henley added on top of it was soft and brushed against her bare back causing her nerve endings to flutter. The sweater would have to come off if she wanted to show off the dress.

She combed her hair and brushed her teeth quickly enough to get back to the kitchen just as the eggs reached a rolling boil. After putting two pieces of the rosemary bread from the night before in the toaster, she sliced a couple of tomatoes and arranged a few on each plate. The skirt of the dress swished as she cooked making her feel sexy and not in a subtle way. The memory of the chocolatey kiss was certainly on her mind. As she sprinkled the toast with olive oil, her phone dinged. And dinged again. And again. Quite a few texts from Claudia, Quinn and Simon, each a little more urgent than the last, filled the screen.

She tapped out, "Slept in. Yes, by myself. Making smashed eggs for breakfast. LU."

"Ugh. At least I know there won't be any romance after you feed him that," came the instant reply from Claudia.

Henley peeled the hard-boiled eggs and set them on the toast. With the prongs of the fork she cut the eggs into pieces and smashed them into the crevices of the toast. After a sprinkling of salt and a liberal dousing of pepper, she carried the plates to the porch where G had repositioned the small table. She went back for glasses of orange juice.

When she got back, G was studying the plates.

"*Che cosa?*"

"It's called Smashed Egg Extraordinaire. My mom made it for me when I was a kid."

He gingerly cut off a piece of the sodden eggy toast. "It's...curious."

"With that encouragement I shall send in my application to the Cordon Bleu." She laughed, falling into an elaborate curtsy.

"There's a lot of pepper. You said your mom made this?"

"Pepper is an essential ingredient. She got the recipe from my grandma who I never met."

"There's a recipe for this?"

"Funny. You haven't even tasted it. You might love it."

He dangled a mushy piece of bread from his fork. "Did your mom cook other things besides this, uh, what did you call this?"

"Mom didn't cook, but I always felt lucky because we got cookies from a stupendous bakery. We got take-out so often I use the phone number for our favorite Chinese restaurant as my password. But she always made dinner seem special by using good china and cloth napkins. She even put candlesticks and a vase of flowers on the table."

"What'd she do?"

"When I was little, she was the principal ballerina for the New York City Ballet, but I don't know much about that part of her life. That all ended when I was really young. Later she built miniature houses and spent long hours in her workshop, so cooking wasn't one of her things."

"Miniature? Like dollhouses?"

"Not dollhouses like the ones for children but small intricate houses, replicas of houses from different eras. Everything she did was true to the era. She built the houses and all the furniture and everything in them, even carving pieces like formal wainscoting, chair railings, balustrades, cornices from pieces of vintage wood she salvaged. I guess you could call her a connoisseur. She had a massive collection of every variety of wood. She's pretty famous for those houses."

"She built little houses, and you build big houses."

"I build buildings. It's not the same." Henley shifted awkwardly on the lounge. After a few moments of silence she said, "What about your family? Are they still in Italy?"

"Yes."

"What part?"

"You know Italy is a boot, yes? I'm from the stiletto." This time he shifted, turning his gaze to the ocean. "Last night you cried out in your sleep and made little whimpering sounds. I tried to talk to you, but you didn't hear me. After several minutes you went back to sleep."

"Sorry." Henley covered her eyes with her hand. "That happens to me sometimes. So embarrassing. I took up yoga and studied breathing techniques to help me go back to sleep. If it happens again, just ignore me. Nights are always hard for me."

"I think that's why I work at night." He paused, his gaze once again drifting to the ocean. "It keeps my mind occupied."

―――――

ON HER WAY back from dropping the breakfast dishes in the kitchen, Henley stopped in the doorway back just a step so he didn't see her. And she watched him. His beige linen trousers were rolled at the bottoms, and his white linen shirt was rolled at the sleeves. Such a superb example of slouchy elegance would have fit right in in Monaco or St. Moritz or the Amalfi Coast. A large sketchpad rested against his thighs as he leaned back on the lounge chair. He was motionless. A charcoal stick dangled from his long fingers. Several minutes later his hand began to move, stroking the paper with a furious energy. She watched as a sketch of her face appeared on the page. Her head was bent, eyes raised, gazing at something in the distance, her hair tossed over her shoulder. She knew the waves were swooshing and the birds were singing, but she didn't hear them because her chattering heart had muffled her hearing.

Watching him secretly was an intrusion into his privacy, and the now familiar feeling of being a voyeur settled over her. As if he could feel her eyes on him, he turned to look at her. Once again, she stepped through a doorway to him.

He offered no resistance when she took the sketchpad and charcoal from his hands and laid them on the table, although his eyes did track her every move. She straddled him, putting a leg on either sides of the lounge chair, and draped her arms around his neck. The skirt of her sundress billowed and flowed around them, covering his legs and falling to the floor.

"*Cara, che cosa?* What is this?" His hands dangled at the side of the chair, his fingers brushing the porch floor.

"Really? You don't know what this is?" She circled his lips with the tip of her finger and kissed him once and again. "No idea?" Her voice was soft and luxurious.

"Are you sure, *cara?*" He drew her body to him but instantly pushed her back. "Wait. No. *Cara*, no. I can't do this."

"You don't want to be with me?" Henley pulled back, a hot flush sweeping up her face. She struggled to stand, but the heel of her sandal caught in a crack on the porch floor, and she couldn't get her foot positioned. She yanked her foot hard, pulling the sandal off and knocking it under the chair.

"Don't think that. This is not about you. You're gorgeous. Any man would want you."

"Just not you." Tears filled her eyes, and she squeezed them shut. She took deep breaths and swallowed hard over and over, but it didn't work and tears fell making the whole awful situation even more embarrassing.

"No, me too. There are just...things...things you don't know. For me it's been a very long time. My life is about my art and nothing else. I can't be with you. I can't be with anyone."

Swiping the stupid tears off her face, she tried to scoot down the lounge chair. She had a plan. Get her phone, call an Uber, get a car, go to the jitney, go home. This man was the last man. The last time. As if she needed another lesson in how bad she was at the crap called romance, this one had done it for all eternity. This qualified as a graduate course in Izzy's stupid school of life lessons.

Her body strained away from him, her muscles taut as she struggled to escape. He tried to draw her to him, but she pulled away. They moved in a slow-motion tango. When he wouldn't release her, she finally raised her eyes to his and instantly stilled. What she saw deep in his eyes was that sorrow she'd seen at his studio. A sorrow she recognized. A pain that was familiar. The kind of pain that enters a person and never leaves. A pain that changes everything. She knew the origins of her own pain but not his. They stared at each other, their breath heavy.

She reached to comfort him and cupped his face in her hands. If she could have taken that pain away from him, she would have done anything, promised anything, given anything. With one hand he swept the hair off her shoulder and slowly kissed her neck as his other hand fumbled with the tiny pearl buttons of the cashmere sweater and slipped it off her shoulders. She gasped as his hand moved along her bare back. Grains of sand on the porch floor dug into the bare soles of her feet. She unbuttoned his shirt and tossed it away onto the sand. He tangled his fingers in her hair warmed by the sun slanting in under the porch roof cutting his face half in shadow and half in light. There were no words. Nothing they needed to say. Their bodies spoke to each other. Their own private language of longing.

They fumbled with clothing—their hunger for each other urgent and volatile. So many sparks ricocheted through her body, she imagined some flying into the air and sizzling in the wet sand. Henley lifted herself and lowered her body down, settling him into her. Feeling him. Learning him. Their bodies melted together, flowed into each other. She leaned forward, touching her forehead to his. Their breathing synchronized, heartbeats joined. And they were still.

Time passed over them. It may have been seconds or minutes or even hours. One of them, or maybe both of them, began a gentle rocking. A quiet lapping like the ebbing tide. The flicker came first. Just a flicker. But it persisted. Quietly. Until one moment it broke into a rebellion of light dancing and weaving to an unheard melody. With the sun high in the sky and the waves rolling out and out, their cries joined together ripping over the ocean.

SITTING on a towel at the ocean's edge, legs crossed in the lotus position, palms upon her knees, Henley tried to center her mind. It was difficult not to slip away into the memory of what happened on the porch since her body ached from him and for him, and she carried his scent on her skin. She tried to follow the instructions from yoga class, acknowledging the thoughts and dismissing them so her mind could clear. But every time she acknowledged one thought and dismissed it, another popped in usually accompanied by images and sensations that sent shudders rippling through her body. She had never experienced anything like that before. Quinn talked about mind-shattering sex, but Henley had never known what she meant. Now it was all she could think about.

The giddy feeling melted into unease. She'd promised—well, actually, she'd sworn—not to get involved with a man. And not to get involved with this man, in particular. She'd just done what she promised herself, and anyone else who would listen, she wouldn't do. She'd trusted her gut about a man. And her gut had been wrong so many times.

Cold waves lapped at her feet, and she scooted back on her towel, repositioning her body before taking a deep cleansing breath. Why was she here anyway? How was she helping with his art? He didn't seem to need her to do anything. Maybe it was just a ruse to get her out here to have sex with her. But that didn't make sense. He hadn't even tried to get close to her. When she made the first move, he resisted.

So he didn't bring her here for sex. Maybe it was for the art. Maybe muses just hang around. She needed a job description. It did seem odd though. Her friends had a point on that. She could tell him she got a text and needed to go back to the city, but the memory of the pain she saw in his eyes stopped that thought before it went very far. She couldn't walk away from him. She wouldn't do that. There was something between them that she couldn't identify but also couldn't deny. And there was that mind-shattering sex to consider. If she got hurt again, she'd just have to add it to her transcript of life lessons. Finally, she granted herself acceptance. She brought her mind back to the center, focused on the sounds surrounding her, the feel of the terry cloth towel under her bare legs, the sun on her shoulders and slipped into a place of serenity.

She didn't notice the sun falling behind the ocean's ledge until water sprayed her warm skin, nudging her back to the present. At the end of the earth, where the land was surrounded by ocean, the sun fell with blazing speed into the water without even a sizzle. This moment was over, and it was time to begin a new one.

Henley grabbed the towel, damp at the edges from the water's reach, and walked to the porch. Pages of charcoal sketches were strewn haphazardly on the porch next to the lounge chair. He startled when she kissed him on the forehead.

"There's a restaurant down the road with an outdoor bar on the beach. Would you like to go get a drink?" She smoothed the curls back from his face and felt herself sink into his haunted eyes.

―――

G STARED out at the dark ocean and the large expanse of white sand Montauk beach. They were the only ones braving the chill ocean wind—everyone else was inside the restaurant. The couches on the stone patio surrounded a fire pit that warmed them, but Henley still snuggled next to him. She traced little circles on the rough fabric of his linen pants sending sensations directly to his center—heart or groin, he wasn't sure. Maybe both. He wanted to put his arms around her and kiss her for hours. He wanted to lose himself in her. He also wanted to get on that bus and go back to the city. He couldn't have her, and he couldn't resist her. Years earlier he'd promised himself he would never love anyone again. He would paint and only paint. And then she appeared in his life. If the gods had sent her, what would happen if he sent her away? Would he still be able to paint without her? He couldn't take that chance. But there couldn't be any more sex. No more sex, he told himself as his erection hardened.

"This is a good rosé. So many of them taste like soda." It was a silly thing to say, but he couldn't think of small talk when his brain was so distracted. Every thought that came to his mind seemed inane.

"This restaurant is known for rosé." Henley kept tracing those little circles on his pants. He wanted to make love to her on that couch in front of that fire. There was no room for any other thought. "It probably doesn't compare to the full-bodied Italian reds you're used to."

"It doesn't have as many layers of complexity, but it's simple and good. Sometimes it's a relief not to think so much, just to enjoy."

"What was it like to grow up in Italy?"

"Good. Great." He didn't look up from the wine glass. He needed to think of something to talk about that didn't include Italy. Maybe he could just kiss her.

"Tell me one good thing."

"Well..." He hesitated. "There was a river behind my parents' house, and every summer they dammed it up to create a swimming hole. Kids came from everywhere to swim. My three best friends practically lived at my house. Their dad, Bastiano, was my dad's best friend. The memory of jumping into that shocking frigid water is so vivid that sometimes I conjure it up so I can relive that time in my life when things were simple and good. We grabbed apples and peaches right off the trees in my mom's orchard."

"That sounds pretty terrific. Claudia's parents have a house at the Jersey shore. That's the only place I ever went."

They sat in silence, lost in thought. It was several minutes before he spoke again.

"At night my mom cooked in a big stone oven on the patio. We used to play hide and seek and tag in the orchard. Sometimes we danced or chased fireflies. My parents would sit on the patio with a glass of wine, watching, always holding hands."

His heart constricted, and he couldn't breathe. He closed his eyes and let the pain wash over him.

"Is the countryside beautiful there?"

He could only nod.

The peace of the evening was broken by shrieks of laughter. A man came up the stairs leading from the beach to the patio with a blonde flung over his shoulders and dropped her legs akimbo on a couch. He glanced at them and broke into a grin.

"Henley," he shouted. "What are you doing in Montauk, and where are your little girlfriends? I have a bill to give to that tiny one. She owes me for a suit."

The man sauntered over to their couch by the fire pit, brushing sand off black linen pants. Only the bottom two buttons of his hibiscus-covered short-sleeved shirt were buttoned.

"Mind if we join you by the fire?" He waved his arm in front of the couches.

"We were just leaving." Henley stood. "Hunter, leave me alone. I don't have anything to say to you."

"Who's your new boyfriend? Should I tell him your secrets?"

"We're leaving."

Hunter stepped in front of Henley, blocking her way into the restaurant. "Maybe I should tell him what to do to make you squeak. I always loved your squeaky 'ahhh...ahhh...ahhh...uhhh...uhhhh.' Or does he already know all about that?"

He turned to G. "Hey, buddy, need any advice on how to please her?"

"I don't know the story here." G stepped in front of Henley. "You shouldn't talk to a woman like that. You need to walk away from her now."

"A woman? Hardly. That's a good one." Hunter snorted. "She isn't a woman. She's just a little girl."

Henley darted around Hunter and into the restaurant. G went after her, catching her outside the front door. He grabbed her hand, stopping her in the center of the dark empty road.

"I don't know what to say. I'm mortified. That was so embarrassing." Her words spilled out in gasps, and she blinked furiously.

He'd buried his emotions for so many years it was a struggle to control them as they rose to the surface. He wanted to smack that pretty boy in the face and throw his stupid Hawaiian shirt in the fire pit. He wanted to take Henley away and protect her, but he also wanted to dive back into his stone fortress where nothing touched him, and he wasn't responsible for anyone.

His eyes caught on her face streaked with tears and drenched in golden moonlight, and his heart stole his breath. He placed his hands on her face and lifted it to him.

He had to choose, and he chose her.

"He's the one who should be embarrassed, not you. I know he's stupid because you are a woman. He behaved like an ass because he knows it too. You are like a nuanced red wine, deep and complex with layers of mystery." He kissed her gently. "Delicious layers of mystery waiting to be discovered. *Mi togli il respiro.*"

She glanced up, her eyes searching his face.

"What does that mean?" Her voice was so soft he had to lean in to hear her over the tide.

"You take my breath away."

"That's beautiful. But I'm such a mess." She hung her head and pulled away walking down the sandy road. "I feel like such a stupid fool."

"In Italy we have a dance you should know."

He stood in the road, waiting.

She stopped. "A dance? Seriously? Now you're making fun of me."

"A dance." He nodded. "It can cure that feeling forever."

She scuffed at the sand with the toe of her sandal. He saw a small smile on her face.

He caught up to her and put his arm around her shoulders. He chose her. He felt his shoulders lift and a smile, a real smile, fill his face.

"Many years ago in Italy we discovered that if a person is bitten by a poisonous spider, they can be saved by dancing the tarantella."

"So it's for spider bites. Not for feeling ridiculous and pathetic."

"The dance is to expel bad things from of your body. It's very fast, so it spins all bad things away. Every evil whirls away. I'll show you how. First you swivel your hips."

"I'm not doing that. You're joking, right? Are you making fun of me?"

"A swivel first and then a shimmy." He held his arms out wide from his body like a director welcoming improvisation. "I'm sure you've got a lovely shimmy, don't you? Show me."

Henley did a little swivel and then a tiny, tentative shimmy.

"That was sad. Barely a shimmy at all. More like a shiver. I know you can do better than that." He took his shoes off, felt the sand squeeze between his toes and dangled them in front of her, daring her to do the same.

Backlit by the gibbous moon, she kicked off her shoes and began to dance.

First she swiveled a bolder swivel then a real shimmy. The sound of the tide crawling back out to the ocean rattled in the distance, and the slightest of ocean breezes tousled Henley's hair. The beach houses were dark and closed for the season, and the road was deserted. They had the whole stage to themselves.

"Better. Now an eight count dance around me." G held out his hand and followed her in a circle. "Good. Now lift your knees like in a big skip and go faster."

Henley laughed and skipped around him. She flung her head back as she threw her arm in the air.

"Now reverse. Faster. You must spin the poison away. Dance fast with extreme urgency. Now twirl. Dance with joy and terror. Joy for life and terror for the poison."

As he watched her dance in the moonlight, feelings he had bottled up for so long coursed through his body with such speed he struggled to breathe. He needed this woman. He wanted her.

Henley's laugh reverberated through the quiet evening as she danced and whirled, the moon creating a perfect spotlight.

"It's time to dance together." He wrapped his arm around her waist and spun her out and back to him. She twirled back into his body and kissed him.

"No kissing," he admonished. "This is important medical treatment."

She danced around him again kicking her legs out with every skip and throwing her arms in the air. She shimmied and gyrated, tempting him with every move, and wiggled her fingers asking him to join. He put his arm around her again, spun her out and away and back again into his arms and covered her mouth with his.

"Now you are free from the poisonous spider venom." His breath tickled her ear, and he set tiny kisses on her neck as he made his way to her mouth. He deepened the kiss, willing her to understand the choice he had made. He chose her. He left his safe fortress for her. He wanted to shout, to laugh, to howl at the moon. He wanted to make love with her for hours and never let her go.

THEY TUMBLED INTO THE CABIN, sandy and out of breath. She took his hand, kissed him and felt his warmth surge through her. He slipped the sweater off her shoulders and reached for the straps of her sundress, but she stepped away from him. She stood in the rays of moonlight that were streaming in the window. Moving fluidly, her eyes on his, she kicked off one of her sandals and then the other. She swept the hair off her shoulder and ran a fingertip down the side of her neck, brushing one sundress strap off on the way. Then the other strap. The dress floated to the floor, just as it always did in the movies. She slipped her hands up her body and cupped her breasts, a smile playing at her lips as she watched his body respond to her.

"*Mi togli il respiro.*" His voice cracked. "I can paint you. I must paint you."

"Maybe some time, but I have other plans for you now." Her sapphire-colored lace panties slid down her legs.

"I must paint you." He left the room.

Henley folded her arms over her breasts. "I don't want to be painted naked. No, please don't." She pulled the quilt off the bed and tugged it around her body.

She was grabbing her clothes from the floor when he returned to the room with a bottle of champagne. He poured one glass and set it on the small wood nightstand.

"No, *cara*." He pulled the quilt from her and dropped it on the floor. "None of that. Don't ever hide your body from me."

He scooped her into his arms and laid her on the bed.

"We're going to study art? *Now?*"

"We are. You are going to be the canvas." Henley tried to imagine what Quinn would do if she found herself lying on a single bed covered with cotton sheets so soft they felt like suede with a man standing over her contemplating her nakedness. The thought flashing through her mind like a neon warning was that she was not, and never would be, Quinn. She rolled onto her side, tucking her arm over her breasts and pulled up her legs. G scrunched his eyes together and scowled.

"You're my canvas. Why are you folding yourself up?"

She stretched her legs out a little and tried again to conjure Quinn. She kept her arm wrapped around her breasts.

He set his iPhone on the nightstand and tapped a button. Violins swelled and were joined by oboes and bassoons and trumpets. Finally, the piano responded with sweet liquid phrases, poignant and joyful.

"I know this piece." Henley's face softened. "It's Mozart's Twenty-First piano concerto."

"We're going to start with one of my favorite artists. Some people think Pollock just splattered paint around the canvas. They say their kid could do it. Pollock's drip paintings are one of the most original types of art."

His unbuttoned shirt hung open, and she could see the defined muscles of his abdomen. The glass of champagne was in his hand.

"Pollock changed the course of art."

He put a fingertip in the champagne then held it over the glass so Henley could see the drops fall into the glass. Her breath staccatoed as her muscles tensed. Her center pulsed with desire.

"Pollock believed that a painting had a life of its own. He thought it was his responsibility to release that life on the canvas. And he liked to work with his canvases on the ground, so this is perfect to have my canvas in bed."

He put his fingertip back into the glass then held it over her chest. One drop clung to his finger and fell, landing on her breast sending little ripples across her skin like a stone thrown in a lake. She tried to wriggle away, but G walked around the bed dotting her skin with champagne triggering ripples everywhere the fizzy drops touched. His movements were slow and contemplative at first, but just like Pollock, became confident and fluid like a dancer, drops swirling and falling as the painting took shape in his imagination.

Pollock painted like the tarantella, Henley realized. She hoped she could retain the thought so she could share it with G later.

Through half-closed eyes she saw him swirl his fingers in the glass and fling his arm in the air like a ballet dancer sending minuscule drips through the air to catch golden moonlight before they sprayed Henley's skin. Her muscles clenched and unclenched in spasms, and she grabbed the sheets in her fists.

"Lovely. This is a beautiful Pollock painting." He stepped back and admired her body. "I'm going to show you a different artist, but first I need a blank canvas."

With the tip of his tongue he slowly circled each breast, licking the champagne from her skin. He worked with slow, deliberate strokes up her belly. Her breath exploded in a gasp and her muscles trembled.

A thought struggled to the level of her consciousness, and she sat up, startling him.

"What?" he asked.

She smiled and lay back on the pillow. She spread her arms open welcoming his lessons. He was giving himself to her in the only way he knew, she realized, through his art, his passion. He was sharing himself and his life through every tranquil stroke and every frantic dot. Once she understood what he was doing, she opened her heart to accept his gift, leaning into his touch, opening her senses to the experience, listening with her body to his story. She heard love and sorrow, heartbreak and joy, fear and loneliness. The depth and value of this gift of himself touched her. She blocked out all other thoughts and opened herself to accept the sensations. She welcomed the touches and strokes, the cold liquid, the tips of his fingertips, the softness of his tongue, and the nips of his teeth. She welcomed every sensation he offered, willingly experiencing each of them, allowing them to build to what she knew would be an ultimate experience.

He told her about Gauguin's theory of synesthesia and explained how Gauguin believed visual art should imply movement. To demonstrate he painted to the music of the concerto as if he were a conductor. He talked about Degas and Rothko, demonstrating on her skin as he talked. After each lesson, he kissed and stroked her body, pushing her just to the point of frenzy and stopping.

"I think this time I'll demonstrate Seurat. Do you want to experience Seurat?"

"Yes," she murmured. "Please let me experience him with you."

He pressed dot after dot of liquid on her eyelids and kissed them away. More dots on her lips and her breasts and her belly, the inside of her thighs, licking each of them away in turn. After dotting the sole of her foot with champagne, he painted a line along the inside arch of her foot with his tongue. She was floating on some plane of existence that she had heard about in yoga class but had never experienced.

"Thank you, Seurat. Pointillism is quite delicious. Who shall we study now?"

"I know who should paint now," Henley murmured. "You."

"Me? Yes, you're right. I should paint now."

Her body shook as he traced the lines in her palm with his tongue.

His wet fingers painted a line down her spine. He drizzled champagne on the flat of her back, and it ran down the sides of her breasts. His tongue brushed up her spine, slowing at each vertebra, teasing the hollows. She rolled onto her back and reached for him.

"Not yet. Soon. This painting isn't quite finished."

He dragged a wet finger from the pulse in her wrist to the center of her elbow where he placed his lips and sucked. Fire shot to her core and sent sparks along her nerve endings. She moaned and pulled the sheets tight in her fists. He stroked champagne along the tender inside of her thigh. Her body rose to meet his fingers.

"The lesson is over. It's time to come inside," Henley whispered. In his eyes she read the emotions that had become familiar to her—longing, then sorrow, always sorrow and what she thought was wariness, but there was something new now, maybe hope, maybe love. With one hand she pulled the tie from his hair, releasing a mass of black curls that fell around his face. She wasn't certain of his feelings, but what she did know was that she would never be able to get enough of him—enough of looking at his face, of feeling his body, of making love with him, and yes, enough of loving him. Henley wrapped her arms around his neck and pulled him to her.

He took his time, teasing and circling her. When he did finally slip inside her, she rocked with the frenzy of the tarantella. He held her body to his, and when she stilled, they began again.

He brought her to frenzy again and again. He finally let himself go, and she felt the final gift of himself. He rocked with shudders, his muscles tensing and releasing as the climax overtook him.

THROUGH THE WINDOW in the little bedroom, they could see black ocean waves tipped gold from the moon. She lay in his arms, their legs tangled on the skinny single bed.

"When did you know you wanted to be an artist?"

"I was born an artist." He paused. "I know that probably sounds pretentious, but it's just who I've always been."

"You never wanted to be a fireman or a doctor?"

"Never. I never thought, 'I want to be an artist.' I *was* an artist. I want to paint like the bird sings."

"That's beautiful." She absently stroked his chest.

"I can't take credit for the words, they're Monet's, but it's what I aspire to."

"How did you get this?" Her finger trailed a red jagged scar that ran under his left nipple and down his side. It was raised and about eight inches long.

"A car accident years ago." He edged away from her body, but she moved with him, keeping her hand on his chest and her legs wrapped around him.

"Where'd that happen?" She kept her voice soft.

"In Italy."

"Were you badly hurt?"

It was several minutes before he answered. "I was cut with broken glass from the window." He paused and his voice dropped. "My sister…my sister was killed."

Henley clasped her hands to her heart. "Oh, my God. I'm so sorry. I didn't know. How old was she?"

"Twenty-two. She was to have been married the following week."

"I'm…I shouldn't have…I…I'm sorry," Henley stuttered.

"Paola was the light of our family. My parents adored her. I adored her." His voice faded like it was sucked away by those golden-tipped black ocean waves and drowned.

"Your parents must have been devastated."

"I have no words to describe their pain."

Henley could feel his heart pound under her hand on his chest. "Do you have other brothers and sisters?"

"One brother."

The pounding in his chest quickened and his muscles tensed. "I can't talk about this anymore. Let me wrap my arms around you and pull your lovely body into mine. I need you to fill my hollows. I want you to fall asleep in my arms, to feel your breath against my skin and your head on my chest."

Henley sighed as she curled into his body, her hand over his heart. The pounding had slowed. "I can do that."

In minutes they were asleep, breathing in unison.

WHEN HENLEY SETTLED into the seat on the jitney, G put his arm around her and almost groaned at how good it felt to feel her body next to his. She fit perfectly against him, melting into his spaces. She tilted her head up to him, so he kissed her and kissed her some more until he felt his body hum and knew he had to stop.

She smiled at him in a way that let him know she had some humming going on too. "Are you happy with the work you got done in Montauk?"

He nodded and rubbed her shoulder with his fingers. "I'll paint from the sketches I made." He noticed a photo on the iPad she had just opened. "What's that a photo of?"

"One of the pieces of jewelry that will be in the store I designed. Isn't it great?"

He nodded. "Do you have some photos of the other jewelry?"

Henley tapped a folder on the screen and handed it to him. He swiped through them pausing at one or two of them and handed it back to her.

"They're nice. I understand what you see in them. Like you said, they're elemental. What's your client's name?"

"Scavo. Andrea Scavo. The business is Scavo Designs. They're from Italy. Do you know them?"

He shook his head. "I don't know that business."

As Henley worked, G leaned his head against the window and stared at some faraway spot as the sun set. Normally, he would have been studying how the orange and yellow rays spilled over the horizon, but instead he was writing his list of never agains:

Never get close to anyone.

Never allow his emotions to escape.

And never—ever—fall in love.

CHAPTER ELEVEN

Henley punched the private code into the panel of the freight elevator in Quinn's warehouse. The door shuddered open and chugged closed behind her. She was anxious to get Bella and to tell Quinn about the weekend and the things she'd discovered. The minute the doors opened on the third floor loft Henley heard Bella's joyous barking. Bella knew her mama had come for her.

Quinn's right arm rested theatrically against the doorframe. Her caftan in a brilliant burgundy silk was struck through with slender threads of gold and flowed around her body. Slits on both sides showed her legs and bare feet.

Bella ran through the door and jumped on Henley.

"Bella, Bella, Bella, I missed you so much." Henley kissed her little head over and over, her laughter filling the foyer as Bella covered her face with sloppy kisses.

"You'd think we beat and starved her the way she's acting—like you're rescuing her from prison." Quinn threw her hands in the air, then glanced at Henley. Studied her. Looked her up and down. And scowled. "You slept with him, didn't you? Damn it, Henley. You did, didn't you?"

"Hello to you too. Yes, Montauk was lovely. No crowds this time of year, and the sky was full of stars. Yes, G did get a lot of work done. Thank you for asking." She stroked Bella's head, tipping her own head back to avoid more of Bella's kisses.

"You did. Didn't you?" Quinn demanded.

"I did. I'm a big girl, Quinn. I can make these choices. It was wonderful. Just so you know I was the one who initiated it. The bedroom had two beds, and the first night we slept in separate beds. He didn't do anything. It was the next day when I—"

"Stop. Stop. Okay, Hen. I'll come around—if he's not an axe murderer, that is. I promise I will, and you can share all the special little details. But not tonight, okay?" Quinn shifted from foot to foot and held out her arm to sweep Henley inside.

"What's going on?" Henley looked up from Bella. "What's the matter?"

Quinn's cat Choo lumbered out from behind one of the loveseats in the loft. Walking slowly and setting each paw down with conscious deliberation, he glanced at Henley with absolutely no interest and curled his lip in disgust at Bella's exuberant display.

"Come sit with me on the couch. We need to talk." Two elaborate damask throws and giant colorful pillows covered the dark green velvet sectional. Quinn patted the spot next to her. When Henley set Bella on the ground, she bounded gleefully over to Choo to share her excitement. Choo stood perfectly still in hopes Bella would mistake him for a piece of furniture, clearly assuming she had the brain of an insect.

"Where'd this table come from? I don't remember it." Henley ran her hand over a coffee table made from a huge stump of petrified wood polished to a high gloss, its crevices inlaid with turquoise. "It's magnificent."

"Dewa sent it to me from Bali."

"Dewa? Which one is that?"

"I bought that gorgeous fabric from him last year."

Henley shrugged and shook her head.

"He's the one with the warm oil scented with hibiscus blossoms."

"Oh, yes." Henley fanned herself. "Hard to forget that story."

"There's something I need to talk to you about. I talked to Izzy."

Henley lowered herself to the couch. Bella jumped up against her legs begging to be picked up. "Why? What about?"

"Since I had Bella, she knew your first stop would be here. She asked me to talk to you."

"What are you talking about? I had dinner with her last week. What's going on?" Bella snuggled as close to Henley's left side as was physically possible as Henley ran her hand down her long body.

"Hen, it's going to be okay. I'm here for you, now and for always. You know that, right?" Quinn put her hand on Henley's shoulder. Tears welled in the corners of her eyes.

"Quinn, you're scaring me. Tell me what's going on right now."

"Izzy's in the hospital." Quinn shifted her weight, visibly struggling for the next words. Her lovely, strong body seemed to fold in on itself. "I need to explain to you what's happening."

"Can Bella stay so I can go there now?" Bella shot a glance at Henley as if she understood and disapproved of such a plan.

"Not tonight. You can go tomorrow. They aren't going to let you in tonight. Tomorrow, first thing."

"What happened? Was she in an accident?"

"She was here in the city for tests."

"She didn't tell me anything about tests. What kind of tests?"

"She didn't want you to worry, and she never expected it to be anything bad. You know her, she's invincible and always the optimist."

"That's part of it," Henley said. "But the other part is her secrecy. She doesn't tell me things."

"She loves you."

"She doesn't tell me things because she loves me? How effed up is that? You know it, Quinn. But that's not the issue now. She was in the hospital for tests. What tests? Tell me. I want to know what's going on."

"She had tests done as an outpatient. It's cancer. Hen, she has pancreatic cancer. I'm so sorry. She went into the hospital for this staging thing so they could figure out what to do next."

Henley's chest constricted, the lack of oxygen making her feel faint. She held Bella to her chest and kissed her head. Bella's body shook from resting against Henley's trembling arms.

Henley stared at the open bookcase separating the living area from the kitchen. It ran the entire length of the big loft and stood floor to ceiling. There were no books. It was a showcase for shoes. Her eyes caught on the pair of lace Jimmy Choos Quinn had worn the time they went to the nightclub with the swimming pool. And the pair of Christian Louboutins Quinn wore to the wedding of that woman they knew from school. At the moment, she couldn't remember the woman's name, but those shoes—the mesh ones with the tiny glass crystals and the high skinny heel—she remembered them. And the ones made from tiny gold chains. The last time she asked Quinn there were over three hundred pairs. Maybe her thoughts could drown out the words pelting her.

The shoes receded. The words broke through. They could not be avoided.

Cancer. It's spread. Pancreatic. Stage 4.

"She started having problems a month or two ago, but she wanted to get her work done before coming home. There's not anything that can be done now. It's too late."

"That can't be true. Please, Quinn, no. Tell me that's not true. Not Izzy. She's my only family."

"I'm your family. And Claudia. And Simon. We're your family too." Quinn put her arm around Henley's shoulder and leaned over to rest her chin on top of Henley's head. Bella stretched up and gave Quinn a kiss. Tears fell from Henley's face, dropping onto Bella's back and rolling onto on the couch. Choo rubbed himself against Henley's legs, first one side of his body and then the other, back and forth.

"Quinn, this just can't be true. I can't handle this."

"We can handle this. Together."

HENLEY STARED AT HER NIKES. They were black with long red shoelaces that dangled down the sides. The top of each shoe was scuffed. As she walked down the hallway, she only looked a few feet in front of her, just far enough not to run into someone but not far enough to see the entire hallway.

She didn't look at the gray walls. She especially didn't look into the rooms or at the people in the beds or at their families. She could control what she saw by keeping her eyes on her Nikes, but the acrid odor seemed to rise from the floors and swish up her pant legs atomizing as she walked. It sprinkled from the ceiling, dusting her shoulders. She tried to take shallow breaths to prevent it from entering her lungs. This smell was burned into her memory from years earlier when her mom was in this same hospital. Proust could go on about the memories triggered by his precious madeleines, but smell was a much more powerful provocateur than taste.

She reached room 527 and kept on walking to the end of the hallway where she stopped and pressed her forehead hard against the wall. *Inhale. Hold. Exhale. Again. Again. Again.* Her fingers sought the sharp meets of the amethyst stone in her necklace rather than the soothing facets. She pushed the soft flesh of her fingertips into them, trying to feel pain. A fresh pain to distract from the pain that was waiting like a criminal lurking in a closet. Back down the hallway, past room 527. And again, but slower. Finally, she stopped at the door and put her hand on the cold knob. Inhaling a deep breath, she tried not to cry.

Henley gently pushed the door open and peeked inside. Several vases of flowers sat on the windowsill. An enormous bouquet of white roses was on the dresser. A tall vase stuffed full of enormous joyful yellow sunflowers was propped in the corner. Two large pieces of bold colorful of art hung on the wall. For a moment, she didn't recognize the woman in the bed. For an instant, she thought maybe it was all a mistake. Quinn was wrong. This wasn't her Izzy. Izzy wasn't sick. Izzy couldn't be sick. She was invincible.

But Henley's gaze lingered on the intricate quilt on the bed. Quinn had bought it in Brazil. Quinn had been in this room. She'd brought the sunflowers and hung the art. And laid the quilt. This was Quinn's work. This was Izzy's room. That *was* Izzy in the bed.

Izzy sat propped up against pillows, looking out the window. Henley's larger-than-life aunt was wilted. Her hair was loose, free flowing over her shoulders in sheets of gray. Henley could hardly remember ever seeing her hair down. It was always pulled back in an elegant twist or chignon. This woman in the bed barely resembled her aunt she had seen just a week earlier. Her typhoon of an aunt had been reduced to a summer drizzle. Was this the effect of knowledge? Did knowledge alter existence?

"Izzy," Henley whispered as she tiptoed to the bed.

As Izzy turned her head to the voice, Henley saw her face flush first with love, then with sorrow, fear and guilt before rearranging itself back into love. She leaned against the bed to stop herself from falling to her knees and wrapped her arms around her aunt.

"I'm so sorry, Henley," Izzy whispered.

"There is not a single thing for you to be sorry for. Don't be silly," Henley whispered back.

"I should have done more for you. I should have been here more. It's like I got whacked by a baseball bat, and it knocked me to my senses. Why in the hell didn't I quit my job? I can't imagine why I didn't. That was awful of me."

"Don't be ridiculous. You should not have quit your job. You know better than anyone the needs of the many outweigh the needs of the few."

"You're quoting *Star Trek* to me, seriously?" Izzy threw her head back onto the pillow and laughed. A deep belly laugh. "Oh, my God, thank you for that. You know how much I love everything *Star Trek*. Jean-Luc Picard was always my ideal man. If I'd found someone half as toe tingling as him, I may have gotten married. In keeping with that theme, let me say to you, I am and always will be your aunt. No matter what, Henley."

"Life by Spock." Henley smiled. "Better than any philosopher."

"He was a philosopher."

Henley sat on the bed and held her aunt's hand. "What can I do for you?"

"Nothing. I have no needs." Izzy paused and took a wobbly breath. "Wait a minute. There is one thing. I would die for a croissant from La Maison du Chocolat."

Henley flinched.

"Oh, that was bad wording. Let me rephrase—I would love a croissant from La Maison du Chocolat."

Henley stared at the thin line of dirt edging the floor tiles along the wall. "Do you want me to get that later? This afternoon?"

"Would you mind getting it now? I'm sorry to ask, but the food here is ghastly. Those croissants are the only thing that sounds good to me."

"Of course. Do you want hot chocolate to go with it?"

"You know it. I'd rather have the Guayaquil than the Caracas but either would be wonderful. Thank you, honey."

When the door to Izzy's room closed, Henley's legs went out from under her, and she fell against the wall, sliding to the floor. No one passing her in the hallway said a word to her.

When she was finally able to pull herself up, she had to lean on the wall. She wasn't strong enough to do this. A world without Izzy was inconceivable. She would be alone. Her whole family gone.

———

ABOUT AN HOUR later Henley maneuvered the tray stand over Izzy's bed and spread a white linen napkin on her lap. She set a small plate with two chocolate croissants on the tray and carefully arranged a steaming cup of hot chocolate.

"I used to dream of these croissants when I was traveling," Izzy said. "The little prop plane would be tottering down a rutted dirt runway in rural Africa, the nuts and bolts shaking so hard I was sure the whole thing would unfold like an origami flower as it lifted off. To distract myself I imagined the first bite of a chocolate croissant, the moment when the chocolate squeezes out. I envisioned the flakes fluttering onto the plate and felt the traces of butter on my fingertips. It always triggered memories of home. And of you. I'd forget about the imminent terror, and by the time the daydream was over, we'd be in the air."

Izzy patted Henley's arm and pulled the tray closer to her. "Thank you for getting these for me." A shiver ran through her body when she sipped the hot chocolate.

"You faced overwhelming problems, and you did so much good. You made a difference in many lives. What's the plan now?" Henley grabbed a chair and pulled it close to the bed. "Have you researched specialists? Are there any drug trials? I read an article about immunotherapy having success fighting many cancers. Should I start researching it or did you already do it?"

"Henley, my precious girl. There's nothing to do. There's nothing for me. It's far too advanced. I don't want to be a guinea pig in some trial. I'm not brave enough."

"Don't be ridiculous." Henley rose from the chair and circled the room. Fury flared so quickly it felt like her chest would burst open. "You survived two plane crashes in Africa, stood down tribal chieftains, were held for ransom in India and woke up with a snake in your bed," she sputtered. "And now? *Now* you're scared? *Now* you aren't brave enough? Get real. You are the strongest person I know."

"I understand how hard this is for you, Henley." Izzy's voice was calm and steady. "I'm sorry to leave you. If there was any realistic option, I would take it, but there's just none. I don't want to be subjected to those treatments when there's so little chance of success. I don't want the indignity of it. I'd like to go on my terms."

Henley pressed her forehead against the cold, hard window and watched the boats on the East River. A rusty shopping cart bobbed along with the current. She stared at the whirlpool vortexes that built and dissolved in the water. This grimy East River with dead fish and mangled trash flowed into the Atlantic Ocean. The same ocean she'd stood in front of just a day before, on a beautiful sand beach, her skin warmed by the fall sun, salt wind in her hair and the delicious scent of a man on her skin, without a thought this was on the horizon. One day and her world changed. There had been no warning, no tingling sensation. Just boom. And life changed. Forever.

She wanted to shout at Izzy. She wanted to scream at her to fight, to rage, to not give up, to beg her not to leave.

"You remember what your mom always said to you?" Izzy asked.

"That she loved me to the moon and the stars and back again."

"Me too. Always and forever. Nothing takes that away."

Several minutes passed before Henley was able to take a deep breath. She wiped her nose on her sleeve.

"I'm sorry. I shouldn't have gotten angry. I'm so embarrassed." A brittle yellow light slatted across the vibrant colors and bold shapes of the patchwork quilt. Henley smoothed it before carefully sitting on the bed, intertwining her fingers with Izzy's.

"Honey, don't be sorry. It showed how much you love me. You touched my heart. Do you remember the poem by Theodore Roethke your mom left for you to find after she passed?"

Henley pursed her lips together, tears ran down her face, and she closed her eyes. "I wake to sleep, and take my waking slow, I learn by going where I have to go."

"That's what I'm going to do. This a life lesson too."

Henley nodded and wiped more tears off her face onto her sleeve. "What's the plan then?" She was bone-weary. Somehow she'd forgotten the exhaustion that accompanies grief. The last time—when her mom died—she hadn't been alone. Izzy had been at her side. Now she was supposed to be the strong one.

"I'll be here for a day or two. They're arranging for a hospice nurse to come to my apartment to help me."

"Bella and I will come and stay with you."

"That would be lovely. How is my dear little Bella baby? That's one of my many regrets in life—I never had a dog."

―――

G HEARD the knocking at the door, and he ignored it. He knew who it was. Henley had left several messages, each a little more desperate than the last. He should have called her. He should have at least texted her to tell her he couldn't see her anymore. But he hadn't. And now she was outside. Knocking. Still knocking. He stood in the middle of the studio, rigid, legs apart, fists on his hips in a fighter stance. She wasn't going away.

He flung the door open with more force than he had intended.

A cold wind was blowing grimy scraps of trash from the street against the buildings. A loose newspaper whipped against Henley's legs. G assessed her as she peeled it off. Her face was splotchy and her eyes red. Her breath plumed in the cold, and her chest rose and fell heavily. His heart lurched to her, but he yanked it back and put on an attitude of nonchalance.

"Is everything okay?" Henley asked. "You didn't...it's just you didn't return my phone calls, so I thought something might be wrong."

"Nothing's wrong." He stood awkwardly filling the doorway. "I'm working. I have to translate all my sketches to the canvas."

"I left you a message. I wanted to talk to you. My aunt's in the hospital." Henley's voice caught, and she choked. "She's...dying."

"I didn't hear the message." Damn. Damn. Damn. He wanted to comfort her. But he also wanted to shut the door. "Do you want to come in?" The words were out of his mouth before he realized he'd spoken.

A glance at his studio made him cringe. It was more of a mess than usual. Canvases filled the space, making it difficult for two people to walk. Trash bags leaned against each other, in danger of falling over. She stumbled inside, seeming not to notice the mess.

"She's not going to fight it." Henley slumped down on the futon. "She's going to die. That's it. She's just going to die..." Her voice trailed off into silence.

He struggled with what to say, what to do, and finally asked, "Is there something I can do to help?"

"Not really."

Her eyes were closed as she talked almost as if she was talking in her sleep. He thought she looked achingly beautiful.

"I wanted...I don't know why I'm here. You're busy. I just can't sleep."

"Would you like to stay here?"

"Bella's home, and I need to get back to her. I came because I was worried about you."

"I'll go with you."

Every alarm bell he possessed clanged in his head. *Don't go. Don't go.* They blared like a fire alarms banging inside his skull.

He put his arm around her shoulders and pulled the door shut behind them.

———

BELLA WAS SNUGGLED into Henley's side under the covers, her little head resting in the crook of Henley's arm. G wrapped himself around Henley, one arm draped over her hip, his hand over hers, which was covering Bella. It was warm under the blankets, and he would keep her safe, but she was antsy.

"You need to get some sleep," he whispered.

"There are so many things to do for Izzy. It's a bad time to take off work, but I want to stay with Izzy. This is my last time with her, and I don't want to miss a minute. I'm so confused. I want to help her, but I don't know how. What to say. What to do. How to be. Lists are swirling through my mind, things I can get to make Izzy smile, things to make her more comfortable, some memories we can make together. My mind won't stop. I can't sleep."

"Close your eyes and listen to me. Shut everything else out and focus on my voice. Engage your imagination."

He lowered his voice to a Barry White gravely bass whisper.

"It's early, the sun isn't up yet, but when I reach for you to draw your body into mine, you're gone. I'm alone in our bed with the big rattan ceiling fan above me, turning lazy wobbly circles. In only boxer shorts, I stumble out to the beach to find you sitting cross-legged on a blanket you borrowed from the closet. Silence hangs in the air since the birds haven't yet noticed the sun waking over the horizon. Tiny waves are nipping at the ripples in the sand. Soft breezes are ruffling my unbuttoned shirt you threw around your shoulders. Your body is sitting on the blanket, on the beach, in front of the turquoise ocean, on a tropical island, but it's obvious your consciousness is floating somewhere peaceful. Serenity envelops you. I'm tempted to tiptoe back to our bed and wait for you to join me but more urgent temptations prevail."

Henley exhaled and her breathing slowed. He thought she might have fallen asleep until she sighed. So he continued.

"Instead of going back to bed, I sit down behind you and stretch my legs out on either side of your body. You lean into my chest and put your hands on my bare thighs. When I rub the muscles in your neck, you moan and stretch, first one way then the other. I run my hands down your sides and stop to caress your breasts. The birds are beginning their wake-up chitchat at about the time you turn around to face me. You wrap your legs around my waist, locking us together. I feel your nipples harden as bare skin meets bare skin."

He considered ending the story, but she moaned and wriggled her body into his curves.

"You reach inside my silk boxers and bring me inside you. The smooth fabric slides against me with every luxurious stroke. Your face is luminous in the dusty golden morning sun. In the distance a steel drum counts the rhythm. The tide has turned and water covers my toes and recedes, onto the sand and back out to the ocean, over and over, but we ignore it because we are all that matters."

He felt her let go and kissed the back of her head. Not daring to move, he stared at the moon's dappled light splattered over the ceiling and the walls. Tracking the moonlight patterns to the dresser, he saw a model of a building that looked like the Guggenheim Museum in Bilbao. Hours later his arm was asleep, and he needed to stretch, but he still didn't move. It had torn him apart to let her go after Montauk, but there had been no other choice. He couldn't continue to see her. Then she appeared at his door once again, and this time she was so broken. How he could he have told her to leave? He wanted to love and protect her. He couldn't leave her, but he didn't know how to stay with her. He wanted to throw something, do something to release his tension and frustration, but he stayed still, his arms around her, shielding her from harm in the only way he knew. His mind was such a tangle of thoughts and emotions he was still awake when her phone rang just before dawn.

Henley jolted from the bed and grabbed her phone from the nightstand.

"Hello?" She balanced on the edge of the bed.

Silence. The room was silent. Henley didn't say another word. Bella rolled over onto her back for tummy rubs, but none were given. G watched Henley's face in profile as it collapsed. He wrapped his arms around her from behind. She dropped the phone on the bed and picked up Bella to cuddle her.

"I'm so sorry." He rested his chin on her shoulder.

"She was going to go home tomorrow."

———

WITH EMOTIONLESS HALF-LIDDED EYES, Henley watched Bella on her intruder search rounds as she sniffed under the black mondo grass that edged the bluestone patio and inspected the base of the Sango Kaku Maple trees proudly displaying their coral-colored bark. Henley noticed the leaves had turned apricot in the fall chill. They would soon fall to the ground and decay, she thought with a heavy groan.

Bella stared at the big boulders burbling water in the center of the garden for several minutes before finally curling up in her dog bed in the sun, apparently confident that her property was secure.

Propane heaters warmed the patio, but Henley pulled her robe tighter as she stared at the row of white birch trees at the far end of her garden sanctuary. Their skinny white trunks stood straight and tall in vivid contrast to the red brick walls enclosing the space. To Henley they usually seemed almost defiant, but today they seemed too fragile to stand guard over this private space. The kitchen was just off the patio where she was sitting with Bella, but the sound of the cabinet doors opening and closing seemed to be coming from far away. Light streamed through the leaf-shaped cut outs in the steel roof covering the patio. Artisans had created the roof from Henley's design using a water jet to cut the pattern into steel. It gave the impression of sitting under a tree.

G set a pot of coffee and four mugs on the table. Henley stared absently at Bella.

He came back with a plate of sliced apples and a plate of chocolate croissants. "There's almost no food in your house." Henley barely glanced at him. "Your refrigerator has maybe five things in it. You have Cheetos and almost nothing else."

"Cheetos are my sad food." She drew her words out slow and heavy.

"Some coffee will help." He poured her a cup and topped it with a swirl of foamed milk. "I found a Jura Giga coffee maker with the instructions still inside it. Have you ever used it?"

"I don't know how to use it. It was a gift from Izzy last Christmas." Tears dripped from her nose. She pressed her hand against her mouth to stop the sobs from escaping. G pulled a chair closer to her and sat down.

"Henley, I don't know how to say this in a kind way, so I'm just going to say it. Is there any way you can think of this as a blessing?"

Her head jerked up. "A blessing? What the hell?"

"Listen, not a blessing she got cancer. Of course not. But maybe a blessing she didn't suffer. Don't you think this would have been her choice? You said she didn't want to endure the indignities of being sick."

"She *never* would have left me without saying goodbye."

Henley walked over to the mandevilla plants that wove along the top of the brick wall and pulled a few dead leaves off them. In the summer they dangled a profusion of flowers over the edge like a lei welcoming visitors to this hidden spot. Now it was almost time to cut the mandevillas back and move them inside, or they would die.

G turned to watch her and seemed to notice the garden for the first time. She glanced back and saw his mouth slightly gaped open and his eyes wide. For several moments he stared at the space, his head moving slowly from area to area. When he turned to her, his face was formed in a question.

"You created all of this?"

She tried to smile at the compliment but only managed to tip up one corner of her mouth. She nodded. "There wasn't anything here when I moved in. Well, the brick walls were here, but nothing else. It was an empty space with weedy grass."

"It's amazing. How did you manage to do all of this? It's like a professional garden."

"I didn't know anything about plants. My friend, Simon, gave me the stag horn fern hanging in the living room. That got me started. Now I'm a plant mom. Simon even gave me a shirt that says *Support Plant Parenthood.*"

"How do you take care of all of it? It must take hours."

"It's not work to me. I love the plants, and they respond to my love by growing and being beautiful. It's satisfying. This garden gives me so much more than I give it."

"What are these plants growing on the brick walls?"

"Mostly sedum."

"That's stone crop, right? I'm familiar with that. How'd you get it to grow on the brick?"

Henley slumped down on the chair with a groan, staring down. "It's not really growing on the brick. I set up a grid system of copper tubing that runs along the full length of each brick wall. Each sedum is in a pocket of wool that hangs from the tubing, and I can water each plant easily through holes in the tubing. Sort of a manual irrigation system."

"There must be hundreds of plants there. Are they all types of sedum?" G sat in front her and held her hands.

"Twelve different kinds of sedum. Croton, dianthus and ferns are mixed in for texture and color." She knew he was trying to distract her, to cajole her out of some of this misery, but she couldn't be cajoled.

"You probably even know all the names of the sedum." He smiled at her. She gave him an exasperated shake of her head.

"I recognize the herbs over there—basil, rosemary, oregano. You've got a bunch of mint that might take over your entire patio. Why do you grow herbs when you don't cook?"

"I like how they smell. There's an herb for every mood. Mint is happy. Basil is contented like comfort food. Rosemary is action. I like to have it around when I have work to do. Quinn comes over and cuts them every week."

He walked to the left side of the garden and fingered a leaf on a tree. "Is it an apple tree?"

She nodded. "There are two of them. The apples you found in the kitchen came from those trees."

"Is it a Melo D'Ezio?"

"It's a Decio."

"It's the same. The Italian name is Melo D'Ezio. I didn't realize what the apples were until I saw the tree." He sat back down at the table and popped an apple slice in his mouth, taking a moment to savor it. "It's named for Ezio, who took the apples from Rome to

Padua when he fought Attila the Hun. The apples are exceptional—crisp and full of flavor. These trees aren't common."

"I wanted a vintage tree, so I could grow something I couldn't buy in the grocery store. How do you know it?" She tilted her head up and studied him through cloudy eyes.

"They're Italian." He pulled a croissant apart. New tears pooled in Henley's eyes when she saw the flakes fall to the table. "These croissants are excellent. Even better than the ones I used to get from Gontran Cherrier in Paris when I was in school. Those used to be my favorites. These are now."

"They're from La Maison du Chocolat. Izzy's favorites. When she was in the hospital, she asked me to get them for her, so I picked up some extras."

He put his hands on her arms and touched his forehead to hers. "I'm going to leave since your friends will be here soon. I wish I could tell you this will get easier, but I won't. You know it won't. It'll become less present though."

———

BELLA HEARD them first and somersaulted from her dog bed. She ran to the kitchen door and leapt into Claudia's arms. Henley didn't get up, so Quinn bent over and kissed her.

"I'm so sorry, Hen." Quinn sat down in the chair G had vacated minutes earlier.

"This sucks majorly. I'm so angry." Claudia plopped down with Bella in her arms. "I'm so sorry, Hen."

"Look what I brought." Quinn pulled a pale lavender cloth from her bag and handed it to Henley, who let it drop on the table.

"What's this?" Claudia asked, running her hand over the lavender fabric. "It feels like flannel."

"Exactly. It's a flannel onesie."

"It's a little small for Henley."

"Come here, Bella baby. Let me show you what Auntie Quinn

brought for you." Quinn took Bella from Claudia. Bella rolled onto her back and let Quinn wiggle the onesie on her sausage body.

"Aren't you darling?" Quinn held Bella up. Henley looked up to see Bella clad in soft lavender flannel, even her little paws. And she laughed.

"That's what I wanted." Quinn set Bella down on the ground and rubbed Henley's back. "It was going to be a Christmas present, but I knew it would make you smile."

"There's coffee." Claudia poured a mug for Quinn and herself and topped off Henley's mug.

"Coffee?" Quinn said. "Did you order delivery? Where did all this come from?"

"I picked up the croissants at La Maison du Chocolat."

"You got them for Izzy, didn't you?" Claudia picked up one of the croissants. "I remember all those times she took us there for hot chocolate."

"It was so wonderful. The croissants. The hot chocolate." Quinn smiled at the memory. "But mostly Izzy. Bigger than life. Laughing. Telling stories. She had always come from some fascinating place."

"And always loving you," Claudia said to Henley.

"Always loving us all." Henley wiped tears from her face.

"She was a huge influence on my life," Claudia said. "I think of her every day. She inspires me."

"Where did the coffee come from?" Quinn asked. "You can't make coffee."

"G."

"G was here today?"

"Hmm." Claudia glanced around as if she was looking for evidence. "Interesting."

"What can we do to help?" Quinn asked, with a quick shake of her head to Claudia.

Henley stared at them. "I don't know what to do."

"It's okay, honey. We'll help with whatever you need," Claudia said.

"I don't know how to ask for help because I don't know what needs to be done. Is there a book or something that lists what to do when someone you love dies?"

Bella went back to her sunshine spot and curled up to sleep, in her soft lavender flannel onesie.

"She was Catholic. So we can start there," Claudia said. "We'll need to choose a church for the service."

"She loved Father Mike like a brother, so his church would be the one. Oh no, he doesn't know yet. I have to call him this morning," Henley said. "I don't want to make that call. He'll be devastated. I don't know if he knew she was sick. Or maybe he knew before I did. Who knows."

"Izzy loved music. We'll need to get a choir. Choose what songs you want them to sing. The songs are going to be important. And arrange for flowers," Quinn said.

"A church...music...flowers. Sounds like someone's getting married." Henley gave them a rueful smile.

Quinn and Claudia looked at Henley, measuring her words. The corners of Henley's mouth turned up just a little, and she put out her hands to her friends, who each grasped one. It was such a slender line between life and death, and she was grasping for life.

"I don't know how to let people know about the funeral." Henley propped her head in her hands. "Should I send invitations? Does Hallmark sell invitations for funerals?"

"I'm not sure, but I think you call people," Claudia said. "Or you can email them. Her foundation should put a notice on their website too. I'll work on a draft for you to review."

"What about her foundation? Who's in charge now?" Quinn asked.

"I was just thinking about that. I'm going to have to call all the board members. They need to know before it gets out to the public. I'll have to work with them on the transition."

"You should put a notice in the paper," Claudia added.

"She knew so many people. I don't know how to contact them

all." Henley got up and picked some dead leaves off a row of white hydrangeas. "Everything in my garden is dying back. I hope they come back in the spring." She wanted to just sit down in the garden and wait for that to happen.

"I can go over to Izzy's apartment and get her address book," Claudia said. "I'll call everyone in the book."

"I can call all her cell phone contacts," Quinn said. "We should compare first though so we don't duplicate calls. Let's make a list and divide them."

"What if she didn't like the person?" Henley asked. "Can you imagine? There's someone in her contacts who she hated, and we call and invite them to the funeral."

"Or old boyfriends," Claudia said. "Maybe it was a bad break-up. That'd be uncomfortable. Maybe you should go through the address book first and weed out the people she wouldn't want there."

"Yeah. I'll know a lot of the people but not the men she dated," Henley said. "She only ever used first names, and I never met any of them."

"And there were lots of men," Quinn interjected laughing.

"Billions and billions of men," Claudia said in a Carl Sagan voice.

"She did tell *stories* about some of them," Henley said. "I just never met any of them. They all just passed…through her life." She threw her arms up in a whoosh.

"She did tell great stories," Quinn said.

"But they were just stories," Henley said. "She never came home to anyone except me."

"How big is Father Mike's church?" Quinn said. "There are probably going to be a lot of people."

"You know what would be great?"

Henley and Quinn turned to look at Claudia.

"A wake."

"A wake?" Henley said.

"Yes." Quinn slapped her hands on the table. "A wake. We can do that later and take time to plan it."

"She was Spanish, though not Irish. Is it okay to have a wake?" Henley asked.

"Of course. It's a big party to celebrate her life. And she loved Irish whiskey, so that makes her honorary Irish," Claudia said.

"And she loved New Orleans jazz, so it'll be an Irish wake/New Orleans homecoming type party with Irish whiskey and a big jazz band," Quinn said.

"Perfect," Henley said. "We can give Izzy a party she would have loved."

CHAPTER TWELVE

Henley knocked on the door and opened it when she heard, "Come in."

"You wanted to see me?" she asked.

Wesley Kahn met her part way into the office and shook her hand.

"Yes. Henley, I'm sorry to ask you to come into the office today. How are you holding up? I was sad to hear about your aunt."

"Thank you." Henley nodded. "It's fine. The funeral planning is done, and I was going to come in today anyway. Was there something you needed to talk to me about?"

"Well, since you're busy with, you know..." He waved his hands around. "I wondered if you might like to hand over some of your work while you, you know, take some time to get your other things done?"

"I appreciate the thought, but I don't need help. I have all my work under control, on time and on budget."

Wesley scrunched up his forehead. "Henley, I was hoping not to have to say this, but I received a complaint."

She stared at him. "A complaint? From whom?"

"Mr. Scavo. He was concerned about that meeting. The one you were late for."

"I was late because the time was changed, and I wasn't told. I can't imagine Andrea Scavo called you about that."

"No." Wesley strung out the word and tapped his forefinger on his chin. "It wasn't Andrea Scavo, it was Stephano Scavo. He said he was speaking for his father."

There was a knock at the door, and Brett stuck his head in. "Is this a good time?"

Henley blinked at him and groaned inwardly.

"Brett, thanks for stopping by. So Henley, Brett offered to pick up some of your work to help ease the load for a while. You know, just until you get through some of your personal things. What do you think? Good idea?"

Henley looked from one smiling face to the other, taking her time to answer so that her voice wouldn't shake with the indignation she felt. When she realized the pause was making them nervous, she waited a beat longer.

"Brett." She put a bright smile on her face. "Thank you—so much—for your concern. Both of you—you're so kind to think of me. But I'm fine. I don't need help with any of my projects. Wesley, would you please call Andrea Scavo and ask him directly if he wants me to handle his project? I am certain that will clarify this issue."

With a quick glance at their slack-jawed faces, she turned and left the office. She wasn't good at smackdowns—never had been—but that felt so good she vowed to do it again. Someday.

HENLEY PUSHED through the carved wood door into Ah Bar and waved to Quinn and Claudia, who were sitting at a table by the window. Simon gave a "just a minute" hand gesture to the two Simonettes who were hanging over the bar displaying their assets. He reached Henley in three large strides and wrapped his arms around her.

"How are you today? Is there anything I can do for you?"

Henley sighed into his shoulder. "You're doing it quite perfectly."

"You need to remember energy cannot be destroyed. It can only be transformed."

"What?" Henley tilted her head up to him.

"It's a law of physics. The law of conservation of energy. It holds that the total energy of an isolated system remains constant."

"Huh? Simon, I don't—"

"Energy cannot be destroyed. It can only be transformed. She's a different form of energy now."

"That's the best thing anyone has ever said to me." Henley hugged him. "She's kicking butt in Africa and in India. Doing good for all those kids. The people can't see her, but they can feel her every time her energy field hits their butt. I love that. It suits her so well, since she was a constant ball of energy. Is it okay if I use the conservation of energy at the memorial service?"

"Anything I have is yours. You know that."

Henley kissed him on the cheek. "You are a prince. You know that, right?"

The blush that spread across Simon's face made him all the more irresistible.

"On a different subject, can I talk to you about a work thing?"

"Sure, if you kiss me on the cheek again."

Kiss bestowed, she said, "Today my boss called me into his office and tried to give my work to Brett. Apparently Stephano Scavo called him to complain about me. I don't think it's a coincidence that Brett and Stephano have become friendly just as Stephano calls my boss. It's not proof that Brett's trying to screw me over but..."

"It's pretty suspicious. What'd you want to do about it?"

"If he's trying to hurt me, I want to stop him. Let's go with the plan we came up with. Will you set it up on my computer?"

"You bet. I'll set it up and give your computer back after the funeral." Simon put his arm around her shoulders and walked with her to the table where Quinn and Claudia were waiting for her. The four of them wrapped themselves into a group hug.

Henley wiped her face and rubbed at the runny mascara under her eyes with a napkin. "You guys are making me cry." A margarita with salt was waiting for her at the table.

"Do you want to go over the service?" Claudia rubbed Henley's arm.

"I think it's under control." Henley took a sip of her drink and tipped her glass to Simon. "Hundreds of people are coming, even government officials and some people from the mayor's office. Even people from the United Nations are coming."

"I'm not surprised. Your aunt was a force of nature," Quinn said.

Henley threw her head back and laughed. People turned around and stared at her. Claudia and Quinn looked at each other. Simon watched from behind the bar and smiled.

"Hen, you okay?" Claudia asked.

"A force of nature. Yes, she *is*," Henley said. "Simon told me the loveliest thing about energy. I'll explain it later."

"He is the sweetest guy." Quinn turned in her seat to watch him pouring drinks behind the bar.

"Not to mention scrumptious," Claudia added. "Sorry, I shouldn't have said that. It's not the right time."

"It certainly is the right time. Izzy loved Simon. She said he was a tall ice cream sundae with whipped cream and a cherry on top. Izzy was a big fan of life. She wouldn't want a mope fest."

"When the funeral is over, we'll work on the wake," Claudia said. "That'll be a blast. We'll make it a party Izzy would be proud of."

"With lots of jazz and lots of Irish whiskey." Quinn clapped her hands.

"The only thing I'm worried about for tomorrow is my eulogy," Henley said. "I just don't want to disappoint Izzy. I'm not as strong as she was."

"You could never disappoint her," Quinn said. "You are strong in soft ways. You're kind and compassionate. That takes its own kind of strength."

"What'd she always say to you?" Claudia asked.

Henley smiled. "That she loved me to the moon and the stars."

"Damn right." Claudia smiled too. "You'll be great."

CHAPTER THIRTEEN

From her spot hidden in the sacristy, Henley watched people flow into the massive cathedral. Her friends were in the front row. The entire board from Izzy's foundation sat together. Brett walked in, along with other colleagues from her office, and she felt a pang about what she was going to do to him. Arrangements of white tulips, roses and calla lilies lined the aisles. Footsteps echoed on the stone floor, and the din of voices joined into an indecipherable low rumble as people squeezed into already crowded pews.

G stepped through the imposing wooden doors and slipped into the last pew. Henley almost didn't recognize him. His hair was combed back, and he had shaved. The dark charcoal suit he was wearing would have been at home in the closet of any investment banker on Wall Street. In fact, it looked like that suit Hunter had been wearing when Claudia pushed him into the pool. He looked aristocratic. Faint whispers of desire rose in her body, but one look at the priest shut them down.

Father Mike, resplendent in his white vestments, motioned for everyone to sit. Henley longed to roll herself into the soft velvet of the liturgical garments draped on clothing hooks around the sacristy and close her eyes until this was over.

The priest said, "The choir will now sing 'Goodbye My Friend.'"

There was a rustling of sheet music and the choir began.

Henley stepped away as they sang and held a tissue to the corners of her eyes. She took slow even breaths. *Inhale. Hold. Exhale.* When she heard Father Mike talking again, she walked back into the hallway.

"I sat down a few days ago to write this tribute to a woman I adored. I loved Izzy. I respected her, and I have to admit I feared her a little. She was formidable. Relentless. Indefatigable. She was Izzy. One of a kind. She led a complicated life that would take hours to explain and to properly extol."

As he talked, he walked out in front of the altar and stood with his hands clasped in front of him in conversation with the mourners.

"She had an extreme relationship with God. She fiercely loved and revered Him, but she also hated Him, probably just as fiercely. She was awestruck by life and people, and animals and the world. She honored God for the creation of such magnificence. But she blasphemed God for the suffering, for allowing the suffering to exist. I was on the receiving end of many of her tearful rants. How could I argue with someone who witnessed such atrocities? I didn't have answers for her. Faith is my only answer and often it wasn't enough for Izzy."

Father Mike walked back to the altar and stood silently for a few moments. He seemed to be struggling for composure. Henley's hands shook, and she stuck them under her arms. Soon Father Mike was going to turn to her, and she was supposed to walk out in front of all of those people and talk about her aunt. She wasn't sure she could even walk to the altar much less speak coherently. She really wanted to be home in bed with the covers over her head.

"We had many heartfelt conversations over the years." Father Mike's voice cracked as he spoke, but he held his head high. "We discussed her work and her recent trips. She always described the children she met in such detail and with such profound love that I would carry them in my heart as she did. Izzy drank tea with men who heralded the birth of a child as another worker for the farm, who ignored that child in life and dismissed that child in death as easily replaceable. She was polite to men who sold ten-year-old girls to old men and who denied girls the right to go to school. She flattered men she wanted to knock down and spit on. She did all this because she loved the children and wanted to help them."

He paused, choked with tears, unable to speak for several moments.

"She had to be a diplomat even though it ripped her soul in half to do it. Every success was buried by crushing sorrow for the children she was not able to save. She was acutely aware she could always walk away. She could get on a plane and fly to New York, but the children couldn't leave. She could not enjoy the successes, because every child she left behind was her failure."

Henley rubbed the amethyst stone in her necklace, pulling the chain so taut it cut into her skin. She couldn't catch her breath.

"Such a life, my dear Izzy. Never feeling like she had done enough when she had done so much. The loss of Izzy in this existence is a loss to me, to her family, to her friends and to humanity. It's not often you can say that about a person."

A flush of shame spread through Henley's body as she realized what she was expected to do—simply open her mouth and talk about her aunt—was so insignificant compared to what Izzy had faced. She had to do this for Izzy.

"There was one child who was in Izzy's heart every moment of every day, her niece, Henley. She would like to say a few words."

The priest stared into the hallway.

Henley held her head high, squared her shoulders and walked to the altar. Her first steps wobbled, but she kept walking. From the corner of her eye she saw the white tulips, roses and calla lilies spread out against the shiny cherry wood coffin and her breath caught. Her legs felt too heavy to lift, but she kept moving forward. When she reached the altar, her head was spinning, and she had to stand for a moment before beginning to read from her notecards.

"Thank you for being here today to celebrate Izzy. I'm touched by your presence and your love for my aunt." She couldn't read the words on the notecard because her hands were shaking.

"I'm honored to talk about Izzy." She paused again and closed her eyes. When Henley finally opened them, she saw her friends in the first pew and breathed their love deep into her lungs. A flood of strength surged through her body. She started again, her voice rang strong and clear. "Izzy was a sponge. She absorbed experiences, facts, places, people, children, all the good things in the world. But she also absorbed all the sorrow she saw. When she saw suffering, she tried to help. She gave away pieces of herself everywhere she went to everyone she met. Like a sponge, every piece she gave away grew back. The more she gave the more she had to give. Izzy will live on in our good deeds. My advice to everyone who loved Izzy is to be a sponge, absorb life and give yourself freely away. You will grow from the experience."

She smiled and blinked away the tears that had pooled in her eyes, sending them running down her face. She proudly lifted her face to the congregation, letting them see the love in the streaks on her face. The board from Izzy's foundation were nodding almost in unison.

"So, yes. What I'm telling you is to be a sponge. Be a sponge for Izzy."

She held her arms out as if she was bestowing a gift, a gift from Izzy. People turned and looked at one another, some smiled, others nodded and some dabbed tears. Henley looked at Simon.

"One of my dearest friends is a physicist who recently explained the law of conservation of energy to me. Apparently you can't destroy energy. Go figure—it's a science thing. Energy can only be transformed. So let it ring loud and clear, Izzy Rana is not gone, simply transformed. So, world, watch out for her. She's not finished yet."

Laughter rippled through the sanctuary and many people turned to their neighbors and smiled.

"One of the things that gave Izzy strength was poetry. That was another thing she absorbed. She tucked poems everywhere. She put them in letters she sent to me and to friends, stuck them in favorite books with the thought she would find them someday and be happily surprised. She hid copies of poems in the backs of airplanes seats and admitted to daydreaming about a person joyously finding one on a long flight."

She laughed and rolled her eyes, and people laughed with her.

"Always the optimist, she left them on tables in doctors' offices and tire repair shops. She thought if she could catch someone bored, they would read anything and figured if they read one poem, they would love poetry for life. She was certain poetry could make the world a better place. From the time I was little she quoted lines to me. I was seven or eight years old by the time I realized it was somewhat unusual for people to speak in iambic pentameter."

More laughter filled the sanctuary.

"There's a special verse I would like to read today with apologies to Shakespeare for the edits. Izzy read it at the funeral for her beloved younger sister...my mother." She cleared her throat and took a deep breath.

"...when she shall die,
Take her and cut her out in little stars,
And she will make the face of heaven so fine
That all the world will be in love with night
And pay no worship to the garish sun.

Izzy quoted that verse to me many times after my mom passed away. She taught me to look for love in the stars. Now I will look for you too, my precious aunt."

Quinn and Simon wiped away tears. Claudia sat straight-backed, balancing on the edge of the pew, feet flat ready to come flying to Henley if needed.

"Another thing Izzy loved almost as much as poetry was *Star*

Trek. So let me end by saying, 'Warp speed ahead, Izzy. Second star on the right and straight on 'til morning.'"

Henley took a seat next to Claudia, who put her arm around her. Simon leaned over and patted her on the back. Quinn was still wiping away tears.

"Now we will close this celebration of Izzy's life with one of her favorite songs," Father Mike said.

The woman who stepped in front of the choir seemed too young and too frail to be a soloist. She stood silently with her head lowered. For an instant, Henley thought she was nervous and looked to Father Mike for help, but she soon realized it wasn't nerves. The young woman was commanding the stage, drawing the attention and waiting for silence. Then she raised her head, nodded to the choir head and began.

"I'll be seeing you…"

Her voice deep, resonating with emotion, seemed to swirl and swoop around the mourners mesmerizing them. Henley closed her eyes and could imagine Billie Holiday standing in front of them.

When she finished, a collective sigh filled the cathedral. Even Claudia sniffled a little.

Father Mike gave the benediction and then said, "To honor Izzy, remember the signature line she borrowed from Edmund Burke and always used on email and letters. 'All it takes for evil to prevail is for good people to do nothing.' Go do something good for Izzy."

———

THE TREES throughout the small cemetery were shades of glorious orange, red and gold. Every autumn her mother would quote Burroughs, "How beautifully leaves grow old. How full of light and color are their last days." Not to be outdone by her sister in their constant exchange of poems, her aunt would respond with a quote of her own from Browning, "Autumn wins you best by its mute appeal to sympathy for its decay." Now they were both gone, and she was alone. She didn't have a poem for that.

Henley leaned around the person in front of her and peered at the crowd lined up at the casket. Her brow furrowed. A stream of people wove through the gravestones, spilling out on the winding cemetery road. Claudia quickly put her arm around Henley's waist, caught her eye and nodded firmly to her. She whispered in Henley's ear, "You got this. Remember there will be margaritas tonight."

Henley shook another hand, listened, nodded, said "Thank you" and turned her gaze to the next person in line. With the precision of a synchronized swimmer, Simon deftly moved each one along with munificent courtesy. A cool breeze whipped through the headstones, and Henley drew the cashmere shawl tighter around her shoulders. The pale taupe silk blouse slid against her skin as she shook hand after hand. The muted color softened the black wool jacket and slim skirt Quinn had left in her bedroom the day before. Henley hadn't even thought about what to wear, but Quinn had. The fine wool jacket had tiny pleats self-belted in the back near the waist, making the suit more feminine and less like funeral clothes. Of course it fit perfectly. The taupe shoes matched the blouse. Henley was surprised Quinn hadn't also delivered underwear.

She caught the odd expression on the face of the person standing in front of her and realized she had been lost in thought.

"I'm so sorry. What did you say again?" Henley roused herself from the stupor she had fallen into.

"It's okay, dear. I understand." The woman patted her arm. "I'm Elena, your aunt's neighbor."

"Her neighbor? Izzy traveled so often, I'm surprised you knew her. It seemed she just dropped in to pick up clothes and was off again."

"I've known her for years. She did travel a lot, but when she was home, it was wonderful. She was always so interesting. And she adored you."

"Thank you. It was lovely to meet you. Thank you for coming,"

Henley said as Simon took one step to his left and put his hand on Elena's elbow gently steering her away.

A young woman wearing a long red sarong covered with bright white patterns threw her arms around Henley.

"Izzy saved my life." The woman rocked Henley back and forth. "My father, mother and aunties all died. I was alone until Izzy found me." She spoke in flawless English, the words tumbling out of her mouth so quickly Henley struggled to catch them all.

"You must be Nomcebo." Henley hugged the woman again. "Izzy talked about you all of the time. I've heard so many stories about you. Your paintings are on the walls of my office."

"They aren't!"

"They are."

"They aren't." Nomcebo slapped her legs. A smile filled her face.

"Really, they are. I love them. They're gorgeous and vibrant, so full of life. Everyone who comes into my office comments on them."

"I can't believe paintings I made in school in Africa are on the walls in your office in New York City. This is such a magnificent life." She laid her hand over her heart.

"If you ever want to become an artist, I know someone who might be able to help you."

"I'm very happy at my job with the United Nations, but thank you for offering to help me."

"You're working at the UN?"

"Izzy got the job for me. I work for the High Commissioner for Refugees."

"What a perfect job for you."

That smile once again overtook Nomcebo's face.

"Izzy was so proud of you," Henley said.

"I just moved to New York City a few months ago. I had dinner with her two weeks ago, but I didn't know she was sick." She put her hand over her mouth. It took a few minutes before she continued. "I was truly devastated when I found out. I didn't get a chance to say goodbye to her or tell her how much she meant to me."

"Her death surprised us all. She knew you loved her. You can believe that without question. She thought of you as a daughter."

"I think maybe that makes us like sisters." Nomcebo's laugh filled the quiet cemetery. People waiting in the long line looked up from their phones and smiled.

Nomcebo hugged Henley again and didn't let go until Simon and said, "Hi, I'm Simon, a friend of Henley's. I'm pleased to meet you." He held out his hand so she had to release Henley from the hug.

"Henley, I'm so sorry." It was Brett who held his hand out to her. He brought her in for a quick hug. She hadn't seen him behind Nomcebo and wasn't prepared for him.

"Thank you for coming," she managed.

"Please let me know if I can help in any way." His smile seemed sincere. She wavered on the plan she had cooked up with Simon. She never had been a good cook.

Next in line was a man with silver hair and a confident, almost patrician bearing, smiling at her. His black frame glasses were decidedly stylish, and his pale gray suit was exquisite. She didn't need Quinn to tell her that. She shot a glance to Quinn, who looked the man over, tilted her head almost imperceptibly and subtly raised one eyebrow. Henley read the code.

"I was very fond of your aunt," he said to Henley as she shook his hand. "Your eulogy was perfect. She was a force. I'm sure she still is, like you said. Believe me, I know all about her power."

"Did you...work with Izzy?" Henley asked. She took a step back when he reached his left hand out to grasp her arm as part of the handshake. She had the feeling he was going to try to pull her to him, maybe hug her.

"I'm Ian McDaniels, the deputy mayor. I had many skirmishes and a few battles with Izzy over the years. I've got the scars to prove it. *No* wasn't a word she readily accepted. Despite those battles, I had great respect and affection for her. Actually, maybe it was *because* of those battles. She was a strong lady."

"I'd love to hear those stories sometime. Thank you for coming." Henley turned to the next person in line. Simon stepped forward.

Ian took one step back, nudging the person behind him aside. He turned his body and faced Henley directly. She felt his cool blue-gray eyes scrutinize her and straightened her posture.

"I'd love to share those stories with you. This is my card. Call me if you'd like to talk. Do you know 'When grief comes to you as a purple gorilla / you must count yourself lucky.'?"

"What?" She looked at him quizzically. What did this man just say to her? Did she misunderstand him? Her mind whirled at the incongruity of the situation. A purple gorilla. Then…

"Oh. Yes." She nodded and smiled. It was a sad smile just the same. "'You must make a place for her at the foot of your bed.'"

"I figured you'd know that Matthew Dickman poem. It made a profound difference in my life. Izzy left it in my office one day. We'd spent quite some time that day engaged in a terrific battle, the kind where no one wins. After she left, I found the poem on my desk." Ian nodded his head to her, turned to walk away but hesitated.

"Anytime. Feel free to call anytime."

As she continued to thank people, Henley watched Ian McDaniels. He paused at the polished cherry coffin suspended over the hole in the earth, then kissed his fingertips and pressed them to the wood. He stood with his head bowed.

HENLEY AND QUINN leaned against each other on the couch in Henley's living room. Bella snuggled between them in ecstasy as both women mindlessly rubbed her soft pink belly. Claudia stood in front of the framed photos covering the exposed brick wall. There were photos of vacations they had all taken together, parties in Southampton, Quinn in her loft before, during and after construction, Simon remodeling Ah Bar covered in sweat and dust, all of them at graduation from Brown, smiling, their arms flung around one another, Claudia spiking the football in the end zone during a football game with her five brothers, and Henley at an awards ceremony for an architecture prize. The photos documented their love and friendship. No matter how many times the friends were at Henley's home, they all stopped in front of the wall to look at the photos. In the kitchen, a blender whirred alongside clanging and clinking.

"I love this photo of us the morning after you first moved in here," Claudia said. "The place was full of boxes and we slept on blankets piled on the floor."

"The photo of us in the morning with the hangovers, looking like zombies?" Quinn asked.

"Except for Henley. She wasn't hung over," Claudia said.

"But she still looked like a zombie after sleeping on the floor."

"Are there more plants in here, Henley?" Claudia waved her hand around the room.

"There are a few more kids. I discovered a new type of philodendron with holes in the leaves. I vined it around a big tube. I hope it's going to climb to the ceiling."

"Pretty soon there's not going to be room for people or dogs. You know that, right?" Quinn said. "I think you have an addiction."

"When you start naming them, we're going to stage an intervention." Simon set a tray of margaritas on the coffee table alongside the platters of food people had dropped off and plopped down next to Quinn.

"I'm not *supposed* to name them?" Henley grinned.

"You created this monster when you gave her that thing." Quinn said to Simon, pointing to the massive staghorn fern dangling above them.

"Did you see the new one? It's got holes in the leaves. She asked me if I could find a six-foot-long clear tube. She stuck it in the pot and threaded a string of those little LED lights through it. Then she trained that plant around the tube. It's ghostly when the lights shine through those holes."

"Yep. I think it might be intervention time." Quinn crossed her arms over her chest and glared at Henley. Who laughed.

Claudia licked her finger and swiped the salt from the rim of her glass.

"This sriracha salt is so spicy. It burns so good," she said stretching out the o's in *so* and in *good* before sucking the salt off her finger.

"These are the best margaritas ever, Simon. You have upped your already great margarita game. What's the change?" Quinn asked.

"It's the tequila. This is Highland Anejo. I've been studying tequila for a new drink I'm developing. The agave is grown in volcanic soil in Mexico, so it's spicy and acidic. I like it better than the fruity tequilas. I'm experimenting—trying to find the right balance."

"I'll try anything you're serving. Especially if it's spicy. You know I love spicy." Quinn winked at Simon, who put his arm around her shoulders.

"*You're* spicy." He smacked her with a kiss on her cheek.

"I thought the service today was lovely. You were perfect," Claudia said to Henley. "Very calm and confident."

"You were dignified but not afraid of being emotional," Quinn agreed. "It showed that you not only loved Izzy but also respected her."

"I love the sponge idea," Simon said. "Sponges are such fascinating Porifera."

"The odd thing is I felt strong. When I was standing in the sacristy while Father Mike was speaking, I was shaking. I wasn't sure my legs were strong enough to walk to the altar. I was afraid I would fall apart in front of all of those people."

"What changed?" Quinn asked. "Did you do the 'imagine them in their underwear' thing?"

Henley shook her head. "It hit me I am Izzy's niece. Something of her must have rubbed off on me. It became a mantra. 'You are Izzy's niece. You are Izzy's niece.' That got me to the altar, but I was still pretty shaky. What really saved me though was when I saw the three of you, I felt a strength seep through my body like it was being pumped through my veins. I got this image of that green monster from some old TV show. I thought of him and felt power surge in my body. It was sort of thrilling."

"Wait. Wait. Wait." Simon jumped up and waved his arms wildly. He stuck his fingers into his hair making his curls to stick out at crazy angles. A frenzied cloud covered his eyes. "There was 'an old TV show about a green monster'? Seriously, Henley? Bruce Banner was a physicist who was exposed to gamma rays and became a *superhero*, not a green monster. The Hulk is a comic book and video games and the Avengers movies and...he's the *Hulk*. Hen, come on. You might have just broken my heart. How have you missed out on the Hulk? You have a gaping hole in your life."

Henley rolled her eyes. "What? This guy's your hero? Is it a physicist love thing?"

Simon turned his back to her.

"Hen, where are you living? The Hulk is fine," Claudia said. "Mighty fine."

Henley looked over at Quinn, who shrugged.

"Don't look at me. I'm with them. I love the Hulk."

"I have a mission." Simon was pacing the room. "You and I are going to have a Hulk marathon. Name your weekend. I'm honor bound to this mission. Hulk must be... well, *avenged*."

"Hey, me too." Claudia raised her hand. "I want a piece of that."

"I'll bring the food," Quinn said. "Everything will be green."

"I'll even create a green drink," Simon said. "You in, Hen?"

"Okay?" Henley looked at them askance not sure if they were making fun of her. It seemed like they were serious about this green stuff.

"Seriously, though. I wanted to tell you that you looked great at the church," Quinn said. "I think your confidence wasn't only the super green blood surging through your veins. It was also your exceptionally fabulous clothes."

"You did look beautiful." Simon flopped down on the couch.

"Thanks, so did you. I don't remember seeing that suit before." Simon jerked his head at Quinn.

"Oh, yes." Quinn rubbed Simon's leg. "I dressed him. I...dressed..Simon. I told him I needed to run my hand up his leg to check the fit, but really, I just wanted to. It was simply delectable."

"Sweetheart, you can run your hand up my leg any time." Simon waggled his eyebrows at her and laughed.

"Just as Father Mike was starting the service G came in and sat in the back row. I thought you could all meet him afterward. The black suit he was wearing was so gorgeous you could have dressed him too, Quinn. I didn't even know he had a suit."

"One point for him. He owns a suit," Claudia said. This time she licked the sriracha salt right from the edge of the glass. "He's still in negative numbers though. He might have rented it."

"Who was the guy with the gray hair in that beautiful suit at the cemetery?" Quinn asked. "The one you gave me the eye about. Nomcebo and I were talking, so I didn't hear what he said."

"He's the deputy mayor, Ian McDaniels. Apparently, he and Izzy had some history."

"Maybe he's one of the many, many men she left behind," Quinn said. "The suit was a Cucinelli. I'd recognize their cashmere anywhere. Definitely bespoke. The pick stitch was sublime."

"Ohhhh, that sounded sexy," Simon said. "Could you whisper that in my ear, Quinn?"

"Come here, Simon. I'll whisper in your ear." Quinn crooked her finger at him. He winked at her.

"I'm not exactly sure what you said, but I'm guessing you meant the suit was nice," Claudia said.

"Very." Quinn nodded.

"Did you see him at the casket?" Henley asked. "He stood there for a long time. Then he kissed his fingers and pressed them to the wood. It was sad and sort of loving."

"It does sound like they had a thing for each other," Simon said. "My Spidey senses are tingling. Something's up here."

"At least it's not your green blood boiling," Henley said. "He said he would like to tell me stories about Izzy."

"That sounds interesting. Imagine the stories he could tell," Quinn said. "Can I come listen?"

"Sure. Wasn't Nomcebo great?" Henley said. "Did you get a chance to talk to her?"

Quinn nodded. "Her laugh made me happy. She spreads happiness like fireworks."

"It's sad to think of all of the children in the world who needed an Izzy and never found one," Claudia said. "How many of them would have been like Nomcebo if they just had a chance."

"Izzy made a difference to so many people, including Nomcebo," Simon said. "She was an example of how to live an important life."

"I wish there'd been more time to talk to everyone who came," Henley said. "So many people loved her."

"Maybe you should contact people and ask for their stories about Izzy. You could put them in a book. Partially to honor Izzy but also to raise money for her foundation," Simon said. "And maybe we could use the stories at the wake."

"What a terrific idea." Claudia laid her hand on Simon's arm. "Not only would you get to hear all the amazing stories and raise money but it's also a way to keep her memory alive."

"I love it," Henley said. "I'm definitely going to do that, but it will have to wait a while. I'm buried at work because of the jewelry store construction, and the museum project for the contest isn't done yet. Things are a mess right now."

"Hen, with all you've got going on and cleaning out Izzy's apartment why don't you give me all the business cards, and I'll start contacting people?" Simon said.

"Are you sure?"

"I'd really like to do it."

"What did I say about him the other day? The sweetest guy? Were those my words?" Quinn leaned over and kissed Simon's cheek.

"I think those were your words exactly," Claudia said.

"And what were *your* words, Claudia?" Henley said.

"Ah...I don't remember." Henley noticed a blush rise up Claudia's cheeks. She'd never seen that before. *Claudia* and *embarrassed*. Those were two words that didn't fit together in a sentence. She owned everything she did.

"Maybe it was something about...hmm...I believe the word was...*scrumptious?*" Henley tilted her head toward Claudia.

"Scrumptious? Me?" Simon aimed his most brilliant smile at Claudia, who buried her head in the back cushion of the couch. "Maybe I could get a little help from my friends to put together the book of Izzy memories?"

"I'll help if you make some more margaritas with spicy salt." Claudia's head was still buried in the pillow.

"That's a deal." Simon hopped up from the couch. "Henley, I put your laptop in your office. I took care of everything."

"It's all set up?" Henley asked.

"Warp speed ahead." Simon nodded. "Are you ready for it?"

"I guess I am. I've had a little bit of back and forth about it. Brett came to the funeral today and seemed kind, so I'm feeling a little squeamish about it. Setting him up like this could ruin his life."

"Who's setting up who?" Claudia asked. "What's this about?"

"One of the guys I work with may have changed the time of a meeting to make me look bad," Henley explained.

"And you're planning ruination for that?" Quinn asked. "I'm sure glad we're friends."

"He tried to get the managing partner to take away my work and give it to him." She looked at Quinn and Claudia. "And he got a client to call and complain about me."

"Okay. That's pretty bad," Claudia said. "But ruination is pretty severe."

Simon turned to face them. "It's only ruination if he's bad. That's the beauty of this plan. His future is in his own hands."

"I'm worried he's going to steal my design for the Calder Prize," Henley said.

"So I'm setting a trap on her computer," Simon said.

"If he's not a thief, then nothing happens." Henley shrugged.

"If he takes the bait and steals the design, I'll be able to track it, and he'll need a fire truck to put out the flames when he goes down," Simon said.

CHAPTER FOURTEEN

"Hey Brett, could you bring the calculations for that load-bearing wall in the back of the jewelry store down to my office?" Henley spoke into her office phone.

Henley paused to listen to his response, said thanks and hung up.

When she heard footsteps outside her office door, she turned her chair around from the door and pretended to talk into the phone.

"You're such a good friend, Claudia. I appreciate your belief in me. The museum design is finished, but I think the entry in the Calder Prize needs the model, and I don't have time to make one."

She paused as if she was listening.

"I know I don't have to submit a model, but I want to. I think it's important. So I'm just not going to enter this year." She enunciated the words slowly and clearly. "I can enter the Calder next year. I'm not going to submit my design this year."

She paused again and turned the chair around to find Brett leaning against the door, just as she expected.

"Hey, Claudia, I need to go. I'll talk to you tonight, okay?"

"Brett, thanks for stopping by."

"Glad to see you're back at work." Brett handed her some papers. "These are the numbers for that wall."

"Thanks. Does it look like we can move it?"

"Yeah, we can move it. You don't really need to look at this stuff, though. I know you're really busy. I promise they're all good to go." Brett made a magician motion and gave her his most winning smile.

"I'm sure they are. No doubt. But my name is on the seal that goes on the drawings, so I need to go through them."

"Of course. I was just trying to help. I'm happy to be working with you even though you're younger than I am." He winked at her. She had to swallow the groan that rose from her throat.

"I appreciate that, Brett. I think I'm only a year younger, so I'm not sure that counts."

"Just let me know if you need anything. Really, anything. I'm here for you."

"Well, thanks. I appreciate that. I need to run to a meeting now."

She left him leaning against her office doorway and walked down the hall—her laptop on her desk.

BELLA SNORED in her little bed and Erroll Garner's piano played from the speakers as Henley got out her tools. Before she started, she ran her finger over the brittle creases in the old photograph and tiny pieces flaked away. In the center of the photo was a two-layer cake with fancy chocolate icing. A pink bakery box with elaborate scroll writing was visible at the back of the table. A candle in the shape of a seven stood in the middle of the cake and a balloon dangled from a chair. Her mom and Izzy stood on either side of her. They had big smiles on their faces—so did she. Smiles engulfed by the sad eyes. She'd never noticed those sad eyes before. Henley gently laid the delicate photo on the corner of her worktable. For the thousandth time she reminded herself to get it scanned to preserve it.

Henley hunched over the table and carved a tiny piece of balsa wood into a miniature railing wielding the X-ACTO knife with confidence and alacrity as the sharp blade stripped precise shavings from the wood. When a hint of geranium floated in through the open window, Henley lifted her head, turning first left then right, trying to catch more of the scent.

Hours later as she glued green cotton balls onto twisted pieces of wire, the sun crept through the windows. She used tweezers to position the last of the trees in the garden on the roof of the model for the children's museum—her submission for the Calder Prize.

When she finished cleaning her tools and putting them back into their cases, Bella stretched and blinked as if to ask if it was finally time to go to bed. Henley stroked her sleek fur and kissed her little head. "Sorry, sweetie. I can't stay home with you. I have something very difficult to do today. I'm definitely going to need some sweet Bella kisses when I get home."

CHAPTER FIFTEEN

The empty boxes in Henley's hands knocked against the small table in the entryway as she came to an abrupt stop. Claudia and Quinn bumped to a halt behind her.

"I don't feel right going in here. She'd hate this," Henley said. "It's such an invasion. She would despise the thought of anyone going through her private possessions."

Henley eased inside and backed against a wall of the living room, surveying the apartment her aunt had called home for over thirty years.

"The thing she would hate the most is putting you through this." Claudia dropped the boxes she was carrying in the middle of the floor.

"I'm sure she planned to have her things sorted, donated, trashed or ready to be given to the people she loved," Quinn said. "These are choices she wanted to make herself. Knowing Izzy she probably planned to write notes to everyone thanking them for being in her life and explaining the gift she was making to them. She wrote beautiful letters. I treasured the ones she sent me. Always with a stamp from some exotic location. They made me feel special."

"Me too," Claudia said. "In high school I kept those letters in a box I decorated with pink and purple hearts. I aspired to be her. Still do."

"She told me she never minded plane rides because they gave her captive time to write notes and make plans without interruptions." Henley dropped her boxes on the floor next to Claudia and circled the room.

"So it's up to us to make those decisions for her." Quinn set her boxes on the couch. "Look at it as a way to honor her. To use what we know about her to make the best choices."

Henley pointed to an exquisite hand-loomed rug on the wall in the living room.

"This apartment is so her even though she wasn't here that often. That Persian rug has been hanging on the wall for years. And those wood carvings on the mantel—she brought them back from Africa. And her bookcases. I never saw her without a book. A stack sat by her bedside in the hospital. Her suitcase is still on the stand in the bedroom. It isn't unpacked, because she planned to leave again."

"We weren't the only ones who thought she was invincible. She thought so too," Claudia said.

"The choice about the furniture is easy. Several shelters for abused women and children said they would love to have it. They'll pick it up," Henley said. "So we need to figure out what to do with everything else. The artwork and all of her books will come to my house. I'll add the wood carvings to the ones in my office. I don't think I have a spot for the Persian rug though. Quinn, wouldn't it look fabulous at your place?"

"Seriously fabulous. Are you sure?"

"I am. Give it a place of honor, and whenever anyone comments on it be sure to tell them how Izzy got it so that story can live on."

"That's one I don't know," Quinn said. "What's the story?"

"Oh, it's a classic." Henley laughed. "She was in Pakistan working on education issues for girls when a tribal elder decided he wanted to take her as his third wife and wouldn't take no for an answer. He gave her lots of gifts, including goats and that rug. It was getting scary for her. She thought she might have to leave the country secretly in the trunk of a car. That would have been terrible for the program she was working on."

"What'd she do?" Claudia asked.

"She agreed to have dinner with him one night. He arranged this elaborate affair in a tent with candles everywhere. Servants rushed in and out with food. She said there were at least twenty-one courses. Through all the courses she smiled at him and batted her eyelashes. He took it as acquiescence and started talking about the wedding. She leaned over, ran her hand up his leg and whispered to him that she was looking forward to taking him as her twenty-third lover. At first he didn't understand what she was saying, but when he realized she was telling him she'd slept with twenty-two men before him, he rushed out of the tent in a panic, rubbing at his hands like they were dirty."

"Totally Izzy!" Quinn clapped her hands. "Brilliant. She turned male chauvinism upside down. What a great story."

"She never saw him again, but she brought the rug home as a memento. That's why it needs to live on. If it hangs in your loft, maybe it will inspire someone else."

"I promise to tell that story with pride and enthusiasm," Quinn said.

"What if we donate her clothes to a charity that helps women find jobs?" Claudia said. "One that helps them build a professional wardrobe."

"Great idea," Henley said. "I want to keep a few things though like her tan cashmere coat. I want to wrap myself in it and pretend it's a shield of protection. There are a few other things too. I'll take a look."

"Should the kitchen stuff go to the shelter too?" Claudia asked.

"No way *Henley* wants it." Quinn laughed.

"Yeah, of course. I wish I'd thought of that," Henley said. "I didn't ask them, but I'm sure they'd be happy to take that too. If there is anything either of you wants, please take it."

"That's a good plan," Quinn said. "Why don't we put everything to be thrown away in big trash bags in the bathtub to get it out of the way? Let's push this furniture to the walls to open some space and put the boxes for things to be donated in the center. The things you want to keep or give to people she cared about can go on the bed for you to go through them."

"Make it so," Henley said.

"Make it so," Claudia laughed. "Warp speed ahead. Izzy's love affair with Jean-Luc Picard really did endure for decades. When she dumped other men alongside the road, he was still standing."

"Hey, he's a hot guy," Quinn said. "I understand Izzy's devotion to him."

"True," Henley said, "but I think what appealed to her was his unwavering sense of morality and ethics. Doing the right thing even when it was difficult was her bugaboo as she used to say. I need to find a way to work that word into my vocabulary as a way to keep her close to me."

———

"HEN, come in here. You've got to see this," Quinn called from the bedroom. Henley and Claudia reached the bedroom at the same time and found Quinn pulling things from a pink shoebox. Photos were strewn around the bed. "I found this on the top shelf of the closet. Look—this has to be your mom."

"I want to see too." Claudia picked up a few photos. "Oh, Hen, your mom was gorgeous."

Henley's hands shook as she moved from one photo to another. They were professional photos taken of a performance. Henley couldn't tell which ballet it was, but there was her mom, young with a vibrant smile Henley didn't think she had ever seen. Claudia was right—she was gorgeous. Henley never knew that woman in the photos.

"There's more. What's this in the bottom of the box?" Quinn pulled out a pile of crushed tissue paper. Henley gasped when two worn pointe shoes fell to the bed. The pale pink satin was wrinkled and stained. She stepped back from them like they might burn her.

"Why did Izzy hide these things away like they were disgraceful?" Henley's voice wavered and cracked. "I asked so many times to see photos of Mom dancing. I'm not sure how to feel about this."

"Like you discovered a treasure," Quinn said. "Because that's what this is. Maybe we'll find some more."

THERE WAS a thump at the door and then a couple more insistent thumps. Claudia stopped sorting kitchen items and looked through the peephole.

"Simon!"

"Food," she shouted. "You're our prince."

Simon set a bunch of brown bags on the dining table and looked around. Several boxes in the living room were stuffed with clothes. Bedding and towels overflowed a couple of others. A mop and broom protruded from one in the corner.

"Look at this." He turned in a circle around the room. "Boxes everywhere. You've gotten a lot done."

"Food." Quinn stormed in from the bedroom. "I could kiss you, Simon. I thought Henley might keep us here until we were done, and I'm starving."

"Me, too." Claudia brought paper plates and napkins from the kitchen. "What did you bring?"

"Thai from Tamarind."

"I really *am* going to kiss you now," Quinn said.

"Come on baby, bring it on. I like me some kissing." Simon held out his arms and wiggled his fingers to Quinn, who threw her head back in laughter, her mass of curls bouncing every which way.

Henley came in from the guest room, her arms full of things she dropped into a donation box. She kissed Simon on the cheek and said, "Food. Bless you, my son." She bowed deeply to him. "What did you bring?"

"He brought Tamarind," Quinn answered, opening containers and setting them on the table.

"You did? My most favorite food." Henley opened a container and inhaled the savory aroma. "Did you get the samosas?"

"What samosas?" Simon said.

"What samosas? You know what samosas," Henley said.

"You mean the ones with fresh pomegranate and those potatoes spiced just the way you like them? *Those* samosas?"

"Yes, those samosas. Did you? Don't joke about those samosas."

"Of course. Would I ever let you down?"

"Never have."

"Never will," Simon said. "Let's eat."

"What did you bring besides samosas?" Quinn asked.

"For you, Quinn, I brought something new. Majjiga pulusu. It's made with green plantains, yams, radishes, white pumpkin, carrots, okra, mustard seeds and curry leaves."

"I love plantains." Quinn scooped food onto her plate and popped a plantain in her mouth. "Tastes like home. We had them in our backyard in Jamaica when I was a kid. My dad cooked them a bunch of different ways, but my favorite was a stew with ginger, cayenne, lemon and garlic. I'll have to make some for you."

"Did you get the naan?" Claudia asked, searching through one of the bags.

"Crap. The naan." Simon buried his head in his hands. "Sorry."

They all stared at him. He smiled and shrugged.

"Of course I didn't forget the naan. There's rosemary naan. And a bunch of rice."

"Think you brought enough food?" Quinn asked.

"I didn't know how long this would take. You could be locked in here for days. How much more do you have to do?"

"I'm almost done in the kitchen. Izzy had some top quality kitchen things, but I don't think she ever used them," Claudia said.

"Aspirational cooking appliances. She bought them with good intentions," Quinn said. "Sort of like exercise equipment."

"For all Izzy's greatness, she really wasn't a cook," Henley said.

"Like someone else I know." Claudia punched Henley in the arm.

"I cook." Henley punched her back.

"You don't," Claudia said. "What you do is not cooking."

"That crazy smashed egg thing of yours does not count as cooking," Quinn said.

"It really doesn't." Simon shook his head vigorously his mouth open in mock horror. "There was this one time in college when Henley stayed with me for a while. She kept trying to get me to eat that smashed thing."

"Hey, it made you feel better," Henley said.

"What it did was make me get out of the apartment so you wouldn't make me eat it again. Getting out made me feel better."

"It's okay after a hangover," Quinn said.

Simon laughed. "Not even then."

"All right then. I won't cook for any of you again." Henley flipped her hand defiantly.

Claudia jumped up and held her hand out to Henley. "That's a deal."

"So how much longer?" Simon asked.

"Most of the bedroom is done. I'm working on the bathroom next." Claudia spoke between bites of food. "The furniture is all going to a shelter."

"Are all these boxes donations too?" Simon waved at the boxes in the living room.

Henley nodded. "The clothes are going to a charity that helps women get jobs. The boxes of bedding and towels are going to the dogs. I'm going to take them over to the animal shelter where Bella came from."

"I can take them over now on my way to the bar."

"Thanks," Henley said, "but I want to do it so I can play with the dogs."

"That's what *I* was going to do." He laughed.

"I'll go with you," Claudia told Henley.

"You just want to play with the dogs too," Simon said.

"Yep." Claudia grinned. "Someday I'm getting a dog."

"Me too," Simon said. "Maybe we could all go together so we can all play with the dogs."

"I'll pass. Choo would think I was cheating on him if I came home smelling of dog." Quinn brushed imaginary dog smell off her shoulder. "He's barely forgiven me for taking care of Bella."

"I still have to go through her desk and files," Henley said. "I'll start on that after lunch. Simon, the things on the bed are for people she cared about. Please take anything you want, but there's one thing I want to give you."

Henley went into the bedroom and came back with Izzy's briefcase. The tobacco brown vintage leather was worn soft with years of travel. She handed it to Simon. "It's a Pineider. She got it in Italy years ago and was never without it."

"She called it her second brain," Claudia said. "When I think of Izzy, she's always carrying that briefcase."

"This is a beauty. She took such good care of it." Quinn stroked the supple leather.

"Hen, are you sure? Don't you want to keep this?" Simon's face had gone pale and tears welled in his eyes. "You should keep this."

"Simon, Izzy not only loved you, she respected you. She saw your future and knew there are big things waiting for you. You're going to need a briefcase like that one of these days. I chose to give it to you because I knew without question that is what Izzy would have wanted."

"I'm speechless. You know everything I have is yours so if you ever want it back..." Simon's words trailed off, and his head dropped.

Henley put her arms around him. "And everything I have is yours...except that last piece of naan." She reached behind him and snatched the last piece from the foil wrap.

"I'll take good care of it." Simon hugged the case to his chest.

"Back to work." Claudia started stacking food containers. "We have more to do if we want to go play with the dogs."

HENLEY WAS SORTING papers when Quinn walked into the living room carrying a simple black jar and rubbing her finger and thumb together. "This is lovely body lotion. I might get this for myself."

"That's Frederic Malle and crazy expensive," Henley said. "It was the only extravagance Izzy allowed herself."

"It's such a subtle fragrance...I can't quite tell what it is."

"Izzy always said it was Turkish rose, but I thought it smelled like geraniums."

"Is there jewelry somewhere?" Quinn asked. "I know Izzy didn't wear much jewelry, but there isn't any in the bedroom, and I don't want it to get lost or accidentally donated."

"Her jewelry is hidden in one of those hollow books—a book of poems in the bookcase. She figured it was safe there because no one would pick up a book of poetry. Much to her sorrow."

Claudia scanned the bookshelves. "There are a lot of books of poems. Which one is it?"

"T.S. Eliot. He was her most favorite poet. Well, and William Carlos Williams, Theodore Roethke and Gwendolyn Brooks. Well, she had a lot of favorites. But it's in the Eliot book."

Claudia found the book and set it on the table.

"Wow." Quinn fingered the small silk bags that filled the book. "I didn't know Izzy had this kind of jewelry. I never saw her wear hardly any jewelry."

"Except those square diamond earrings. She always wore them," Henley said.

Claudia and Quinn removed all the bags from the book and laid them carefully on the table, all the while oohing and ahhing over the contents.

"Rubies and sapphires and diamonds, *oh my*. Is there a gemstone she didn't have?" Quinn dangled a pair of pearl and diamond earrings. A waterfall of diamond strands cascaded from a center pearl that was surrounded by petals of diamonds. Each strand of diamonds finished with a plump waterdrop diamond. "Gorgeous, but I just can't see her wearing something like this."

"This jewelry should be in a safety deposit box," Claudia said. "Look at this necklace. Is this real? Ten rubies and ten diamonds, and they're big stones. Movie stars borrow this kind of stuff for the Academy Awards."

"I think she trusted Eliot more than a bank," Henley said. "She saw firsthand the harm that big banks and corporations do in the world."

"Where did all this come from?" Quinn pulled a pair of sapphire earrings from a bag.

"Men she dated, I assume. She wouldn't have bought it herself. I didn't realize how much jewelry there was, but I'm not at all surprised." Henley held one of the necklaces to the light and watched the rubies sparkle. "It's all beautiful...but does it seem sort of sad? Now that I think about it, I'm not sure she ever had a serious relationship."

"She did it her way," Quinn said. "She had a good time."

Henley started to answer but paused. "Maybe. I'm not sure. Maybe she led such a busy life to distract herself from being lonely."

"She didn't seem unhappy." Quinn moved on to a long stand of black pearls with a diamond drop and clasp. "In fact I've always admired her not only for all of her accomplishments but also for living life on her own terms. Not everyone wants the prince and the castle and the dwarfs like you."

"I don't know. All of this makes me sad." Henley swept her hand over a table covered with gemstones. "Maybe jumping from one man to another was driven by something deeper. Some fear or sadness. Or maybe she was searching for something, someone she couldn't find. She didn't even wear this stuff. I don't think it meant anything to her."

Henley shook her head like she was trying to shake away the thought and walked back to the desk covered with papers. Over her shoulder she said, "What should I do with it? I'm certainly not going to wear it. I only want those diamond studs."

"You should get it appraised and rent a safety deposit box," Claudia said. "I'll put all of it back in the book, but you should take it home with you. Maybe I should hire a Brinks truck to follow you."

———

WHEN HENLEY STOOD to stare out the rain-streaked window, papers fell from her hand and fluttered to the floor. Darkness covered the city and traffic was piled up at the red light on the corner. She pirouetted like a ballerina and swung her arm flinging the papers stacked on the desk through into the air. She grabbed the remaining papers and threw them against the window. The scream that filled the air was guttural—she was still screaming when Claudia and Quinn reached her. The last paper was crushed in her hand when she crumpled to the floor. Quinn put her arms around her as the screams dissolved into gulping cries.

Claudia knelt next to Quinn and smoothed Henley's hair.

"We know how much she meant to you," Claudia soothed.

Henley glared at Claudia so furiously she withdrew her hand. "Henley, what's going on?"

Henley didn't answer for several long moments as Quinn and Claudia exchanged worried glances.

"I hate her." Henley spit the words out so sharply her friends jerked away.

"Wh-What?" Quinn stammered.

"My dad isn't dead." Henley slumped against the window, exhaustion overtaking her fury.

"What?" Quinn and Claudia said almost in unison.

"My. Dad. Isn't. Dead." Her voice was dead.

"What?" In unison again.

"Ian McDaniels is my father."

"Why do you think that?" Claudia asked.

"Izzy has my mom's important papers. Ian McDaniels was married to my mom. They divorced when I was four. Izzy knew he was alive. He's not only alive, he's here in the city." As she stood the anger rose again. "They told me he was dead." She screamed and slammed her fists against the window. "Why in the hell would they do that?"

"I don't know," Claudia said quietly. "I can't imagine why. He's deputy mayor. It's not like he's a criminal they wanted to protect you from him."

"Well, he is a politician," Quinn laughed.

"At the funeral he said he had a lot of stories about Izzy. I'll *bet* he has a lot of stories. All these years he's been right here and never contacted me. It was so awful after Mom died. I was lost and alone. Izzy sent me to boarding school and went back to work. I didn't have anyone, and he never even called."

"I hate to throw this into the mix." Claudia grimaced and looked to Quinn for reassurance. "But he could have been married to your mom but yet not be your dad. I mean, you know it's possible."

"Do you think they kept it quiet because of his political career?" Quinn asked. She sat down on the couch next to Claudia. Henley finally turned and looked at them.

"Why would that matter? All kinds of politicians are divorced. Why would all three of them—him, Mom, Izzy—why would they keep this secret for all these years? And after Mom died, why didn't he contact me then? My mother was dead. My aunt was gone. I was shipped off to boarding school when my father was right here close to me."

Quinn gathered the papers from the floor, straightening them as she worked. "Did you look at these papers?"

"I saw some of them. I stopped when I found the marriage and divorce information."

"These are invoices." She shuffled the papers as she thumbed through them. "And there are canceled checks to Brown and to Columbia from Ian McDaniels."

"What?" Henley's voice cracked. "I didn't see those. He...paid for my education?"

Quinn nodded, still reading. "It looks like it."

Claudia picked up some more papers. "And he paid for Miss Porter's and even school trips. So I guess if he's paying your bills, he probably is your dad."

"Why would he do that?" Henley buried her head in her hands.

The three women sat in silence. Even the city street sounds seemed to dissolve.

CHAPTER SIXTEEN

"Henley, you need to slow down. I can't keep up with what you're saying." G sat on the couch watching Henley fold clothes. Bella nestled on his lap as he stroked the little crease between her eyes with one finger. She was hypnotized.

"My father is not dead." Henley threw her hands to the ceiling and danced around in a circle. "It's a miracle." She folded a towel into a square and slammed it down on the table. "He's been here all the time but never said a word to me. Everyone I loved lied to me."

"How'd you find this out?"

"Papers in my aunt's apartment. If I had known about those papers, I would've rifled through her desk a long time ago. I had a key, and she was always out of town, so I could have found out the truth about my life many, many years ago."

"Who is he?"

"Ian McDaniels. He's a deputy mayor for the city. I met him."

"You went to see him?"

"No, he introduced himself to me at the funeral. Told me his name and his job and that he respected my aunt. Forgot to mention the 'I'm your father' part." Henley slapped another folded towel on the table. "He even offered to tell me stories about Izzy. I guess he was going to leave out the part about 'I was married to Izzy's sister who just happened to be your mother.'"

Another towel smacked the table.

"What are you going to do?"

"I don't know. Quinn says I should ignore him forever. Forget about him the way he forgot about me." More folded clothes hit the table. T-shirt after T-shirt added to the pile.

"Would you please stop folding and come over here to sit with me?"

"I don't think I can sit still. The one truth of my life is that it's a lie." Henley took in a long breath and released it in slowly. "Claudia thinks I should confront him. Maybe publicly. Take him down. Ruin his career."

"You're not going to do that. That's not you."

"It's not me? Really? Maybe it is me. If it's not me, maybe it should be me."

"Please come here."

Henley stopped folding, blew out a deep breath and sat on the couch. He handed Bella to her.

"Turn your back to me so I can rub your shoulders."

His fingers kneaded her shoulders so gently she had to relax to feel his touch. As she calmed, her breathing steadied. His fingers moved down her spine applying pressure to the muscles on each side of her vertebrae. Finally, she moaned with relief.

"That took a while. You resisted." His breath was warm against her ear. "Relax into my touch."

"I'm so confused. And so sad. These people who I loved, who I thought loved me, lied to me. Their lies have cost me so much."

"It's time to stop thinking about it for now. It needs to settle before you make any decisions. Just breathe and feel my hands on you."

Henley stroked Bella's soft hair. "I can't stop thinking about it."

"I have ways to take your mind away from your thoughts, *cara*," G whispered. "I have my paintbrush. I could paint you."

"You brought your paintbrush? You come prepared."

"I come hopeful." He kissed her neck and ran his hands over her breasts. "What artist do you want to study tonight? Maybe Monet? What do you think?" He kissed the palm of her hand, and she shivered.

"I think I like his water lilies."

"He used very rapid staccato brushstrokes to create many of his paintings."

"Hmm. That sounds like a class I should take." Henley stroked her hand along his thigh. "I need to box my model for the Calder Prize first. Tomorrow is the last day to submit entries. Do you want to see it?"

G PUT his hand on the small of her back as they walked up the steps to her office.

"This is my first time in your office. It's a great workspace. A little cleaner than mine."

"The subway is cleaner than your workspace." Henley laughed.

"This antique letterpress cabinet is in beautiful condition."

"It's one of my favorite things. Izzy gave it to me when I got my architecture degree." Henley pulled open a drawer. The old letter compartment was filled with several sizes of OLFA knives and an assortment of replacement blades. Another drawer contained rolls of thin wire organized by graduated size.

"May I?" G glanced at Henley, who nodded.

He opened another drawer, which held various sizes of tweezers and nail files. And another with chips of glass arranged by size and color.

"This organization makes me queasy." G laughed. "I feel faint."

"I like organized. I use a lot of stuff. It's quicker for me to know where everything is." Henley rubbed her head against his shoulder.

"You have some beautiful tools."

"Izzy gave me some of them to me. Others were my mom's."

"Your mom used these tools to carve the pieces in her houses?" Henley nodded.

"This is the children's museum you designed?" G bent to peer inside the windows of the model building. "It's round."

"It's more accurate to say it's rounded. There aren't any corners in the building. I thought it would amuse the kids and encourage them to walk around the rooms and see more art. There's something sort of subliminal about running into a corner that inhibits creativity. I was influenced by the curving spaces in the Guggenheim Museum in Bilbao, Spain that Frank Gehry designed."

"That's the model on the dresser in your bedroom, right?"

She nodded. "That building has been…I don't know…it's been important in my life."

"You have tiny pieces of art on walls with labels hanging next to them. That's really detailed."

"All of the art in the museum will be hung at the kids' eye level. The labels will explain the art and the artist in a funny way—jokes or even emojis—something that will grab their attention. In every room there will be an open area where the kids can draw on the walls. They can imitate the art in that room if they want. The walls will be erasable."

"Did you carve these little pieces like the railings or did you buy them?"

"I carved them. I started doing that in architectural school. It helps me think through the design and how all the components work together. My favorite part is the roof. See, it's a cloud forest. For inspiration. I think it's an aspect of art often overlooked when teaching about art. How does an artist decide what to paint? What motivates them? The kids can come up to the garden and experience nature. The roof will be sort of like a muse." She was glowing as she talked.

"I can't remember inspiration even being discussed in art school." G was bent over peering into every corner of the model. "Aristotle said that art takes nature as its model, so the cloud forest is perfect"

"I like that. I think I'll put that quote on a plaque at the entrance. It took me a long time to think of the design for the roof. At first I wanted to create an imaginary world like Narnia or Neverland, but I really wanted a nature theme. I sketched out a bunch of designs, but nothing worked. One night I was looking at the photos on the wall downstairs and noticed one of my friends and me lounging in the hot springs at the Arenal Volcano in Costa Rica and voilà—an idea."

She threw her hands out to her sides.

"There's a cloud forest there called Bosque Eterno de los Ninos. A bunch of kids from Sweden founded it, but kids from all over the world donated to it. It's enormous—I think maybe it's the largest private reserve in Costa Rica. It seemed appropriate to choose a cloud forest protected by kids as an inspiration for kids. I discovered that the most magical world is a real one."

"That looks like a hanging bridge." He pointed to a spot on the roof.

She nodded. "We walked on a bunch of them in Costa Rica. I found them pretty terrifying, because they span valleys thousands of feet down. Every time someone walks on them, they sway. One of the photos downstairs is of Claudia doing a cartwheel on one. I never let go of the railings. I was holding on so tightly I had creases in the skin of my hands. This one will only be about two feet in the air. Do you see the animals hidden among the plants?"

He peered more intently into the garden. "Yeah. They're going to be fake, assume?"

"Fake. I thought about real butterflies, but I can't figure out a way to make that work, so there will be lots of butterflies, especially those magnificent blue morphos, but they won't be real. Birds will be everywhere along with their song. They won't be real either. I'm looking into video projection. If I can make the projection realistic enough, that might be exceptionally cool. There will be one animal that will be real, poison dart frogs. The most poisonous animal in the world. One drop of their venom can kill you. That'll get their attention."

"Poisonous frogs and kids. What could go wrong?"

Henley laughed. "The kids won't be able to touch the frogs, only look at them. The frogs aren't poisonous in captivity anyway. It's something about the food in their natural habitat that makes them poisonous. They're so beautiful and unique and the whole most poisonous animal in the world thing is sure to be a big selling point. The frogs will be in a massive vivarium full of plants so the kids will have to look closely to find the frogs. I hope it will teach them to pay attention to detail."

G examined the plantings in the model forest. "You made each of these trees and the plants?"

"They're made from dyed cotton balls, twisted wire and bits of moss."

"Did you spray them with fragrance?"

"I didn't, but what a cool idea. I might do that. Sort of subliminal messaging. Why? What did you smell?"

"Geranium."

A smile flashed across Henley's face but quickly disappeared when she remembered her aunt. And all of her lies.

"Time for Monet?" G held his hand out to her.

CHAPTER SEVENTEEN

Henley met Andrea at the door of the new jewelry store and handed him a pair of safety glasses and a hard hat.

"It's only electrical crews working right now, but I don't want to take any chances."

"Thanks for looking out for me," Andrea said. "By the way, you should know that Brett handled things at the job site well while you were out."

"What? No. Andrea, I was never out. I was at this job site every day and answered questions constantly no matter where I was."

"I should have known better. I meant no offense. I was only trying to compliment your team. Stephano told me Brett was running the project."

Henley felt like steam was blowing out of her ears and had to evoke her yoga lessons to calm down. It wasn't Andrea's fault—it was Stephano's, and probably Brett's. Every time she turned around she found Brett's fingerprints.

After spending two hours walking through the store looking at everything big and small, they left the store together. Andrea ran his hand over the rough walls of the cave on the way out.

"I'm so pleased with the progress. This has turned out beautifully. I felt a surge of anticipation when I walked inside the store even though I knew what to expect. It will all be surprise to the customers. They will be intrigued from the moment they walk in."

"It worked out just like we planned. It will be an adventure for the customer. I think they're going to love it. The final inspections are set with the contractors and the city. Everything is on schedule."

As they stepped outside Andrea put his hand on Henley's arm. "I was sorry to hear about your aunt."

"The flowers you sent were quite exceptional. Thank you."

"How are you doing? Do you have friends who support you? Maybe a boyfriend?"

"My friends are terrific." The question did give her pause—was G a boyfriend? They hadn't talked about that kind of stuff. He was, she supposed. And why did Andrea want to know?

Andrea nodded slightly. He seemed to be waiting for more.

"I've been struggling with some complicated feelings and trying to find answers in poetry. My aunt and mom loved poetry. They quoted it to each other and to me from the time I was little. Poems hung from refrigerator magnets and were stuck to mirrors—pretty much anywhere you could hang a piece of paper there was a poem. I'm glad to have poetry as a legacy from them. Poems show me I'm not alone in my feelings—that other people have felt the same way."

"If you get through life without great grief, then you've gone through life without great love," Andrea said. "In the beginning it's like a massive gorilla is sitting on your chest and every breath is a struggle. Every day he sits there he loses a little weight, and breath comes with a little more ease. Pretty soon he's standing by your side. You can breathe, but he's holding your hand. He's always holding your hand in his big hairy hand."

"Yes." Henley's eyes glittered with tears. "That's exactly how it is. That's beautiful. You could be a poet. You know a lot about grief."

"A gorilla walks by my side and holds my hand."

"I'm sorry."

Andrea nodded. "Me too."

They stood in silence for a few moments.

"I'm looking forward to seeing you at the dinner next week. Will you be bringing a companion?" he asked.

"No, only the people from the firm who have worked on this project will be coming to the dinner."

"Remember my invitation to Italy when this project is over. Should I ask my wife to invite some eligible young men over while you're there?"

Henley blushed. "I'd love to talk to you about a trip when the project is over."

"I'll look forward to it." Her blush deepened when he winked at her.

CHAPTER EIGHTEEN

EVEN THOUGH THE autumn air was crisp sweat beaded on Henley's skin as she strode down the street. The ornate details of the historic City Hall building sharpened as she got closer. Her momentum halted by a red light, she looked back north towards her office, her home and her friends. This was the compromise she worked out with Claudia and Quinn. She'd confront Ian McDaniels at work but not in front of people. In his office. Just the two of them. There wouldn't be any stories about Izzy or her mother. She told Quinn and Claudia they couldn't come with her. It would be just her. And him.

In the elevator she checked her hair in the security mirror and tried to smooth the peach fuzz frizz on her waves. Stepping to the side of the camera she used a rumpled napkin from her purse to mop the sweat from under her arms. She pulled her shoulders back, lifted her head and took a deep breath as she fingered the amethyst around her neck. *Inhale. Hold. Exhale. Repeat.*

The sound of her shoes on the marble floors echoed in the cavernous space. She slowed her pace to try to keep the heel of her shoe from hitting the floor.

"I'd like to see Mr. McDaniels, please."

The woman seated at a large intricately carved walnut desk in the enormous reception area stared at Henley with the finely honed expression of all receptionists that said, *Surely you're joking*. She hesitated for a moment to enhance the seriousness of the breach of protocol.

"I don't see an appointment for Deputy Mayor McDaniels on my calendar." She waived her exquisite manicure in front of her computer screen to prove there was obviously no appointment.

"I don't have an appointment, but he'll see me. Please tell him I'm here. My name is Henley Rana."

"That won't be possible. Mr. McDaniels only sees people with appointments. I could schedule one for next week. What is the subject?"

"I'd like to see him now. I'm not going to leave until I talk to him." Henley's heart skipped and fresh sweat popped under her arms. She wanted to yank off her shoes and run but forced herself to stand still.

"I've explained it's not feasible. If you don't leave, I'll call security."

"Just ask him. Is that so difficult? Would you rather make a scene than make one simple call? If he says no, I'll leave."

The woman's lip curled ever so slightly and she reached for the phone her long, shiny frizz-free hair swinging just exactly as it was coiffed to do.

"There's a young woman to see you, but she doesn't have an appointment. She refused to leave until I interrupted you." There was a pause while she listened. "She said it was Henley Rana." While the receptionist studied her manicure, Henley swiped at her hair fuzz again and straightened her already straight jacket.

Another pause. The receptionist tapped a single red nail on the desk. Then she frowned, "Yes, sir. Okay, sir."

The office door opened, and Ian McDaniels strode out. His jacket off, he was holding the black-framed glasses in his left hand. His iron-gray pants had a perfect crease and not a single wrinkle. The white button-down shirt looked freshly pressed. A red tie, because what man could be a politician without a red tie? Henley could not read his face. An excellent politician, she thought. Inscrutable.

"I'm so glad to see you." Ian extended his hand to her. "I didn't expect to see you so soon after the funeral. Please come into my office."

The receptionist looked like she'd swallowed a bug.

Ian followed her into his office. It was formal, like the building itself, with high ceilings, fancy cornice moldings and ornate dark wood paneling on the walls. A massive mahogany desk with curved legs and claw feet stood in the middle of the room. The desktop was clean except for a document he had obviously been reading. Photos of New York City throughout the years covered the walls—but no family photos. There didn't seem to be anything personal in the entire room.

"Can I get you something?" He was flipping his glasses around in his hand. "Coffee? Water? I can probably find some tea. What do you like to drink? I'm just surprised to see you here. It's so unexpected." The surprise seemed to have knocked a little of his cool off. He looked as nervous as she felt. "I think there are some cookies in the office kitchen. I can check if you want. Would you like that?"

"No, I won't be here long." She took her time and stared at him.

"Well... Okay. Tell me what I can do for you. Do you have a parking ticket or a garbage problem I can help with?" His laugh sputtered like a choking car when he saw her face. "Please, sit down." He gestured at the chairs in front of his desk. She remained standing so he did too. He was still spinning those glasses.

"Do you want to explain to me who you are?"

"Who I am?" He put out his hands, palms up as if to say, *I have no secrets.*

The gesture caused Henley's anger to flare. "Yes. That's what I'm asking. Who are you?" She said it slowly enunciating each word.

"I introduced myself to you at the funeral. I'm not sure what you're asking."

"I know your name. I want to know who you are. I thought I

should give you the opportunity to speak for yourself, because if I spoke for you, let's just say, I don't think anyone would vote for you again."

"This isn't an elected position."

She noticed the tiny stutter in his voice.

He dropped the glasses on the desk and picked up a pen to twirl between his fingers. "The mayor appointed me." He wasn't looking at her anymore. "Your aunt was a friend of mine. I explained that. I'm still not sure what you're asking."

"I found some papers when I was cleaning Izzy's apartment. You owe me some answers."

That was the first blow. It glanced off of him. Ian steadied himself, palms down on the heavy wooden desk.

"I...we...I don't know..." he stammered. "Tell me what you know." He dropped into the leather chair.

"What I know? Seems I'm the last person to know anything." He was staring at her but seemed lost in a faraway thought. After several seconds of silence she said, "You aren't even listening to me." Her face flushed as her voice rose. "I want to know if you were married to my mother. Is that a clear enough question?"

"I was."

Just that simple.

She pressed on. "Are you my father?"

"I am."

"You're alive. Imagine my surprise."

This blow hit home. Ian looked like he'd been slugged with a baseball bat and was going down for the count. He slumped to the side of the leather chair. With great effort he pulled himself straight, put his elbows on the desk, buried his head in his hands and rumpled his silver hair.

"Would you please sit down so we can discuss this?" His tone was plaintive.

"I won't sit down. You left us."

"Henley, it wasn't like that."

"No?" she scoffed. "Really? It seems that way to me. Where have you been all these years? You know Mom died when I was fourteen? You knew that, right?"

Ian nodded. He stared at her with eyes now red and drowning in tears.

"And I was alone. Izzy sent me to boarding school. On Parents' Day no one visited me. Claudia always took me along with her family, but it wasn't the same. Izzy tried to get back for my graduation, but she missed a plane connection. I had no one in the audience when I graduated. Do you know what that feels like? Where were you?"

"Miss Porter's." His eyes were half-closed and his arms hung loosely at his sides. His mouth gaped open.

"Yeah, Miss Porter's. I get it." Her voice a low hiss. "I know. Izzy kept you informed. You got updates, but you were too busy to visit me. Too busy to be my father. Too busy to love me. What'd you do just throw some money at Mom and Izzy? Was I politically inconvenient? Was that it?"

Ian's head jerked up. "No, that's not true. Please let me explain. Henley, please sit down. This isn't how I wanted to tell you. Please give me a chance."

"You didn't give me a chance. I'm not going to give you one *now*. I'm going to leave you just the way you left me. I don't want to see you or hear from you again."

She slammed the door on her way out. The sound echoed down the hallway.

CHAPTER NINETEEN

Henley leaned over to Andrea, who was sitting to her right at the large, round wooden table in the back dining room of Gramercy Tavern. The heavy velvet curtains separating them from the main dining room swayed as the restaurant staff moved in and out of the room. Lit only by candles on the table and by low floor lighting, the room felt comfortable and welcoming. Stephano and Brett were deep in a conversation, interrupted only by laughter and the occasional fist bump or shoulder slap. Their behavior helped alleviate any lingering guilt she felt about what she and Simon had done to Brett.

"I'm just going to eat this sour cherry jam all night. I don't need anything else. This might be the single best thing I've ever tasted in my life." She spread a red dollop over a slice of goat cheese on a paper-thin cracker.

"I think this jam is made from amarena cherries," Andrea said. "They're Italian. I favor them because they're a little sweet but not too sweet. I like to put the jam on vanilla ice cream with a tiny drizzle of balsamic vinegar. Perfect on warm summer nights. This jam is good, very good, but I have tasted better."

"Impossible." Henley smiled. "Where?"

"My wife makes the most extraordinary jam. It starts with the cherries she picks from the trees in her orchard. They're special trees. Rescued trees."

"Rescued trees? How do you rescue a tree?"

"She saves trees from extinction by growing them in her orchard. She calls it *arboreal archaeology*. Many species of trees are going extinct, so we're losing unique flavors of fruits. The fruit in the grocery store all tastes the same now, flat and bland. When people eat a piece of fruit that has no flavor, their brain actually supplies a memory of the flavor, so they don't realize what they are eating is so... how do you say it? *Blah*."

"*Blah* is the perfect word for that fruit." Henley laughed.

"My wife searches for trees in hidden spots all over Italy, old fallow fields, farms, churches, cemeteries, anywhere time has left behind. She takes cuttings from them, grafts them on new seedlings and plants them in her orchard. After she researches each tree, she documents it in her database."

"How many trees does she have?"

"I'm not sure. About 500? Maybe more. Stephano, how many trees would you say Mamma has in her orchard?" Stephano interrupted his conversation with Brett and turned to his father.

"Mamma's trees? How many? Who knows? She keeps adding more. She cares for them like babies." Stephano threw his hands in the air. "The only thing that would take her away from her beloved trees would be a grandbaby. Don't look at me for that."

Andrea turned back to Henley with a smile. "It's true, she does baby them. The fruit and jam are extraordinary with the complexity of a fine wine. For her cherry jam she uses cane sugar from Mauritius and lemons from the trees in our yard. Sometimes she fights the birds for the fruit. One year she had trees covered with peaches the size of baseballs—butter yellow with delicate pink streaks. She visited the trees several times a day, squeezing the peaches tenderly to decide if they were ready to pick. She wanted them to stay on the tree as long as possible to settle the sugar into the fruit. One evening she told me, in a hushed voice like it was a secret, she was going to pick them the next day."

"And the next morning the trees were stripped bare," Stephano said. "I didn't get any pie that day."

"That's awful. What happened?"

"Stolen. My wife obviously was not the only one waiting until the peaches were just right. The birds, the squirrels, maybe deer were waiting too. I was still in bed when I heard swearing from the orchard. Now, my Maria, she does not swear. I didn't know she even knew such words. I went to the orchard and put my arms around her. It took a while, but eventually we both laughed."

"Andrea, I could listen to your voice all day. It transports me to a big stone villa next to an olive orchard where I'm eating pasta and drinking wine and then dancing under a harvest moon." Henley smiled. "I'm afraid that movie *Under the Tuscan Sun* had a terrific impact on me."

Andrea laughed. "I think it helped Italian tourism immensely."

Henley noticed Stephano sneering at her. "I'm sorry, Stephano. Did I say something wrong?"

"I'm so tired of Tuscany, Tuscany, Tuscany." He sighed elaborately. "We're not from that part of the country."

"What part?" she asked.

"Tuscany, of course." He glared at her. "Your imaginary Italy. We're from Puglia. It's the heel. It's the best part."

"The heel?"

"Puglia is in the stiletto. I think it's the best part too, but Tuscany is lovely also." Andrea quickly stepped in, ever the gentleman. "Everywhere in Italy is lovely. You will see when you visit."

The waiter placed bowls of sunflower-colored bisque in front of each guest. "This is puree of summer squash served with a swirl of pressed and minced currants and a dot of crème fraiche. Be certain to eat the squash blossoms that are on top. They are delicious."

The velvet curtains billowed open, letting in a flood of light as

Wesley Kahn bounded in, arms flying, his face red. Henley and several other young employees of the firm jumped up.

"Mr. Scavo, I'm so sorry to interrupt, but I have such exciting news it just couldn't wait." He stopped and took a deep breath. "I received a phone call from the president of the Calder Foundation. They have chosen a winner of the Calder Prize." He raised his arms in a triumphant touchdown pose, an endearing silly grin on his face.

"We could not be prouder to have one of our own honored once again. It's the sixth time." He paused, looking at each of the eager faces, clearly delighted to have an audience for his announcement.

"Congratulations..." He looked around the room once again. "Henley. Congratulations, Henley. Another prize to add to your impressive list of accomplishments. We're so proud of you." He one-arm hugged Henley, whose head only reached his armpit.

Andrea hugged Henley next, pulling her close and enveloping her in the scent of sandalwood. "I'm so proud of you. Congratulations." He kissed the top of her head. Henley thought she saw tears shimmering in his eyes, which caused her own tears fall.

"Henley, this is good news. Don't cry. You won." Wesley laughed and pumped her hand. "I don't want to interrupt your dinner any longer. I just couldn't wait to tell you the news. Henley, order a couple of bottles of champagne to celebrate. Nice to see you, Mr. Scavo. I'm glad you were here for this wonderful announcement. This is fabulous. So proud. So proud."

Wesley bent down to speak to Brett, who looked like he'd been trapped by the reaction shot cameras at an Academy Awards ceremony. He nodded and followed Wesley to the corner of the room.

Keeping an eye on Brett and Wesley, Henley asked Andrea, "Will your wife be coming to the opening of the store?"

"Our niece is going to give birth to a baby girl at about the time the store opens, and she wants to be there to welcome the baby. This will be the first baby in our family in a long time. My wife is very excited for a grandniece and looking for every possible way to spoil her. There's also the orchard. She hired several men to help her with the pruning and needs to be there to manage them."

"The orchard sounds amazing. Is it on your property?"

He nodded. "In the back where there's a river. In the summer, when the children were small, we dammed it up on two ends to create a pool of water. It was such a joy to watch them splash and play."

Across the room, Wesley leaned against the wall, his arms crossed in front of his chest, nodding as Brett talked using his hands for emphasis.

"Is that a common thing to do in Italy? To dam up rivers to make swimming pools?"

"Very common in our area. The rivers are so clear and blue they make lovely pools."

Brett walked to the table, his head held high, chin up. He clapped Stephano on the back and walked out the door.

"My wife cooked in a giant stone oven on the patio. Every evening in the summer we would have a feast. The children played games in the orchard. They would pick fruit right from the trees."

"Your children ate fruit from the trees in your wife's orchard?"

"Yes. Of course."

"Does your wife soak pasta in red wine?"

"Oh, yes. Delicious. She's a wonderful cook. After dinner the children would dance, and I would share a glass of wine with my wife. Those are my most treasured memories."

"The kids d-d-d-danced after dinner in the orchard? "

Andrea didn't seem to notice the tremor in Henley's voice.

"What did they dance?"

"The children? Usually the pizzica."

"The pizzica?" Henley nodded. "I don't know that dance."

"Either that or the tarantella. The tarantella is an exciting dance, full of passion and energy. The dance is frantic so the little ones put their hearts into being as wild as possible. There's an interesting story behind that dance."

"The spider bite." Henley saw the waiter from the corner of her eye carrying a tray of food. Her vision cracked and images broke into faceted pieces of vivid colors like a Chagall stained glass. A figure lifting a fork to his mouth shifted against a woman laughing, her head thrown back, her mouth open all in sharp lines. As a man picked up a water glass, it caught the candlelight and reflected it like a blinding spotlight. Sounds and smells split away into separate components. The images zoomed and clashed in a jangle.

"Henley. Henley. Are you okay?" Andrea put his arm gently around her shoulders as she swayed in her chair. "What's the matter?"

"I didn't realize you had other children besides Stephano."

Her voice sounded tinny and distant like it was echoing down some eternal cavern. In her kaleidoscopic vision, Andrea's sad smile shattered into shards arranging and rearranging themselves as her stomach roiled.

"Henley." Andrea's voice was filled with kindness. "I think you know my other son."

"What?" Henley's head shot up. "No. No. I don't want to hear this."

"His name is Gustavo. He's an artist here in New York City."

"Gustavo." Henley carefully pronounced each syllable, feeling the name as she said it, her eyes locked on Andrea. "G."

"She knows Gustavo?" Stephano leaned over, pushing into Henley as he spoke to his father. She didn't look at him, but she felt the pressure of his body, and she smelled him, cologne, bourbon and sweat. "How does she know him?" He pushed her into Andrea, whose eyes never moved from her. He spoke to her as if Stephano wasn't there.

"I've been waiting for the right time to tell you this. I'm not sure now is the right time, but I have no choice. I knew you were seeing Gustavo when I hired you."

"How did you know that?" Stephano spat the words out so loudly people at the table turned to look at him.

Andrea kept speaking to Henley. "I had a person here who watched out for Gustavo. To make sure he was safe. He told me about you. I had some, ah"—he waved his hands in the air—"research done. I learned about you."

Tears rolled down her face. She didn't even try to wipe them away and didn't care who saw them. She had no words. Well, there were words in her head, but they were jumbled, and she couldn't form them into sentences. She clamped her mouth closed because she was afraid if she tried to speak some gnarled primeval sound would escape.

"Please, Henley, try to understand. I'm sure this seems like an invasion of your privacy, but I did it for my son. I was trying to protect him in the only way I knew. I had already lost a daughter. I was trying to protect my son."

"Paola," Henley whispered.

"Paola." Andrea nodded.

"That's why the gorilla walks by your side?"

He nodded.

"Is that why you hired her?" Stephano slammed his hands down on the table. His black eyes flashed with anger. "That's why, isn't it? It wasn't because of all those things you said about her work in that meeting. It was because of him. Everything is always because of him."

Still speaking to Henley, Andrea said, "I needed an architect for the store. I didn't like the work the original firm had done. Your firm is well regarded. You worked there. It worked out. It just..." He shrugged. "It seemed right. At the time."

The words in her head finally formed into a sentence. Henley pushed her chair back from the two men. Andrea reached for her hand, but she pulled away.

"You didn't hire me for my talent. I'll ask to be replaced on the project. It's been a pleasure working with you."

Stephano slammed his hands on the table again causing Henley to jump. "He abandoned his family to come here. You haven't heard a word from him, but you do all of this for him."

"Stephano." Andrea's tone was sharp. Conversation around the table ended and people began backing out of the room. "I won't stand for you talking badly about your brother."

To Henley, he said, "I didn't know you when I hired your firm, but it's different now. I was so worried about him. Gustavo locked himself up in that horrid studio and cut himself off from all of his friends. I was terrified for him."

"For six years?" Stephano shouted. "You've had someone spying on him for six years?"

Andrea stared at the floor.

"Have you?" Stephano demanded.

"Have you?" Henley whispered.

Andrea looked up at her and nodded. She reached for her purse and turned to leave.

"Please don't go," Andrea begged. "I was only protecting my family."

Henley nodded. She understood. He loved his son. How could she fault him for that? He was a good father. But to her, he was just another person who lied to her.

HENLEY KNOCKED on the door to the studio. Without waiting for him to answer, she pushed it open.

A large canvas covered with black paint stood propped against the wall. The paint was crusted into hills and valleys, pushed into mounds and crevices. It looked topographical, riddled with tiny slashes that cut through the paint and the canvas. Henley recoiled from the anger she saw in the painting and a tremor shivered through her body. He turned from the painting to her. She couldn't read the expression in her eyes. Maybe resignation, as if he'd been expecting this.

"Is your name Gustavo?" She pounded her fist on the wall. "Are you Gustavo? As in Andrea Scavo's son? My client, Andrea Scavo? The jewelry store I told you about. Are you a Scavo?"

There was complete silence almost as if the garbage trucks, taxi horns and ambulances were holding their breath.

"Yes."

"I'll tell you what else you are. You're a liar. My mom, my aunt, my father and now you. Even your father. Everyone in my life is a liar. After all the things you know about my family and their secrets... I cannot believe you would lie to me."

She grabbed the knob of the dingy door and flung it shut behind her. The glass panes in the front window rattled.

———

GUSTAVO RANG Henley's bell again. Waited. Rang it again. He pounded his fist on the solid oak door. Bella barked on the other side.

"Henley, I'm not going away until you talk to me. I'll stand here all night ringing this damn bell. I'll wake up your neighbors."

When Henley opened the door, Bella jumped up on him wagging her entire long little body. He scooped her up, and she gave him kisses.

"I don't have anything to say to you." Henley folded her arms. "You can leave."

"You talked, but you didn't listen."

"There isn't anything you have to say that I want to hear. You're another liar."

"You remember in Montauk when I told you I couldn't talk about the night my sister died? That's what this is about. I started to tell you about it, but it's...complicated. There's more that you don't know. *Cara*, you're so important to me. Please."

She hesitated and tried to avoid being sucked in by the sorrow she saw in his eyes.

"Okay. Two minutes." She moved back inside and sat on a chair. "And don't you ever call me *cara* again. Give Bella to me."

He put one hand under Bella's chest and another under her plump bottom and set her carefully on Henley's lap. He sat on the couch leaning his body toward Henley.

"I have never lied to you."

"That's what you want to say to me? I agree to listen and that's what you say?" Her voice exploded.

"I haven't lied."

"You haven't told me the truth. It's the same thing. You knew I was working for your father and didn't say anything. You didn't even tell me your real name."

"I *have* told you the truth. I just didn't tell you everything. These are difficult things to talk about it. I was going to tell you, but Montauk was our time together, and I didn't want to spoil it. I was born Gustavo, but I left Gustavo behind in Italy. When I met you, I was G. That was the truth. Since I didn't tell you everything, my entire life story, right when we first met, that makes me a liar? Is there a rule for when to tell someone about the very worst thing in your life?"

He got up from the couch and circled the room stopping at the window. Finally, he turned to her. She exhaled and nodded for him to continue.

"I told you my sister, Paola, died in a car accident. But there are things I didn't tell you about that night."

Pained silence continued for several seconds. He sat down on the couch.

Finally he said, "My sister, Paola. She...um...she..."

"One minute left."

Bella looked first at one then the other.

"I dread going to sleep because I know the accident...I'll dream it. It stalks me. The car swerving back and forth on the road, careening down the hill, rolling and rolling and smashing into a big olive tree, the screams and the blood. Sometimes I dream of Paola in her wedding dress or my mamma walking a grandbaby in the orchard, but it always ends with screeching tires, screaming and blood. The grief was this blazing pain that seemed to engulf my body, but then it turned to frozen numbness. So many times I think I'd rather have the fire."

He stood so abruptly that Bella startled from her warm spot on Henley's lap and barked at him. He walked to the door and rested his forehead against the hard surface. He groaned and hit his head against the door. Henley watched his shoulders shake with silent tears. Her anger dissolved. Henley set Bella on the couch and put her arms around him, resting her head on his back.

"The mountain road curved back and forth. There was a large rock in the center of the road. I couldn't avoid it. I had to choose between hitting the mountain and swerving around the rock on the right. The wheels went off the side of the road, and I lost control."

"You were driving?" Henley gasped.

Gustavo talked to the door. With her head on his back she could feel his ragged breathing.

"It was so dark. When the car stopped, I was hanging upside down from my seat belt. Blood was running down my body from the cut in my side. My brother, Stephano, was out of the car crouched by a tree, screaming and crying. I could barely see into the back seat. The car was sort of caved in around Paola, who was upside down in her seat belt. Her long hair was hanging straight down. I was able to unlatch my seat belt and crawl through the car window to get out. I had to go through the side window to reach Paola. I couldn't get her seat belt unlatched, so I cut it with my Swiss Army knife. She dropped into my arms."

His breath grew raspy, and his shoulders heaved.

"Her head fell down onto her chest. Her hair was wet. I couldn't see the blood, but I could taste metal in the air. It was atomized like perfume. Stephano was still screaming. I knew she was dead, but I sat on the ground holding her in my arms. Our family was over. My parents could never survive the loss."

"I'm so sorry." She kept her arms wrapped tightly around him.

"At the hospital when I was getting the cut on my side cleaned and stitched, Stephano told our parents the accident was my fault. He told them I could have avoided the rock."

"Your parents love you. You must know that."

"Every time he told the story he became louder and kept adding more details and became more vitriolic. He made it seem like I did it on purpose, like I was criminal. I don't think...I've gone over it and over it. I don't think I could have avoided the rock. I just don't think I could have. I could have run into it or hit the side of the mountain. Those were bad options too."

He hit his head on the door again. And again.

"Come sit on the couch with me." Henley tugged him away from the door.

He leaned against her as they walked to the couch. Bella climbed back into Henley's lap.

"Later I started thinking Stephano did it because he thought our parents always favored me. This was his way to be the *primo* son, the first son. He wanted to run things, to take over from our father, to cut me out. This way they would blame me for Paola's death. An unforgivable sin."

"I can't imagine Andrea blamed you."

"They...they...every time they looked at me there was such pain on their faces, such oppressive sadness. Every time I walked into a room, it would go silent. No one knew what to say to me. I thought maybe if they didn't see me, maybe it would help reduce their grief. The sorrow on their faces when they saw me shattered me, over and over. I was the living reminder that Paola was dead. The thing that was the hardest wasn't the sorrow, it was the forgiveness. That destroyed me."

"When did you find out I was working with your father?"

"On the bus on the way back from Montauk. When you showed me the jewelry, I recognized a couple of Paola's designs."

"You asked me the name of my client. I told you Andrea Scavo, and you never said a word."

"After I found out about my father, I knew I couldn't see you anymore. I thought you would lead me back to them, and I just couldn't go there."

"You couldn't see me anymore? What? You dumped me? You didn't tell me that. You dumped me and didn't even tell me I was dumped? You walked away from me without a word."

"I'm sorry. It was wrong. I was going to talk to you, but I couldn't figure out what to say."

"But you did see me again. The night I came to your studio. You came home with me that night. The night Izzy died. I'm not sure I understand. Did you dump me or not?"

"Your aunt got sick, and you were so devastated, I couldn't leave you then."

"You felt *sorry* for me?" Henley's voice crept up a notch. "You didn't care about me. You stayed with me because you pitied me?"

"I cared about you more than you know. I just couldn't go back and open those wounds. I left that all behind. You were a door back into it, all that pain, and I couldn't open that door. It was a mess. You were so sad, I couldn't leave you. But I couldn't be with you. I didn't know what to do."

Henley got up from the couch, Bella still in her arms, and opened the front door.

"What kind of person does that? You made love to me in Montauk. You danced with me in the sand." She stopped and stared at him, realization coming slowly. "You gave me art lessons." Her voice dropped to a whisper. "You painted me. And then you dumped me without telling me and ghosted me. I didn't even know I was ghosted. If I hadn't come to your studio when Izzy got sick, would you have ever called me again?"

He stared at her.

"Tell me the truth." She was shouting now.

"No." He shook his head. "I wouldn't have called you."

"You can leave now."

As he stepped out of the door, she said, "*Culo*." She regretted it the instant she said it.

He lifted his eyes to her. There was no anger, but the pain on his face sliced through her.

Gustavo kissed Bella on the head and left.

Henley kissed Bella on the same spot where Gustavo had just kissed her. "Traitor," she whispered.

"Guess what?" Henley said to the air. "I won the Calder Prize."

CHAPTER TWENTY

Simon pointed to Henley, who was at the end of the bar with her head and arms sprawled out across the shiny wood. A dribble of drool ran down her chin. "She's drunk."

"She never drinks more than two," Claudia said. "She knows she's a lightweight."

"That's why she's drunk. She came in here at about eleven and started drinking. She's had four in two and half hours. I only served her two, but she got two more from Jordan when I was in the back."

"Oh, my God. She's never had four drinks in her life. What happened?"

A guy walked over to Henley and leaned his head down parallel to the bar to look at her face. Simon rapped his knuckles on the bar. When the man looked up, Simon shook his finger like a metronome.

"As far as I can tell, she found out tonight the artist guy is the son of her client, that jewelry guy, Andrea, she's always talking about."

"Andrea Scavo of Scavo Designs? The artist is his *son*? What?"

"Yep. It's a long story, and I didn't follow all of it, but it's something like he dumped her, and then she dumped him. I'm not sure. And the dad, Andrea, lied to her. And speaking of dads she confronted hers a couple of days ago. I don't think that went well. And she says everyone lies to her."

"Well...that is a lot. I understand why she's drunk."

Henley lifted her head from the bar. She pointed a wobbly finger at Claudia, shouted her name and promptly laid her head back down on the bar.

"And she won the Calder Prize."

"What? She won?" Claudia bounced on the balls of her feet like a five-year-old. "That's incredible. We have to celebrate."

Simon looked at Henley, who was moaning. "Maybe we can do that next month."

"I'll take her home. Thank you, Simon. You're a prince."

Claudia stood on tiptoe to kiss him on the cheek.

"You keep saying that." He kissed her forehead. "Let me know if you need help. I'm pretty sure you have my number even though you never call."

HENLEY OPENED ONE EYE. Sunlight streamed joyously into the room, little dust particles dancing in the rays. She looked at the comforter and recognized it as hers. The weeping fig standing in the corner was one of hers. She closed the eye. She felt Bella nuzzled into the curve of her body and laid a hand across her little belly.

"Awake?"

She opened both eyes and saw Claudia sitting on a chair next to her bed.

"Claudia." She tried to roll over toward her and groaned. "What are you doing here?"

"If I weren't here, you'd still be at Simon's passed out on the bar."

"I went to Simon's bar? I don't remember that. There was a dinner meeting with the Scavo people. You won't believe what happened at the dinner."

"You found out your artist is from the Scavo family?"

"How do you know that?"

"Simon told me."

"How did Simon..." She tried to sit up but fell back down on her pillows. "Never mind. My head feels like it's stuffed with stones and weighs a hundred pounds."

"Simon gave me some tomato juice with Tabasco last night. I'll get it and some water," Claudia said on her way out the door.

"Aspirin too, please." Henley moaned, closed her eyes and stayed perfectly still. If she didn't move a single muscle, not even her eyelids, the pounding in her head might stop. Bella stretched, then climbed onto Henley's chest. She sniffed Henley's face, did not offer kisses, turned round and round and lay down with her head tucked under Henley's chin.

Henley sighed.

Bella sighed.

"I remember you were a traitor, little one." Henley stroked Bella's head. "You love him, don't you?"

Claudia set the tray with tomato juice, water, a bottle of aspirin and buttered toast on the nightstand.

"Before you ask," Claudia said, "I refuse to make that silly smashed egg thing of yours."

"I can't even think about food much less eat it. Nobody told me a hangover makes you feel like you have the flu and got dumped at the same time." Henley lifted Bella off her chest and reached for the aspirin bottle.

Claudia sat down on the bed. Bella instantly rolled over so her belly could be rubbed. She gave Claudia's hand a little thank-you kiss.

"So what happened?"

"It's coming back to me gradually, but I'm not sure whether the things I'm remembering happened, or I dreamed them. What I remember is pretty bad."

"You talked to your dad? Did you call him or meet him in person?"

"I stormed into his office, made a scene and stomped off. Then I marched forty blocks back to my office in a fury."

"Well, that's one way to do it. I'm proud of you for standing up for yourself, though. What'd he say?"

"Nothing."

"Nothing? Really?"

"I didn't give him much of an opportunity. I asked if he was married to my mother. He said yes. I asked if he was my father. He said yes. Not much more. I told him I didn't want to see him or hear from him ever again. I said I was leaving him the same way he left me."

"You pretty much knew that stuff already. He just confirmed it. Didn't you have other questions you wanted to ask? Like about the stuff he paid for? Like why he left? Maybe the big one—why they told you he was dead."

Henley sat up in bed and took a sip of tomato juice.

"I know. I screwed up. I had questions but got overwhelmed and a little drunk with anger. All these people lied to me. Mom, Izzy, him. After he confirmed what I found in Izzy's papers, I stormed out and slammed the door behind me."

"Maybe you could try talking to him again."

"He called me a bunch of times and left messages," Henley said.

"What'd they say?" Claudia asked.

"I don't know. I deleted them."

Claudia sighed. "So what about the artist?"

"There was a dinner with the Scavo's at Gramercy Tavern. Andrea started talking about his family, and I realized G was his son. Oh, his name is Gustavo. He didn't even tell me his real name. And, they didn't hire me because I was *sooooo* talented. He had a private investigator type watching over Gustavo who saw me at his studio. They gave me the job so they could spy on him and me."

"That's creepy. Did you talk to...Gustavo?" Claudia said the name hesitantly.

"I went to his studio and confronted him. I said, 'You're Gustavo.' He said, 'Yes.' I said, 'You're a liar,' and I left."

"So...that's the end of him then?"

"Then he came here. Bella kissed him."

"What?"

"Bella's a traitor," Henley said. "She loves him."

"*Henley*, what?"

"Bella loves him."

"What are you talking about? You said he came here? Why?"

"He came to tell me about the night his sister was killed—he was driving. It was an accident, but he blames himself. He felt seeing him caused his parents so much pain, he left Italy. So that's why he came here."

"Stop. Take a breath." Claudia held her hands out palms up. "That'd be an entire season in a soap opera. What a mess. His sister was killed, and he lost his family and even his country."

"And he lied to me. And you know what else? He knew I was working for them, so he dumped me, but he didn't tell me."

"He dumped you?"

"Yeah, but like I said, he didn't tell me. But it's over with him. I told him to leave."

"This is way too much stuff," Claudia said. "There's a lot to talk about here, but I have to go to work, and I need to stop at home first. We can have dinner later to talk about it if you want."

"Dinner, yes. Drinks, no. Never again." Henley rubbed her temples and groaned.

"We probably need to go over the final arrangements for Izzy's wake," Claudia said gently.

"I don't want to do it. I can't celebrate her after she lied to me. She let me think my dad was dead. Is that really forgivable?"

"I don't know. It's pretty bad. Do you really want to cancel the wake?"

"Yes. I really do."

"Okay." Claudia put on her pensive accountant face. "We'll have to find a way to take back all those invitations."

"They already went to all the people on the board of her foundation." Henley grimaced and rubbed her temples with her knuckles. "No, I can't cancel it. That could hurt the foundation."

"Quinn, Simon and I can take care of the rest of the planning. All you have to do is show up and smile."

"I want to do that about as much as I want another drink."

"I'll call Quinn. It'll take all three of us to get through all this mess," Claudia said.

"I'm going to Izzy's to finish sorting the last of the paperwork in the files and give the keys back to the landlord. We could meet there."

"Okay. How about five o'clock?"

"I love you, you know."

"I do know." Claudia kissed the top of her head. "See you at five."

HENLEY ANSWERED the door at Izzy's apartment, looked at her friends and shook her head. "It just keeps getting worse." She walked back into Izzy's living room and flopped down on the couch burying her head in her hands.

"What happened now?" Claudia draped her arm around Henley's shoulders and looked up at Quinn, who picked up a pile of papers and thumbed through them.

"These are receipts for $5000 a month. What are these?" Quinn asked.

"It looks like he pays my rent." Henley's voice was muffled.

"He pays your rent? How's he do that and you don't know about it?" Claudia asked.

"From what I can tell he pays Izzy who pays the landlord." Quinn thumbed through more receipts.

"I didn't know Izzy paid your rent," Claudia said to Henley.

"I would give Izzy $2200 a month. She told me I was subletting it from a friend of hers who was out of the country. It was a rent-controlled deal. It was supposed to be a secret, so I never talked about it."

Quinn shuffled through more papers and handed a stack to Claudia.

"Your place is amazing," Quinn said. "I didn't know what you were paying for it."

"In a terrific location. It couldn't be $2200 a month." Claudia sorted through the papers.

"I know. I'm a fool. I should have known something was off. Izzy told me it was a special deal, so I thought someone was doing a favor for her. I believed whatever Izzy told me."

"Hen, I don't think he's paying your rent." Claudia handed a couple of pages to Quinn.

"I saw the receipts. He pays $5000 a month. That means my place costs $7200 a month. A month! Can you believe that? No way can I pay $7200 a month. I'll have to move. I'll lose my garden. I'm gonna be sick."

"Yeah. He's paying $5000 a month, but it's a mortgage. You *own* that brownstone," Claudia said. "Well, you and the bank."

"What are you talking about? That makes no sense. I have a father who never saw me or spoke to me or hugged me, but he's buying me a brownstone. Why would he do that?"

"You'll have to ask him," Quinn said.

"I can't face him after the things I said. I was awful. I could send him a letter and offer to sell the brownstone. Or I can hire a lawyer and have them send him a letter to sell the brownstone. That seems like the best choice. I'll do that."

"Hen, I understand you don't want to, but I think you have to talk to him," Claudia said. "Don't go to his office and yell at him again though. This time use a smile as your weapon and listen to what he says. Gather information."

"I'll screw it up again. I was so awful to him."

Images of the meeting in his office began flashing through her mind. She could see his expression when he rushed from his office to greet her. Now she could see how pleased he was. She'd missed that at the time, but now in her mental replay she could see it was there. She must not have wanted to see it at the time. The images continued to flash—his expression became worried, then somber. When she told him she never wanted to see him again, he was devastated. She had done that to him. She realized it now. She'd never hurt anyone intentionally in her entire life, but she had hurt him. And she'd done it with malice. To hurt him the way he hurt her. There was no satisfaction in that. She felt hollow. But his lies were so awful.

"You said he's been calling you?" Claudia asked.

"He's left lots of messages on my phone."

"So you didn't screw up too badly," Claudia said. "He still wants to talk to you."

"I'm a little behind here. You confronted your dad in his office?" Quinn asked Henley. "You went to City Hall and yelled at the deputy mayor?"

"Yep, she did," Claudia answered. "And you know what else?"

"I'm afraid to ask."

"She got rip-roaring drunk, inebriated, blitzed, hammered, juiced, crocked ..."

"Please go on Webster. How many other words can you dredge from your memory for *drunk*?" Henley said.

"Okay, let's see, she got gassed, clobbered, soused, shizzatoed, buuuuuuuttered..." Claudia sang.

"Okay. Stop. We all get the picture." Henley put her hands on her head.

"Henley did? No." Quinn stared at Henley. "Henley, who only has two, two's my limit, no-more-than-two-for-me Henley? She got sizzled?"

"Dead drunk, passed out on the bar at Simon's."

"I can't believe you did that."

"She was lying on the bar."

"Just my head," Henley said.

"She was sprawled out on the bar, her arms flung out, drool running out of her mouth."

"Thanks for that description, Mouse," Henley said. "I'm glad you didn't take a photo."

"I didn't? Ohhhhhh, *really*?" Claudia pulled her phone from her jeans.

"Claudia. You didn't."

Henley's horrified expression was enough for Claudia to shove the phone back in her pocket.

"Of course not."

"One thing I can't figure out is how Ian McDaniels—i.e., your father—could afford all of that," Quinn said.

"Good point," Claudia said. "You're an expensive chick, Hen. Get it? Chick. Hen. Ha."

Henley smirked at her. "You should do stand-up."

"Imagine a mortgage with a $7200 dollars a month payment. That doesn't even consider how much of a down payment he made on the place," Claudia said. "Your education was a fortune. I don't know how much deputy mayors make, but it can't be that much. Wonder what the rest of the story is."

"Maybe he was a pirate," Quinn said. "And your brownstone was paid for with gold doubloons. That would be a pretty good story. Maybe that's why he was never around."

CHAPTER TWENTY-ONE

Despite the blisteringly cold wind, the wail of the saxophone drew people together outside the window of the pub where a brass band was playing "In the Sweet By and By." A trombone, clarinet, sousaphone and a tuba joined the soulful sax. The band moved on to Green Day's "Good Riddance." Quinn's playlist was filled with a mix of upbeat, spiritual, mournful and celebratory music.

Smiling photos of Izzy and some of the children she had helped over the years covered the walls. Guinness was on tap and a server carried a tray of shot glasses and a bottle of Midleton Dair Ghaelach through the crowd. The place was filled with people but not crowded just as planned. The three friends stood together off to the side of the room and watched the crowd who were all bedecked in brilliant colors. The invitation had asked guests to wear joyful clothing, fitting for a celebration. Henley leaned toward subtle, but Quinn convinced her to wear a bright red dress with a purple jacket and red heels. When she saw herself in the mirror, she smiled. Quinn was right about the happy clothes.

She shot a glance at Claudia. She and Quinn had both tried to get Claudia to wear a beautiful sky blue silk dress with a flowing skirt. They thought they had been successful until she walked through the door to the pub…in her little black dress.

Quinn had outdone herself with the food. Henley smiled at the long tables groaning with the weight of comfort food. In the middle of the table were four copper and porcelain pots filled with Kerrygold Irish cheddar cheese with more than a touch of Guinness and Irish whiskey blended through it. Around it were enormous platters piled with apple slices, cauliflower, zucchini, broccoli, peppers, pineapple, cherry tomatoes and various types of bread for dipping. Quinn had put a new twist on the traditional potpie by using puff pastry and cooking them in mason jars, and now rows of the golden-topped jars stood on heating trays. There were nine loaves of what Quinn called Almost As Good As Sex Bread displayed on glass trays.

Servers passed through the crowd of people carrying trays of Reuben fritters, garlic-roasted cabbage rounds and mini potato pancakes topped with a thin slice of cheese, a dollop of sour cream and a sprinkle of green onions. People quickly grabbed the food from the trays, and the servers had to refill often.

Henley nodded to Simon, who was wearing a green and yellow plaid shirt with green pants. He walked to a small stage area in the front of the room.

"Thank you for coming to celebrate an extraordinary woman. Izzy loved people, a good party and good Irish whiskey, so let's make Izzy proud. Is there anyone who would like to share a story about her?"

Elena stood and looked around to be certain she hadn't jumped up in front of anyone.

"Come on up." Simon waved her to the stage. "I'd like you to meet Elena. She was Izzy's neighbor for many years. Imagine the stories she can tell." Simon laughed and the crowd joined him in clapping. They raised glasses in a salute.

"This was probably fifteen years ago when my husband was still alive." Elena stopped to take a sip of her beer. "One morning there was frantic pounding on my door. It was early, about six. I looked through the keyhole, and there's Izzy waving her arms at me. I didn't even know she was back in the country."

Servers made their way through the crowd with more food.

"I yanked the door open, and Izzy flew inside in a tizzy. An absolute tizzy. Her arms were flying, and she's pacing around. She's talking, but I can't understand her. There had to be something really wrong because Izzy was normally unflappable. She stops pacing and bends over at the waist. So I say, 'What? What? What's wrong?' In gasps she tells me she ran up the stairs rather than take the elevator because she was trying to beat someone to the apartment. Then she says, 'I need to borrow your husband.' *Borrow my husband.*" Elena repeated with considerable emphasis. "Well, I loved Izzy, and she was a fun neighbor, but I didn't want to give her my husband." She paused and winked at the crowd. "I didn't know if I would ever get him back."

The crowd nodded knowingly. Several people raised their glasses to her again.

"After I heard what the problem was, I agreed she could have Ed." She paused. "For a few hours." She paused again. "In the daytime."

Servers moved through the crowd with trays of golden macaroni and cheese balls. Henley snagged a couple from a tray and handed one to Simon, whose eyes rolled back with the first bite.

"So I got Ed out of bed and sent him to Izzy's house. He was still in his PJs. He was...curious, but I have to admit, clearly not reluctant. Twenty minutes later, I hear pounding on Izzy's door, so I look out the peephole and see this important-looking man in a long white robe with a red headband. Lots of men in black suits swarmed around him. They all had those black earphones with the curly wires in their ears. Ed answered the door. I couldn't hear what the man said, but Ed says, 'What do you want with my wife?' He says it in a deep, intimidating voice. My Ed was a gentle man, so this was surprising. After a lot of shouting, the man stormed down the hallway with his white robes flying and his entourage running behind him talking into their sleeves. Since you know Izzy, you can probably figure out what happened. That man was a prince who didn't take no for an answer. Everyone loved Izzy."

Elena stepped down from the stage to applause and walked over to hug Henley. One person shouted, "Did Ed come back home?" Laughter arose from the crowd.

"He did." Elena laughed. "Izzy probably sent him home."

Simon asked if anyone else had a story to tell. Nomcebo came forward.

"My story isn't funny like Elena's, but it has a happy ending. My father was killed in the war in Rwanda, and my mother died from AIDS. I lived with my aunties, but then they too died from AIDS."

Nomcebo paused, noticing the stricken faces in the crowd.

"It's okay. It really does have a happy ending. I was alone after my aunties died. I was nine. People were nice to me and gave me food most of the time but not all the time. I did go to school, which I liked very much. But there was a crisis. My only dress got a hole. It was a hole in a very bad spot."

She cupped her hands around her mouth and stage-whispered, "It was at my bottom, so I couldn't go to school anymore."

Ian walked into the pub while Nomcebo was speaking. Henley noticed him and looked to Quinn, who nodded to her. Ian spotted a server, picked up a shot glass of Dair Ghaelach, tossed it back and promptly picked up two more.

"I invited him," Quinn whispered. "It seemed right. You don't have to talk to him if you don't want to." Henley gave her a beseeching look and shook her head no.

"On the day I met Izzy." Nomcebo was still talking. "I did not have any food, so Izzy gave me her lunch, but what she really gave me was life. She drove me to a private boarding school and paid the fee. Without her I probably wouldn't be alive today. I certainly wouldn't be in New York City drinking this lovely Irish whiskey and talking to all you wonderful people who I count as my family since we all loved Izzy."

Nomcebo held up her glass. "To Izzy. I love you." Many people in the crowd wiped tears from their eyes as they raised their glasses. "To Izzy."

Quinn and Simon quickly hugged Nomcebo. Simon stepped back to the front of the room.

"Is there anyone else who would like to tell a story?"

"I would," Ian said.

Simon shot a worried glance to Quinn, but he nodded to Ian and moved to the side.

Ian set two shot glasses and a white box on a small table near the stage.

"I'd been in California for a couple of years trying to become an artist." Henley's chin came up, her eyes riveted on him. "That's what I said I was doing anyway. If I was honest, I'd admit I was surfing and hanging out with my friends. On my last week I drove up to Big Sur, set my easel up, put on the Eagles and painted the coastline and the wild ocean. In hindsight, I think I was painting that view of California to keep as a memory of where I came from and to remind myself if my move to New York City didn't work out, the ocean would always welcome me back."

Ian was wearing dark gray jeans and a crisp white shirt but no jacket or tie. Henley wondered if he missed the dress code for the night or if those *were* his joyful clothes. He didn't look like a politician, but he handled the crowd like a master, walking back and forth and talking directly to each person in the pub.

"That night I walked into the bar at one of those Big Sur hotels and my heart stopped. I was a dead man. Two of the most gorgeous women I had ever seen were sitting at the bar. They weren't just beautiful, they had some kind of aura...I don't know. Confidence, charisma, maybe just jaw-dropping, teeth-melting raw sex appeal. I'm ready to signal for a defibrillator when one of those women notices my distress and slides over to me. She puts her hand on my heart. That woman was Isidora—Dori. She became my wife. Isabel, Izzy, was her sister. Dori and Izzy, what a pair. They entered my life and nothing was ever the same. My God, I loved them and would have done anything for them."

Ian picked up the shot glass of Dair Ghaelach and threw it back. Henley stepped away from her friends, who had closed ranks around her. Her heart was beating so fast she couldn't swallow and felt like she was going to choke. She had to force her hands to remain at her sides so she didn't stick her fingers in her ears like a child.

"Like her sister, Izzy was brilliant, funny and possessed of an inner spirit that always seemed to be bursting from the seams."

No more, Henley thought as she pushed through the crowd. She needed to get outside. She needed cold air. She needed to get away from his words. She didn't want to hear his happy stories. Probably more lies. She was just steps away from the door—soon she wouldn't be able to hear him anymore.

"But everything changed though when our baby, Travis, died." Ian paused. Henley felt the collective intake of air in the room. She turned around to see Ian staring at her.

"Dori and I lost him to crib death when he was six months old. A death like that changes everything. Dori...Izzy...me. None of us was ever the same. Izzy was there when we faced the worst. She stood with us in the face of shattering heartbreak. When confronted with sorrow, Izzy became even stronger. I don't know how we would have survived without her."

The guests shuffled and glanced around unsure of how to react. Ian cleared his throat, his eyes on Henley.

"The only thing that never changed for us was our love for Henley. We were all certain she was the cleverest, most talented, sweetest, most beautiful child who had ever been born. And as her father, who has watched her grow into a magnificent young woman, I can attest that we were all correct. Thank you for listening." He raised a shot glass. "To Izzy." It took a few beats, but the crowd returned the call.

Ian walked to Henley, who was wiping her face on the sleeve or her jacket. He handed her the white box.

"These are yours." He kissed her on the cheek and walked out.

Quinn signaled the band, who played the Beatles song "In My Life." Her friends circled Henley. Simon put his arm around her as Quinn grabbed her hand. All four of them watched the door close on Ian. They stood leaning on each other as the band continued. Following the playlist, the tuba thumped and the trumpet blared as the band swung into a New Orleans favorite, "As I Lay My Burden Down."

Several servers fanned out carrying trays of desserts. There were more stories and more songs, more Irish whiskey, more laughter and more tears.

ONLY A FEW STRAGGLER cookie pieces lay scattered on the table as Simon took center stage again and said, "This has been a wonderful night. Thank you for making this evening so special. Henley would like to say a few things in closing."

"Thank you for coming. Tonight has been an almost perfect evening." Henley stared out at the crowd. She couldn't remember what she planned to say and wondered if she could just say, "Thanks again" and sit down. She had a brother. Nothing would ever be the same. Her foundation had cracked and shifted. Simon touched her arm, startling her back to the present.

"The only thing missing is the woman who would have loved it the most. I...uh...there are a couple of gifts for all of you on the table in the back. Please pick them up when you leave." She couldn't remember what else she had intended to say and stood silently in front of the crowd.

Finally her brain kicked in, and she continued, "There are small jars of Izzy's favorite lotion, Frederic Malle. Every time I catch a whiff of her geranium fragrance it makes me feel like she's at my side. Maybe it will do the same for you. There are also boxes of her favorite chocolate croissants from La Maison du Chocolat. Indulge tomorrow morning. It will make your day happy. And there's a book of poetry." She paused and shook her head. "I know. I know. Don't groan. Imagine how happy Izzy would be if you read even one of those poems. Since Izzy has been transformed into energy, imagine that ball of energy pulsing a vibrant happy purple. I want to end with a quote from Jean-Luc Picard, 'Live now, make now always the most precious time. Now will never come again.' Thank you for coming."

The band played Izzy's favorite song, "My Way."

The Frank Sinatra version.

―――

THE LAST BOTTLE of Dair Ghaelach sat on the table ringed with shot glasses. Five shot glasses and five women. Five women dressed in red, fuchsia, yellow, purple and…black. They looked like a human pinwheel.

"I'm starving." Quinn grabbed the last loaf of Almost As Good As Sex Bread and a knife. "I cheated and tucked a loaf behind the bar."

"That bread is to die for," Elena said. "Literally. I had to stop at two pieces because it is a coronary on a plate."

"I took a boule of bread, cross-hatched it, poured melted butter, garlic and Guinness into the crevices, as if that weren't enough, I stuffed it full of cheese. I don't know why you think this is unhealthy," Quinn laughed and pushed a plate of sliced bread to the middle of table along with a stack of napkins.

"No wonder it's so good." Nomcebo put a slice on a napkin.

Claudia nodded to the white box in Henley's lap. "Are you going to open it?"

"You should open it while we're all here," Quinn said.

Henley took a knife from the buffet table and cut the tape on the sides of the box. Before she lifted the lid, she glanced at Quinn, who nodded. Peeking out from under the edges of the white tissue paper were red sequins. Her dream flashed through her mind, and she knew instantly what was in the box. Her hands shook as she lifted the paper. Snuggled safely inside the tissue paper was a red taffeta dress with a satin sash and little red sequined shoes. She held them to her chest, her eyes closed, head lifted to the heavens.

"He kept them for all these years," Claudia mumbled with her hand over her mouth.

"They're darling." Elena cast a worried look around the table. "Were they yours?"

"It's complicated. I wore this dress when I went to see my mom dance in *Swan Lake*. That man who spoke tonight is my dad, but I never knew him. Izzy and my mom told me he was dead. I only found out about him a few weeks ago. And now, tonight, I found out about Travis. My brother. I'm so confused. And so sad. Apparently he kept my clothes for all these years. I don't know what that means."

Henley lowered the dress and shoes back into the tissue paper and put the lid back on the box.

"I don't know the answer to that, Henley. I wish I did. That's too much for anyone to deal with." Elena put her hand on Henley's arm. "What I can tell you without reservation is that Izzy loved you. When she talked about you, which was all the time, she glowed. She used to say, 'I love that girl to the moon and the stars.'"

Henley raised glistening eyes to Elena. "Thank you."

"She did love you." Claudia nodded. "It was obvious. I don't have an answer for all of the rest of this stuff, but I know she loved you."

"Yep," Quinn said. "And I think your dad did too. Tonight was heartbreaking. I felt like he opened an artery and bled all over the stage."

"I had a brother...Travis. Who I didn't even know about. My mom had a baby who died and no one talked about it." Henley put her head in her hands. "All of these people lied to me because they loved me?"

"Yeah. In their own effed-up way." Claudia nodded. "That's what happened."

"That's life." Elena shrugged. "It's messy and often doesn't make sense."

"They lied to me." Henley picked up the box and smacked it on the table.

"Remember that black coat you used to wear in college?" Quinn asked.

"What are you talking about?" Henley's voice rose sharply.

"The black coat with the inverted pleat in the back."

"Yeah. The one that swayed when I walked. I loved that coat. Why?"

"Horrid."

"It wasn't horrid. I still miss that coat."

"It made you look like a ghoul or an undertaker or maybe a Sherlock Holmes groupie. It was massive and it overwhelmed you. You're small and it billowed. You say it swayed when you walked, making it sound all romantic. It billowed like a cloud of coal dust enveloping you. Think Pig-Pen from Peanuts, not *French Lieutenant's Woman*."

Henley's cheeks flushed bright red. "You never told me."

"Because every time you wore that stupid coat you glowed. It made you feel good, and I wasn't going to take that away from you. So sometimes lies are just—I don't know—kind."

"I think I would have still worn the coat even if I'd known what you thought of it."

"Maybe, but you wouldn't have glowed."

"Your point?"

"Lies are complicated."

"Next time would you tell me if I wear a ghoul coat?"

Quinn shrugged.

"Maybe." Nomcebo's voice was quiet but carried wisdom and strength. They all turned to look at her. "Maybe... the focus should be on the love and not the lies."

Henley grasped Nomcebo's hand. "Maybe," she said softly.

"Your mom, dad and Izzy were all just trying to protect you," Quinn added.

"I don't know how those lies protected me. From who? From what? And then there is G and his father. They lied to me too. So many people have lied to me."

"Look, I realize I'm coming in on the middle of the play, but it seems like your artist just didn't tell you his worst stuff," Elena said. "Imagine if we all opened that suitcase we have packed in the back of our closet that's filled with all of our grief, regrets, doubts and failures. We'd scare everyone away. That stuff has to be dished out in little bites. Like this, what'd you call it? Better than sex bread?" She winked at the women, waggled a piece of bread and popped it into her mouth.

Henley looked around the table. Claudia and Nomcebo nodded. Quinn shrugged. "G built an alternate existence in another country across an ocean. The death of his sister. The grief of his parents. He's from a rich Italian family, and he was living in a crappy studio. He closed himself off. What would any of us do if those things happened to us?"

"Now you're in favor of him after all the times you told me to stay away from him?"

"I'm not in favor of him, and I wasn't against him. I was against him hurting you. I was trying to protect you from getting hurt by another stray jerk."

"That's harsh."

"It's true. You told me I should tell you when you wear a black ghoul coat."

Henley sighed. "I should walk away, then?"

"Actually, I think you should hear him out. I hate the word *closure*, but if you don't talk to him, it will bother you. You'll be one of those seventy-year-olds trying to find the one who got away on Facebook."

"Thank you all. I'll think about everything you've said. Before we go, I have a gift for each of you from Izzy." Henley handed each of them a mauve-colored velvet bag. The four women stared at the bags.

"Should we open these now?" Claudia asked.

"Oh, my God," Nomcebo squealed. "What is this?"

Henley put her hand on Nomcebo's arm.

"Izzy wants you to have them. She loved you."

"I can't accept these." Nomcebo pressed her hand firmly against her mouth. "I just can't. It's too much."

"I agree." Claudia held a pair of sapphire and diamond earrings in the palm of her hand. "I can't accept these."

"Listen, I chose a few pieces to share with the women Izzy loved. All of you. The rest I'm going to sell and put the money into the foundation to help more children. Some of her jewelry needs to stay with her family though. You are her family."

Nomcebo blew her nose. Elena wept, her shoulders shaking.

"I'm honored." Quinn held up a pair of pearl and diamond earrings to her ears. "Thank you. I'll wear these with pride and always try to be worthy of them." Quinn leaned forward and kissed Henley on the cheek.

Henley reached for their hands. After several minutes, Claudia grabbed the last bottle and poured them each a shot. "To Izzy." They clinked and drank.

———

HENLEY KNOCKED on the door of the studio. Snow squalls swirled around her legs. The knock echoed through the hollow space. She peered in the windows. No canvas. No messy futon in the back. No sprawled bedding. No hot plate or little refrigerator. It was a dirty, dark, dingy studio.

An *empty,* dirty, dark, dingy studio.

———

HENLEY WALKED in to find Simon hunched over the bar, typing on his laptop.

"Thank you for everything you did for the wake last week. You were an excellent master of ceremonies. Izzy would have loved it."

"It was a group effort, although most of the credit goes to Quinn. Hey, what happened with your dad? That was pretty heavy. You okay?"

"Still processing. I don't know what to feel. Should I be angry, sad, maybe happy that I have a father again? I really don't know. We're going to go to the exhibit at the American Folk Art Museum together to see my mom's little houses."

"Sounds like a start. You'll figure it out as you go."

"What's this I hear about you having a new addition to your family? Claudia texted me a photo. I can't wait to meet him. How'd that happen?"

"He's at Claudia's now, but I'll get him tonight. We worked out a visitation schedule. The day we all went to the shelter to give them the bedding I fell in love that little tricolored Australian Shepherd. Later I found out Claudia did too. So we figured out together we could take care of him. He has two homes and two people who love him."

"And he didn't even have to go through a divorce to get two homes," Henley said. "He's a lucky guy."

"And Claudia is helping me with the book about Izzy, so when I'm at her place working on the book, we're all together. We take breaks and walk him at the dog park around the corner. There's a restaurant that allows dogs a block over, so we go there because he gets his own meal. He's so great with everyone he meets. And of course he's brilliant."

"It's sort of like you and Claudia are parents. That's interesting. Bella's excited to meet him. He's welcome to stay with us whenever you need. What's his name?"

"Neut."

"Newt? Like a lizard?"

"Like neutrino. A type of particle."

"You got Claudia to agree to that?" Henley asked.

"I think she might be calling him Garfunkel or Gar."

"Garfunkel? Why?"

"Because Simon and Garfunkel, get it?" Simon smirked and shook his head. "So what'd you do with the artist?"

"I went to his studio to talk to him, but it's empty. He's gone."

"So that's it? It's over?"

She shrugged. "Quinn thinks I should talk to him so there aren't any feelings swirling around that will whip around and try to strangle me in my sleep."

"She's got a point on that. It's hard to get past the past. I'm the bug in amber on that problem. In the grand scheme of things, I don't think their lies helped anyone, but since they intended to help, maybe you have to put the needle on the intention rather than the outcome."

"You should be a philosopher." Henley put her arm around his shoulders.

"I am. I'm a bartender."

"Simon?"

"Yeah?"

"Why are you a bartender?"

"I'm a good bartender."

"You're the best bartender. When will it be time to do something else?" Henley asked.

"Time is an interesting concept."

CHAPTER TWENTY-TWO

"I'm having trouble getting used to you being alive." Henley side-glanced Ian as they stood in line at the American Folk Art Museum on the Upper East Side not far from where she lived.

"I have a lot to explain. I didn't know if you would ever be able to forgive me for the secrets. You slammed the door to my office so hard it rattled the windows in the building. People probably thought there was an earthquake. I'll tell you, for me, your visit *was* an earthquake."

Henley gestured at the museum. "Have you seen any of Mom's houses before?"

Ian shook his head. "Only in photographs. She started them after I moved out."

Henley nodded as they moved forward. The line was impressive, snaking up six steps and down a long hallway to the exhibit. The anticipation of seeing her mother's work again made her feel shaky, like her legs might fold in on themselves, dropping her to the ground. Waiting in line made the nervousness worse.

"When was that? That you moved out, I mean?"

"You were four. I see you're wearing the amethyst necklace. It looks beautiful on you."

Henley touched the stone, her fingers comfortable on the familiar facets. "Izzy gave it to me after Mom died."

"I gave it to Izzy to give to you. Amethyst is known as the protective stone. It was one of the ways I watched over you without being there."

Her brain stumbled and had to reset. The ground shifted under her feet once again. She struggled to understand what he said. Her heart ached for the sweet lovingness of the gift, but bitterness was mingling there too. It was another lie to add to the blazing bonfire of her life. Remembering what Claudia said about bringing a smile to the battle, she bit back the bitter. It took some time, but finally she said, "I wear it all the time. Thank you."

The smile he gave her would have burned a hole in her heart if she hadn't quickly turned her head away.

"Are those Izzy's earrings?"

Henley touched the square diamond earrings at her ears and nodded. "I kept these because Izzy wore them all the time."

"The governor of California gave them to her. He wasn't governor then, of course. It was a long time ago. She was dating him when I met your mom. It was a glorious week." He was lost in a memory, and a smile flitted over his lips. "We drove down the coast highway together—the four of us. The roof of the convertible down, the sea air in our hair, and the Eagles on the radio. Those earrings were supposed to be a pre-engagement gift. They planned to get married at some point. Izzy was setting up her foundation, and he was running for state office. They wanted to get those things done first, and then they planned to be together."

"What happened?"

"I'm not sure. Neither of them would talk about it. They were apart a lot. She was traveling overseas, and he was always running another campaign for some office. I wondered if they grew apart, but I don't think so. I think they would have found a way to be together if Travis hadn't died. Izzy was so devastated, just as your mom and I were. She saw what it did to your mom, me, you. I think she was afraid."

"Izzy? Afraid? I can't believe that."

"Izzy saw how great a pain can be when you give yourself to someone. Your mom and I adored each other, and we were nuts about you and your brother. She saw the greater the love, the greater the pain... maybe she never wanted to face that. I don't know. I do know that she rarely spoke to him after Travis. But she always wore the earrings."

"They're the only jewelry I ever saw her wear. I always thought she was holding out for Jean-Luc Picard, but maybe it was the governor."

"He was heartbroken when I told him she passed. For him hope really did spring eternal, now it's too late. I'm sure you have questions. Ask anything." Ian held his arms out in a *search me* stance.

"Did you pay for Miss Porter's?"

"Yes."

"And Brown and Columbia?"

He nodded.

"And where I live, you're paying for that too?"

"Part of it. You pay for part."

"And it's not rent. It's a mortgage?"

"Yes."

Henley paused in front of the craft display that lined the hallway, taking time to phrase her next question.

"What I don't understand is why you would leave me, never see me again, and yet pay for all of those things. You let me think you were dead. Was it guilt? Did it appease your conscience for leaving me and Mom?"

"Guilt? Well, in a way...yes...I suppose. But before I explain, I need to correct one thing you said. You said I never saw you. I did see you every time I could."

"I didn't see you."

"I was at your high school graduation and your graduations from

Brown and Columbia and all the little things in between. When you played Emily in *Our Town*, I was in the audience. I clapped like a madman. I was at all of your violin recitals until you gave it up. I gotta agree with you on that one. You weren't Suzuki material."

He smiled at her, but she stepped away, unable to look at his earnest face.

"I was at every concert, play, track meet, fencing bout, recital and graduation. Izzy gave me your schedule, and I sat in the audience like every other proud father."

"What about when Mom died? Where you there then too?"

"I was at the funeral and watched you standing with Izzy. The black coat you were wearing had buttons almost all the way to the bottom, and your black boots came up to your knees. It was frigid that day, and the wind kept blowing your hair over your face. You never let go of Izzy's hand. I wanted to grab you and run away somewhere I could keep you safe."

"I don't think you can imagine what it would have meant to me to have heard those words when I was ten or twelve. It could have changed my life."

His face instantly shifted from earnest to crestfallen. "I'm sorry."

They turned into the exhibit room, which was lined on each side with nine elaborate miniature houses. Henley stopped to steady herself. She hadn't seen these houses in many years. Memories of her mom flooded back. The emotions were so conflicted they seemed to wind around her, slowly engulfing her.

"Do you know how your mom chose what kind of house she built?"

She was grateful for the question. "I don't. She built grand manors, Edwardian homes, English country homes, Hollywood bungalows and even a log cabin. My guess is when she saw something she liked, she built it. I don't think there was anything more to it."

When they reached the first house in the exhibit, Henley's heart pounded. She knew this house well. Images of her mom flew through her mind. Full-color images of her mom bent over the house, her hair in a ponytail, the big white button-up shirt she always wore flapping as she moved around her work, scraps of wood scattered on the table and the floor. Henley stood still in front of the house for fear her feet wouldn't move. She could almost smell the glue and turpentine and feel the sawdust under her feet. Finally forcing herself forward, she waived to the second house.

"This house is a replica of the Farnam Mansion in New York. I watched her build this house. The roof tiles were hand-cut from big pieces of slate, maybe ten by ten. She used tile cutters to break them into small pieces, then she sanded the edges until they were smooth. It took forever, but I'm not sure she even noticed time. She slipped away into her work. Those decorative cornice brackets and the ornate pediments were all carved out of mahogany like the original house."

Ian leaned close to the house to inspect the details. "There's a tiny rolling pin on the counter in the kitchen, measuring cups and mixing bowls too. Are they carved from wood?"

"Sometimes. Occasionally, she could find authentic replicas in metal. See the books in the library? Each one is carved, and the spine is painted with the titles. She sewed the curtains from velvet. She spent so much time on the details. One time I heard her tell Izzy that the mark of a good con is in the details. I've thought about that comment many times over the years, but I still don't know what she meant. Who was conning who?"

"Maybe she was conning herself. Henley, did you see the paintings on the walls in the rooms?"

"She carved the frames and painted the art herself."

"But did you see the paintings? They're Degas. His ballerinas."

"I didn't realize that. I never noticed."

"They're on every wall. Every painting is a ballerina." Ian's face was ashen. The crowd behind them was getting pushy.

"And that's your bedroom." Ian's voice shook as he pointed to an upstairs room.

Henley bent to look inside.

"It's pink with a purple giraffe on the wall." She faced him. "The giraffe was Wilbur."

Ian nodded. Henley pointed to the other bedroom.

"And that was Travis's room. Blue, with elephants on the walls." She was momentarily triumphant with recollection.

Ian nodded.

"They had their trunks in the air. Oh, my God, I remember Travis." Her face crumpled. "His tiny fingers and toes. I remember kissing the bottoms of his little feet."

She clasped her hand over her mouth with such ferocity her teeth bit into the inside of her lips. She didn't cry, but it felt like her internal organs were dissolving into woozy jello. Ian grabbed her arm as she swayed.

She looked up at him in horror. "You screamed at me. It's you I see in my dreams."

"We need to leave." He steered her out of the room.

HENLEY WRAPPED her hands around a glass of red wine and watched Ian stare into his glass of Maker's Mark, jiggling the single ice cube against the crystal. They hadn't spoken to each other since walking into the club, both lost in their thoughts.

Ian shook his glass rhythmically so the ice cube hit the side over and over. Henley wondered if he was trying to break the glass. After several minutes of silence, he said, "Your mom was trying to find her life in those houses. Her dancing, her children, her home, her life. She was trying to find what she lost. It kills me to see her loss laid out like that for people to gawk over." His voice was choked with tears.

"I don't think anyone else would know the meaning of those things. People are impressed over the artistry. We should be proud of her," Henley said softly. "Would you tell me about my brother?"

He stared at the ceiling and shook the glass a few more times before answering her.

"Travis was a precious baby, so sweet. He never cried, not from the first day we brought him home. I'd come to his crib, and he'd be lying there smiling, babbling, grabbing his feet, putting his toes in his mouth. Not like you, I'm sorry to say."

"So he was Boston cream pie. What was I? Dill pickles?"

Ian's smile was tinged with sadness. "You were a pill." He nodded his head. "You screamed for a few years. I'm not kidding. It was years. But you were so beautiful. The baby intercom would jangle with your screams at all hours of the day and night. I'd tell your exhausted mother I would get you, and I'd drag myself out of bed and trudge down the hallway to your room. There you'd be, standing in your crib holding on to the railing, rocking back and forth, beet red, tears and snot covering your hands and running down your cheeks. The second I saw you, my heart melted. When you saw me, you'd stop crying. Being alone was the worst thing for you. We loved you so much."

A few simple images of her brother flashed through her mind—his little fingers and toes, the way he smelled like milk and sugar, how he blinked at Henley, and his little blue socks. There weren't many images in the mind movie, but each of them was like a punch in the chest. She wanted to know more, but she was afraid of what she would hear.

"But Travis was an angel?"

"He really was. Maybe he was never meant for this world. When I can't sleep, I tell myself he was always an angel who was never meant to stay. It doesn't really help to think that, but I can't think of anything better. I suppose because there is nothing that will ever help."

"Please tell me what happened to Travis."

"Your brother, Travis." He looked at her to be certain she really wanted to know and on a deep breath out went on in a soft, monotone voice. "He died in his sleep when you were four. It was the first night your mother danced after he was born. She didn't want to leave you with a babysitter, so I agreed to stay home. When I checked on him an hour after she left, he was blue. I pulled him from the crib, laid him on the floor and called 911 while doing CPR."

Henley listened with her eyes closed, allowing the words to wash over her. The soft jazz and murmured conversations in the background registered faintly, but she kept her eyes closed trying to keep her breath steady and even, trying to keep her heart from breaking out of her chest.

"You woke up and came into the room and started crying. That's when I screamed at you. I shouted at you to shut the fuck up. Shut...the...fuck...up." He slowly enunciated each word, making a popping sound in this throat on the last word. "Those words still haunt me. I never screamed at you and certainly never swore at you. Your face twisted in fear. You were afraid of me. I see that image like a photograph when I close my eyes at night. I'm so sorry for that. I would give anything to take back those four words."

They both looked up from their drinks and stared at each other. Cigar smoke wafted through the room. Ice cubes in crystal glasses rattled sharply over conversations around them.

"I kept doing chest compressions on his tiny fragile chest. I was afraid I would break his ribs but also afraid it wasn't hard enough to get his heart to beat again. You shot from the room. The EMTs came, but he was gone. They tried, really tried. The men who were there that night worked so hard to bring him back, but they couldn't."

"And you called Mom to come home?"

Ian dropped his head again and closed his eyes.

"I couldn't find you. We lived in a big loft in SoHo so the space was pretty open. You weren't in your bed or behind furniture. I knew you'd been in my studio because paint was thrown on the walls and the floor and several canvases were on the floor. I finally found you in a corner of your closet buried under a pile of clothes, not making a sound. I carried you to the couch in the living room and held you. Eventually, you fell asleep sucking your thumb, which was something you stopped doing years before."

He looked up at her. She read his pain and knew he didn't want to continue, but she pressed anyway. She needed to understand. "Please, I need to know about Mom. She came home and learned baby was dead?"

"I..." Ian slapped his hands down on the arms of his chair, and Henley thought he was going to get up and leave, but he didn't. "I called the director of the troupe and told him there was an emergency. I asked him to tell Isidora to come home the second she came off the stage."

"He told her to go home. Nothing else? He didn't tell her what happened?"

"I didn't tell him what happened. Isidora tore into the apartment like a tornado. She had pulled a coat on over her costume, and it was buttoned wrong. I remember seeing her burst through the door and turn to me. I thought, *Your coat is buttoned wrong.* What a thing to think. It's stayed with me all of these years. That coat. Her stage makeup was smeared all over her face. She had tried to call me, but the phone was off the hook. The more times she tried, the more frantic she became. She didn't know what the emergency was, but she knew it had to be bad." His voice was so heavy it fell on her like wet snow.

Ian rubbed his face with his hands. A waiter veered to their table, but Ian stopped him with shake of his head.

"She found me on the couch holding you. One glance at me and she knew. She ran to the baby's room. There was medical stuff scattered on the floor, stuff left by the EMTs—plastic tubes, needles, wrappers, so much trash. They tried so hard. The crib was empty. She stood in the middle of the floor and screamed. Of course, you started screaming again. There was screaming everywhere. It seemed to be coming from all directions like a foghorn."

He slumped in his chair, head dropping, glass tilted and spilling bourbon.

"Maybe we should stop. This is enough for now." Henley set her glass on the small table and leaned forward. She regretted pushing him.

Ian shook his head. "She didn't stop screaming. She was curled on the floor, keening. I tried to hold her, but she screamed and tried to scratch and bite me. A doctor came to give her a sedative. She woke up screaming the next morning. She was committed to a psychiatric hospital for three months. Izzy visited her. Every time she saw me it dumped her into such a well of sorrow...I couldn't visit her. This woman I adored, couldn't stand to see me."

"It wasn't your fault. There wasn't anything you could have done to prevent it, was there?"

Ian shook his head no.

"I sensed the sorrow in Mom, but I didn't grasp the importance. Now I understand the pervasive sadness that covered our lives. But why did she tell me you were dead?"

"She said it was my fault Travis was dead. She said I should be dead instead of him. I wanted me dead too. She said I couldn't come anywhere near you. When she told you I was dead, I just didn't fight it. I threw away my paints and burned my canvases. I never painted again. I went to work on Wall Street. Can you imagine a more soul-sucking job than that? At least it gave me the money to pay for the things I wanted for you. I stayed there until you graduated from Columbia."

Henley set her glass on the table, straightened in her chair and repositioned her body, readying herself, for what she wasn't certain. She forced herself to continue, to ask the question that had been hovering over her life since she learned he was alive.

"You could have fought back. You could have gone to court to get to see me. You could have called me after she died. But you just let me go. Why didn't you fight for me?"

"I should have. I suppose I was so buried in grief I couldn't think straight. I told myself you would be better without me. I felt guilty. I was there when he died. I should have checked on him sooner. Intellectually I know it wouldn't have mattered, but I can never convince my heart of that. When she said I was guilty, I believed her. Guilt and grief are a lethal combination. Afterward, I regretted not fighting for you. With all my heart. But it was done. I couldn't figure out how to take it back. The deal I made with myself was that I would watch you and as long as you were happy and safe, I would stay quiet."

"But those lies hurt everyone. You, Mom, Izzy, me."

"We all tried to protect you because we all loved you. We were wrong, but the lies were born of love."

"If you had it to do over, you would have done it differently?"

"Absolutely. Regret is a bastard."

He laid his hand palm up on the small table—an invitation...a hope. She put her hand in his. His wrenching gasp sent reverberations through her body. She felt the love and grief and dreams and sorrow burst the damn he had created and surge through that simple touch.

And she thought of gorillas.

The purple gorilla Ian McDaniels, now Dad, talked about at Izzy's funeral—the one you must make a place for at the end of your bed. And Andrea's gorilla—the one that sat on his chest so he couldn't breathe. The one that, with time, walked beside him, holding his hand. And she understood everything. Grief is strong because she is love. You can't bury grief. If you try, she'll reach her hand out and grab you by the throat when you're standing in the grocery store. You can't ignore grief. If you try, she'll bring you to your knees whenever she wants. You can only live with her. You have to give her that place at the end of your bed and let her walk beside you. There is no other choice. Her mom, dad, Izzy—they hadn't understood that.

CHAPTER TWENTY-THREE

Andrea grabbed Henley's hand as they left the jewelry store. "Could we please talk?"

"We'll be finished with those items we discussed shortly." She slipped her hand out of his and kept walking.

"Henley, please stop with the project talk. I'm grateful you agreed to finish the store, but I want to talk about us. How do I make this up to you? I didn't see how it could hurt you to give you the project. It seemed like a win-win to me. You got a good project that could further your career."

"And you used the job to spy on me. It's creepy. Knowing that you were doing it to protect your son, doesn't make me feel less dirty."

"I'm sorry. It's easier to be thoughtless when you don't know the person. I'm not proud of that, but it's true."

"I'm constantly thinking about the places I've been and wondering whether someone was watching me. Did they stand outside my house?"

"No, they didn't. They saw you when you went to his studio."

"They only saw me when I was with him?"

"For the most part."

"For the most part? What's that mean?" She glared at him, her voice rising.

"At first when we found out about you, he did a little research to find out what your motivations were. It all checked out, so he didn't watch you anymore."

"I checked out. Ohhhh, I'm so thrilled. I passed. Did I get five stars or an A or an A+? Did I get an A+?" Her voice was drenched in sarcasm. "Is there a review I could put online?"

"Stop. It wasn't like that. I only wanted to know you weren't out to hurt him. Please, *cara*."

"Don't you call me *cara*. Don't you say that again." Her expression instantly turned from anger to dread when a thought formed in her mind. "Did you have someone watching us in Montauk?"

He wouldn't look at her.

"Did you?"

Andrea nodded, his head down, eyes closed.

"I can't believe this." Henley walked away but turned around and came back to stand in front of where he was slumped against the outside of the building.

"What did he see?"

Andrea shrugged.

"What did he tell you?"

"That my son found a woman he loves." When he finally looked up at her, he was crying—not just tears at the corners of his eyes but full fat tears unashamedly rolling down his face. "That's when I told him to stop following Gustavo. He had you. He would be safe with you."

"But he doesn't have me."

"What?"

"We're not together. He dumped me when he learned I was working for you."

"You're not together anymore? I didn't know. I didn't have anyone watching him any longer." It was Andrea's turn to look horrified. "I caused this. How can I fix this?"

"I don't know if it can be fixed."

"Henley, I know what I did was wrong. I would take it back if I could. I didn't know you. By working together, I grew to respect you. And then to love you. My feelings for you have always been honest. I was so tangled in grief over Paola, and then my son was gone off to another country. I wasn't thinking straight. It wasn't meant to hurt you."

Her anger softened. His feelings were believable to her because she felt them too. She had initially respected and appreciated him but had grown to love him. And grief. Well, she understood that too.

"Please. What can I do?" Andrea pleaded. "Just tell me. I'll do it."

"I don't know. It might be too late."

CHAPTER TWENTY-FOUR

G was already at the restaurant when she arrived. In his black jeans with a white linen shirt under a black cashmere jacket, he didn't look like a starving artist anymore. His hair was combed back into a ponytail—only one unruly curl escaped. He rose instantly and helped her with her coat. The hug was as brief as the kiss on her cheek.

"I was so glad to get your phone call. Every day, every night, I hoped you would give me a chance to explain." He looked straight at her as they sat down at the table.

Henley longed to reach her hand out to him, to feel his touch. The desire to kiss him almost pulled her up and out of her chair. She wanted to crawl over the table, grab him by his cashmere lapels and kiss him for the next hour. She twined her fingers together and averted her gaze from him to the restaurant with its crisp white walls and sharp red accents.

"You look beautiful. Your dress looks like a Matisse painting with the bold simple colors."

She pulled her eyes back to him, and the desire rose again. She knew what he was thinking—*he's an artist we haven't studied.* She managed a "Thank you" that came out in a deep, sultry voice she hadn't intended.

"How's Bella?" His question drew her back from the thoughts of art class.

"Sassy as always."

"I grew attached to her. I miss the way I could hypnotize her by running my finger down the crease of her long nose."

He could not have said anything that would have touched her heart more. "She loves you. There aren't many people she trusts."

"Can we talk about what happened?" G leaned forward on his elbows almost as if he was going to kiss her.

A server appeared at the table and set menus in front of them, giving her a chance to mentally scold all those pulsing parts of her body and tell them to knock it off.

"I do understand why you didn't volunteer the information about your life. I'm sorry about what happened with your sister and your family. It's heartbreaking. I overreacted on that. It seemed to me that everyone knew things I didn't. It seemed the same as with my family, but it wasn't. My family lied to me."

"I would have told you about what happened. I just needed to find the right time."

"I get that. That's not the issue. Once I realized what happened with your sister, I understood why you didn't tell me. But G, you dumped—"

"Gustavo," he interrupted.

"You're Gustavo now?"

"I'm not running from who I am anymore. That's why I left that awful studio."

"I thought you didn't pay attention to where you lived?"

"We can all make ourselves believe anything if we try hard enough. That place was a dump. I suppose I was punishing myself. I want my life back. And I want you in it."

"I don't know how to trust you. You dumped me without even

talking to me. You made the decision and that was it. I didn't even know about it. You didn't text me or leave me a letter on the counter, or even a Post-it-note on my computer. Any of those things would have been cowardly, but you didn't even do one of them. You canceled me."

"I couldn't believe you were working for my father. It caused my brain to go haywire. My instinct was to run. I'm sorry."

"And the next time there's a problem, is your brain going to go haywire again?"

"The only honest answer I can give you is that I don't think so. This was a unique situation. I'm aware of the reaction, so I think I can stop it from happening. I hope that if it ever did happen, you would see it for what it was—fear—and give me the time to deal with it and come back."

After they gave the waiter their order, Henley said, "Can I have some time to think about all this?"

"Of course. What happened with your father?"

"It's a long, sad story, but we're trying to make a life that includes each other."

"That's great. Do you want to talk about it?"

"Not today, maybe someday. How about your father? Have you talked to him?"

"No. Paola is still gone. I would cause them pain. There isn't anything I can do to take change what happened."

"I've known your father for a while now, and I can tell you that he loves you. He's grieving for Paola, and I'm sure he always will, but he loves you. Your absence makes the loss of Paola worse, not better. You can't protect him from the grief. He has to live with it."

They sat quietly, both lost in their thoughts. Henley wondered if she should tell him about the man Andrea hired to follow them. She didn't know whether he would find it loving or invasive. She couldn't take the chance, so she waited for him to talk.

"I have a show." His words were quiet but his face betrayed his excitement.

"A show? Of your art? You always said the art would tell you when it was ready. Did she tell you?"

"She's been a talkative brat recently—pushing me to do all sorts of things. There's a special piece I want you to see."

"When is the show?"

An idea took hold in Henley's mind. An idea that could lead to tears of happiness or sorrow. She needed to carefully consider how to manage it.

CHAPTER TWENTY-FIVE

STANDING on the street corner where the delicate fragrance from flowering trees mingled with savory odors from the various food carts, they watched people file into the building across from them. In the large window facing Fourth Avenue a painting she knew well filled the entire space. It was as mesmerizing as the first time she'd seen it. It was the blue painting, and it stood like a beacon calling her.

"Henley, I don't think this is a fair thing to do to him," Andrea said. "It's not right to surprise him in front of so many people on such an important night. We should wait until another time. You can call him and ask for a time to come here in private."

"I've thought a lot about this. You've lost too much time already, Andrea. And he should get to share this huge success with you. You don't want to miss this. Look at that crowd. This is an amazing night for him."

She sounded much more confident than she felt. It certainly *could* go all wrong.

Inside the gallery people balanced little plates of food and wine glasses as they talked and pointed to various paintings with their chins. She didn't see Gustavo.

"You look gorgeous tonight, my dear," Andrea said. "I've never seen you dress like that before."

She wasn't wearing one of Quinn's designs tonight, but Quinn helped pick it out from one of the design houses on Seventh Avenue. Quinn's discount was the only way she could wear an Alexander McQueen original. The sleeveless dress had a fitted black ribbed top that cinched at her waist with a wide black belt. An intricate pattern of butterfly wings in a rumble of glorious reds filled the skirt that draped over her hips and fell just to her knees.

"I didn't tell his mother I was going to see him. If I lose him again, I don't want her to know. I can't have her heart broken again." Anguish filled his features, but in the beam of the streetlight Henley saw hope sparkle in his eyes—hope and unbounded pride.

"You won't lose him again. I promise. Come with me."

HE SAW her open the gallery door out of the corner of his eye. He'd been watching for her, anxiety building as the minutes wore on. All day he made adjustments to the exhibit, anticipating her reactions when she saw the paintings. He hung the information card for the last painting himself, not trusting anyone else to do it. Over the objections of the gallery owner, he insisted on choosing the music. When everything was in order, he waited and paced, barely able to talk to people interested in purchasing his work. He hoped this was the way to convince her of his feelings.

As he watched her walk through the door, two thoughts filled his head. If he could paint the emotion he was experiencing, it would be the pinnacle of his artistic career. And he loved her.

"I'm so glad you're here. I've been waiting for you." Gustavo took her hands in his and kissed her on both cheeks. "*Cara.*"

Behind her he saw his father. His father was standing in the doorway. With Henley. His father.

"I'm sorry," Andrea said to Henley. "I shouldn't have intruded." He opened the door to leave.

"Papá? Papá, what are you doing here?"

The door closed behind Andrea. Gustavo spun around to Henley.

"You brought my father? What were you thinking? What gave you the right to do that? Why didn't you tell me?"

"You would have told me not to. Don't let him leave. Go talk to him."

Gustavo stared at Henley then looked out the door at his father, who was on the street corner hailing a cab.

"Gustavo, don't let him go."

He bolted out the door.

SHE WATCHED Gustavo run to Andrea, watched him put his hand on his father's arm to stop him from getting into a cab. The two men faced each other. It didn't seem like they were saying anything.

Henley stepped away from the door and wandered through the gallery. Gustavo's paintings hung on six parallel walls of glass that rose from slots in the floor and reached about fifteen feet in height and stretched maybe thirty feet in length. The walls looked like ordinary clear glass, but she figured they were probably high-density plexiglass, just like the roof in her office building and in her museum design. She examined the edge and bent down to see how it was anchored to the floor. Lighting at the bottom of the panels inside the slots was directed up, causing the glass to disappear and creating the impression that the paintings were hanging in midair. She glanced up from inspecting the base of the wall to see a small group of people staring at her. She tipped her glass of champagne to them.

Gustavo and Andrea had come inside and were involved in an animated conversation, both gesticulating wildly with their arms.

Henley started with the glass wall closest to the window, the one where the blue canvas was hanging. The first time she saw the painting in his old studio, she'd been transfixed by the sense of movement, but now she realized it was more than that. It was motion, but that motion was frantic and multidimensional, striking out in every direction. The painting was emotion. The words etched on the glass by the painting said, "Turmoil" by Gustavo Scavo. Henley walked to the opposite side of the first glass wall and found a painting vibrating with reds and blacks titled "Anger." Around every corner was another emotion—shame, grief, fear, disgust.

Sensory overload forced her to step out of the maze of walls. Gustavo caught her eye for just a moment and nodded before responding to something Andrea was saying. She thought the nod was encouraging, like he was asking her to go on, go further, to see the rest.

The din created by people talking over one another added to the emotion of the paintings like a movie score. Behind the din she could hear music. After several seconds with her head tilted, ear to the speakers in the ceiling, she was able to distinguish Mozart's Piano Concerto no. 21. Memories of Montauk swelled with the music.

The walls surrounding the room held smaller paintings. The first group were of the ocean, some tempestuous with wild strokes of color and others lolling and peaceful but all with texture and depth. Following along the wall the next group were sand paintings with raised dots of sand glinting in the bright sun. She looked at the painting from different angles even pressing her head against the wall trying to see how he created the sand effect. "Pointillism," she whispered as a thrill surged through her nerve endings as they vividly remembered the dots of champagne.

These were the Montauk paintings. Love and lust were cresting and filling her heart when she turned a corner to find a painting hanging alone in an alcove, and she was instantly repelled. It was the angry black painting. The one in the studio the night she confronted him. Sickened by the sight of it, she turned and walked away, only to catch Gustavo watching her. The disappointment and hurt in his expression stopped her retreat.

She faced a choice, leave and escape the anger and lies she saw in that painting or trust another man and risk being played the fool, again. She slowly turned to the alcove, taking slow even breaths, and confronted the painting.

The nighttime sky spread out in front of her, full of glorious swirls of amethyst, sapphire and emerald, dotted with sparkling silver and gold and topaz. The effect was immediate and knee weakening. Henley reached for something to hold on to but grabbed only air. *Inhale. Hold. Exhale.* She found her own strength and walked to the canvas, feeling Gustavo's eyes on her every step.

Hundreds of tiny multicolored lights behind the painting leaked through the slashes in the canvas hitting the crusted mounds of black paint, creating the impression of a night sky with dancing stars of fluctuating intensity. It was their Montauk sky. The information card said, "Henley's Sky." Below it was another tag that said, "Not for Sale." He had given her the stars, and she saw love in the stars.

"I'm sorry to interrupt." Henley put her hands on Gustavo's arms. His expression of hope and longing was more poignant than any poem or any painting. She put her hands on either side of his face and looked into his eyes. And then she kissed him.

"*Cara, mi togli il respiro,*" Gustavo whispered as he wrapped his arms around her.

Andrea's face was like sunshine in the rain. He was smiling and crying at the same time.

CHAPTER TWENTY-SIX

The line to get into the new Scavo Jewelry store went down the street and around the corner. Henley heard gasps, laughter and clapping from inside the store. She was outside where it was a little quieter so she could talk to reporters. Quinn had suggested having food and drink delivered to the people standing in line so servers in black tie carried trays of champagne and various types of canapés. Wesley Kahn was strutting like a proud peacock in and out of the building shaking every hand and telling everyone that this was his favorite project. Henley smiled every time he said it. Last time she saw Stephano he was scowling in a corner drinking champagne.

The white linen dress Henley was wearing was gathered at the waist and flared out flowing just below her knees. The fabric was embellished with flowers of such a pale pink they were just a whisper, more a sensation than a presence. Quinn's magic again.

As Henley was finishing her sixth interview, she saw Simon, Quinn and Claudia coming down the street and forced herself to resist the urge to run to them. She wanted to jump up and down and scream like a four-year-old who just found out they were going out for ice cream.

As soon as the reporter said, "Thank you for speaking with us tonight," Henley did run down the street and was engulfed by her friends. She managed not to jump up and down or scream.

"This is quite a shindig," Simon said. "This is huge. Look at all those people waiting to get in. It's like a massive conga line. Maybe we could start a dance. It'd be cool to have a flash mob in the street. A flash mob conga line." His eyes lit up. "Let's do it."

"I love a conga line. Why don't you start it, Simon?" Quinn rolled her eyes to Simon and hugged Henley hard, let her go, and hugged her again. "This is simply outrageous."

"It's pretty great, but just wait until you get us all into the Met Gala." Henley laughed and spun around in circles with her arms swinging out wide.

"I'm so proud of you." Claudia lowered her head and swiped at her face.

"Claudia, what's the matter?" Henley put her arm around Claudia's shoulders and bent down to look at her. "Are you crying?"

"I...I...I'm just so proud of you," Claudia stammered.

"I've never seen you cry before," Quinn said. "Not for anything. Not even when you broke your arm in tenth grade."

"Come here, sweetie." Simon opened his arms and hugged Claudia. "I'll make it better. It's hard to watch our little girl grow up."

"You're going to make me cry, and I have more interviews." Henley laughed and hugged Claudia, who was still in Simon's arms. "I love you all."

"Is that Ian talking to Andrea?" Quinn asked.

"Yeah. They've become buddies. It's surreal. Ian says he's going to Italy to visit them. Andrea's wife, Maria, is determined to find him a lovely Italian woman."

"Is Gustavo here yet?" Claudia asked.

"He's inside. I'm sure he'll be out in a minute. He and Andrea are pretty inseparable these days—making up for lost time. Usually they both have silly grins on their faces."

"So Gustavo...he's pretty delectable," Quinn said. "Henley, could I have him for a little while? Maybe for a weekend? Just a loan?"

"You know everything I have is yours," Henley said.

Quinn smiled in the way only Quinn can smile.

"...*except him*." Henley laughed. "Anyway, aren't you meeting that sexy Frenchman Pierre Comtois at some fancy Caribbean resort?"

"Maybe," Quinn purred. "If he's very, very lucky."

"There's a lot of food and drink when you get inside. Don't leave without telling me," Henley said.

"We're not leaving until it's over," Quinn answered. "Not until everything is over."

Henley screwed her face into a question. "Whatever you say. Gotta go, my public calls." She offered a silly curtsey and danced away to another interview.

―――

HENLEY CONTINUED THE INTERVIEWS, answering the same questions from another reporter. "Where did she get the idea? What was the cave made from?" As the reporter walked away someone tapped Henley's shoulder. She turned and found Brett, his hand extended to her.

"Henley, it's a great launch, don't you think?"

A dozen responses flashed through Henley's mind, but unable to extract one, she settled for gawking at him.

"I'm thrilled to have played a role in the creation of such an unusual store. This press is great for them, but also for us, don't you think?" He clapped her on the back.

Finding her voice, Henley said, "Brett, thanks. I'm a little surprised to see you here."

"I wouldn't have missed this. It's important for the firm that we all support each other."

"The firm?"

"Our firm. Of course. Ah, you're worried about that little kerfuffle with the Calder Prize. Henley, thank you for your concern. I'm touched."

"I wouldn't describe it as a kerfuffle. I...ah...I heard you submitted a Frank Gehry drawing in the contest. I guess I thought you, I don't know, maybe there would be consequences. There weren't?"

"It was a little dicey there for a while. I explained to Wesley that I accidentally clicked on the wrong folder on my computer when I submitted my entry. He understood how that kind of thing can happen."

"And you accidentally submitted the Gehry drawing for the museum in Bilbao, Spain?"

"Yeah, isn't that just a laugh?"

Brett's grin was a big as it was fake. Henley tried to duplicate it.

"Yeah. That's a laugh, all right." She stepped away from him. "I haven't seen you around the office recently."

"Well, yeah...I've been onsite at a warehouse project."

"Oh. Eek." Henley grimaced. "That sounds...exciting?"

"Work is work. Always glad to do my part. So did you decide at the last minute to enter the contest or had you been planning to enter it all along?"

She just smiled at him.

"I didn't realize you were such a fan of Frank Gehry," Brett said. "Hey, no hard feelings, Henley. Maybe we can get a drink sometime?"

As she walked away, she said over her shoulder, "Nice to see you, Brett."

WHILE A FEW SMALL groups of people mingled, the cleaning crew gathered the last of the detritus of the evening. Henley chatted with Andrea and Gustavo. Her friends were huddled in a corner talking. It looked conspiratorial so she walked over to check it out just as

Stephano and Brett walked out, laughing and nudging each other like frat brothers.

"It's okay if you all leave," she told the three of them. "I'm just finishing up. I'll meet you somewhere."

"No, we're not leaving," Simon said.

"Nope, we're not." Quinn shook her head. "We're not going anywhere."

Ian appeared at Andrea's side out of breath with a bottle of Cristal in his hand. He dug his cell phone out of his pocket.

"I didn't miss it, did I?" Ian asked Andrea.

"Miss what? You brought Cristal? We still have some champagne left if you want some," Henley said. "Do you want to stop someplace for a glass of wine to celebrate?"

Everyone took a step back. Henley glanced at them her brow furrowed. "No? You don't want to?"

Gustavo took a small black box out of his pocket.

Henley looked around the room as her heart pounded in her ears. Her friends were grinning at her, their cell phones in their hands, facing her. Her father's arm was slung over Andrea's shoulder, both of them smiling like goofy puppies. She looked back to Gustavo, who was reaching out to her.

"Gustavo?" she whispered.

"One evening last fall, I was in my studio lost in a painting when I heard a crash outside. I was so frustrated by the painting and caught in a spiral of turmoil and hopelessness, I almost didn't turn around. I did though and found you battling a cardboard box. When you looked up at me, I saw wonder and curiosity and...well, appreciation in your eyes. You saw the me I wanted to be. You are my muse and my love. I want to paint you through all the seasons and all the years. Will you marry me?"

She nodded, exhaling the breath she'd been holding in a long whoosh.

"Is that yes?" He laughed.

"Yes. Absolutely yes. You can paint me for the next thousand years."

Gustavo pulled her into his arms. Andrea and Ian hugged them both. Simon, Quinn and Claudia circled them all. It was a big ball of human hug.

"Wait a minute," Henley said from the middle of the hug. "What's in the box?"

"This was made for you by my family." Gustavo looked at his father as he opened the box and struggled to get enough space from the hug to hold it to Henley.

"It was made for you with love by *your* family," Andrea said.

A strand of rose gold and a strand of platinum twisted around each other to create a band that was embedded with rose-tinged diamonds. In the center was a yellow diamond, it's facets and planes sparking in the light.

Henley blinked but did not reach for the box.

"How big is that?" she finally stammered.

Andrea laughed. "The rose gold in the band is you and the platinum is Gustavo. The ring symbolizes the intertwining of your lives, and the yellow diamond in the center represents your love and the joy this has brought to so many people."

"And the pink diamonds in the band represent babies." Ian grinned. "Grandbabies."

As Gustavo slipped the ring on her finger Andrea and Ian wiped tears from their eyes, her friends had their arms slung around each other, their faces lit with happiness. And love filled all her lonely spaces.

CHAPTER TWENTY-SEVEN

Henley watched from a window of the villa as Gustavo and Maria moved from tree to tree, weaving tiny lights through the branches. She didn't know what they were saying, but Maria's smile was as bright as the morning sun shining down on the orchard. Gustavo stepped off the ladder and swept his mother into an embrace.

"I wonder if Andrea and Maria would adopt me so I could stay here in Puglia, live in this outrageously fabulous villa and eat Maria's cooking all day long?" Claudia plopped on the big four-poster bed in the room that had been dubbed "Henley's room."

"I could move my studio here," Quinn said. "We could all stay here. It's big enough for all of us. Have you decided if you and Gustavo are moving here?"

"We agreed to three months here, three months in New York City, three months here and three months back there. I convinced my firm that Puglia will inspire my creativity, so I can design while I'm here and meet with clients back there."

"Do you have more opportunity to call the shots now that you're a partner in the firm?" Claudia asked.

Henley smiled mischievously. "Now that I control the Scavo

Industries architectural work, they do seem to listen to me a little more closely."

"Can you fire Brett?" Quinn asked.

"No, but I can make his life uncomfortable." Henley smiled.

"Should we go down and help with lunch?" Claudia asked.

"Let's wait a little and give them some time to finish the lights. They were going to hang those lights for Paola's wedding, so it's one of those bittersweet things for them. Oh, Maria offered to teach me to cook."

Quinn and Claudia stopped what they were doing and stared at her open mouthed.

"Don't worry. I told her not cooking was a family tradition. Anyway, Gustavo is a fabulous cook. He's almost as good of a cook as he is an artist." She winked at them. "He's even better at other things."

The relief on their faces was apparent. Bella jumped up against Henley's legs asking to be picked up.

"Where is Bella's dress?" Henley asked with a wink to Claudia. "I hope we didn't forget it."

"Really? You think I might have forgotten her dress?" Quinn said. "That dress took hours to make. Your dress took—"

"—five people over a thousand hours each to hand sew thousands of tiny crystals," Claudia finished. "I've heard that somewhere."

"Me too, maybe a few hundred times." Henley laughed as she snuggled Bella. "It is the most magnificent wedding dress in the history of wedding dresses."

Quinn nodded. "You bet it is."

There was a rap at the door and Simon walked in.

"What if we'd been naked?" Quinn asked.

"You aren't naked." He fell on the big bed next to Claudia.

"I know, but what if we had been?"

"That's hypothetical. Did you know there's a river behind the orchard? After lunch they're going to damn it up so some of the kids can go swimming this afternoon."

"And you're going too?" Henley said laughing.

"Of course. Wouldn't miss it. Anyone want to join?"

"Nah. Hair. Make-up. Nails." Claudia tilted her head at him.

"Oh, yeah. I'll tell you how it is. Are you coming down for lunch? Maria cooks like a five-star chef. It's set up on the patio," Simon said.

"If you think lunch looks good, wait until you see what Maria has in store for dinner after the wedding," Claudia said. "It'll knock your socks off."

"That'd be cool. I'll go put some socks on." Simon jumped up from the bed. "See you downstairs."

―――

FULL FROM LUNCH, some people lounged on chairs trying to keep their eyes open while others gathered in small groups talking and laughing. Shrieks of laughter rose from the river. When a baby wailed from a carriage, Maria and her sister both bent to soothe her. Claudia played lifeguard at the river while Quinn checked each stitch of the dress.

Fall sun warmed the three levels of stone patios that were terraced into the hillside leading down to the orchard. A huge stone oven sat next to the second patio. Empty pans and discarded plates covered tables on the patio closest to the house. Enormous pots of white orchids lined the edges of the stone patios—each spike was covered with over twenty bird-shaped flowers.

Henley and Bella walked toward the orchard. Big pots of tulips, the symbol of perfect love, stood in front of the orchard like sentries. Ian broke away from a conversation, put his arm around Henley's shoulders and said,

"She walks in beauty, like the night
Of cloudless climes and starry skies;
And all that's best of dark and bright
Meet in her aspect and her eyes."

"Lord Byron. That's a beautiful poem. Thank you for that. I miss Mom and Izzy, especially today. That helps me feel closer to them."

"I miss them too. Always. They would be so proud of you."

"Was that Stephano leaving?" Henley asked.

"Yeah. Nothing you need to worry about."

"Is he coming back?"

"I don't think so. No worries."

"What happened?"

"Well... he grabbed Claudia's, uh...*derriere* and she kicked him in his, uh...private parts."

"Dad, I'm thirty. You can use those words in front of me."

"Okay. Well, he grabbed Claudia's ass, and she kicked him in the balls. He stormed off in that little blue sports car."

"Sounds about right," Henley said.

"I'm so thankful to be here," Ian said.

She nodded. "Me too. I dreamed about a life with a man I love and a big family, but I never really believed I would have it."

GUSTAVO STOOD in front of an arbor of roses, his artist's eye absorbing every luscious detail. To his side stretched the orchard of rescued trees decorated with lights and ribbons and behind him the Adriatic Sea glistening with all the colors of the sunset. He wore a black tuxedo with a platinum stripe up the side of the pants and a platinum tie. Standing next to him were his childhood friends, Raoul and Mattia. Under the watchful eye of their father, Bastiano, they quietly clasped their hands behind their backs and struggled to keep a serious expression on their faces. Bastiano and Andrea had been best friends since babyhood—as had their fathers and their fathers and so on. Bastiano sat next to one of sixteen pounded silver bowls filled with flowers that stood on pedestals lining the aisle. They were his work, exquisite from generational knowledge.

Andrea and Maria sat half turned in their seats, nearly sparking with happiness, waiting to see their new daughter walk down the aisle. Bella sat on Maria's lap decked out in a rose satin dress, her head held high as if she understood she was getting a dad that day.

Gustavo inhaled the subtle fragrance from the flowers gently blowing in the breeze. His arms were loose at his sides, his feet firmly planted on Italian soil. He felt the strength of generations of his family. He treasured this life, its value seared into his soul by its loss. He had given her the stars, and she had given him life. Peace flowed through his body as he waited for her to come to him.

She came into view just as the string quartet began to play. She was everything he had ever wanted. Tonight's art class would be especially sensual. He would show her the depth of his love.

———

QUINN, Claudia and Simon helped Henley lift her dress from the ground as she carefully walked along the narrow path from the villa to the hill overlooking the Adriatic. When she saw Gustavo standing in front of an arbor covered with roses her heart broke into its very own tarantella. Ian was waiting for them behind the last row of chairs. He wore the same expression she had seen so many times that week—like he just couldn't contain all of the emotions he was experiencing. She saw the look in Gustavo's eyes and knew just what he was thinking. For as much as she loved all of the people who were smiling at her, she longed to be alone with him. He had given her the stars, and she would love him forever.

Quinn's satin sleeveless trumpet gown matched the rose gold in Henley's ring. She kissed Henley on the cheek and began a slow walk down the aisle in her inimitable style. Her curls ruffled in the sea breeze, and Izzy's pearl and diamond earrings sparkled on her ears.

Claudia followed, her long black hair glimmering against her platinum gown, accented by Izzy's sapphire and diamond earrings. She wobbled a little in the five-inch heels she insisted on wearing.

Simon was next, elegant in his black tuxedo with the same platinum stripe and Vans on his feet. When he reached the altar, the three friends linked arms.

Henley turned to her dad and held out her hand. Together they walked down the aisle, Mozart's piano concerto no. 21 floating with them. The LED lights hidden in the base of all of the pots embraced the flowers in a heavenly glow. Tiny platinum and rose Swarovski crystals covered the nude bodice of Henley's dress and swept out and down one hip of the full diaphanous chiffon skirt in a glorious flourish. She wore the amethyst necklace, Izzy's diamond earrings and Gustavo's ring. They caught and reflected the light along with the crystals on her dress like thousands of little stars.

After the walk down the petal-strewn aisle, time moved quickly. Gustavo extended his hand. Ian placed her hand in his saying, "Her mother, her aunt and I do." Andrea and Maria both stood and hugged Ian when he sat next to them alongside Bella. Henley and Gustavo promised to love, treasure and respect each other for the rest of their lives. When Gustavo added that he would paint her, people laughed. If they only knew. Gustavo and Henley kissed. People clapped. The sun set.

STARS EXPLODED like glitter in the Italian sky, and the orchard transformed into a magical kingdom with silver and rose silk streamers fluttering in the trees and thousands of tiny lights twinkling. Music and laughter swooped around and over the trees and the night filled with love. Gustavo and Henley, their bodies fitted together like a puzzle, carved out a spot on the crowded dance floor and swayed as the band played "At Last."

In the middle of a song, Simon barged onto the dance floor waving his hands. "Wait a minute. Stop the music. I've just learned there's a dance that promises medical benefit. The tarantella? I think this requires a scientific experiment."

Henley raised her head from Gustavo's shoulder and smiled at Simon.

"I'm in," Claudia said.

"Me too," Quinn said. "Show us this dance."

The crowd cleared the floor. Gustavo bowed to Henley, who nodded and began slowly with a shimmy and a swivel.

"I can do that." Quinn chose a gorgeous young man from the crowd. She swiveled. *That* was a swivel. Andrea and Maria joined them. Ian bowed to a dark-haired beauty with a lily tucked behind her ear, and they joined in. Simon extended his hand to Claudia and wrapped his arm around her waist, drawing her into him. Children ran in between the dancing couples dangling silk ribbons behind them. Fireflies flickered gold.

Henley's family and friends laughed and danced and loved. Stars sparkled in the sky, and geranium floated on the air.

PRAISE FOR AT LAST

"I read it straight through as I couldn't put it down! No words can express the emotions I am feeling. The plot twists, the fierce friendships were amazing. This a novel that is now one of my favorites—and that is really saying something."

~ READER KRISTI F.

"This is a profound story of loss and grief and the power of love. I had tears running down my face while my heart was smiling. So beautifully written, I saw myself in the words and learned some valuable lessons. It filled me with hope that love always finds a way."

~ READER JOYCE K.

"The relationship between Henley and her artist certainly caused some sparks to fly for me. I need to find someone to paint me! I really want to know more about Simon—the adorkable bartender. I want to take him home with me! I loved her dog Bella so much I'm going to the shelter to adopt a dog myself."

~ READER JUSTINE M.

"I was charmed by the devotion between the three friends. The strength and power and glory of female friendship is touching. It reminded me to tell my women friends how much I cherish them. Women are a ferocious force of nature."

~ READER BROOKE W.

ACKNOWLEDGMENTS

First, thank you to my family.

And thank you to my community whose support was crucial.

Rosann Brooks, Kristi Freischmidt,
Adrienne Moss, Shelly Karver, Sue Slezak,
Wendy Marcelli, Janel Evans,
Gretchen Armstrong, Janet Stack, Dan Lasley,
Darlene Korenberg, Rachel Folmar,
Phyllis Roberts, Sara Bleemer,
Elizabeth Munson, Janet Hall, Gerry Shaw

Since *At Last* is my first book, I didn't have a group of people to ask to read my book. I reached out to my community in Pennsylvania and asked if anyone would help. The response was thrilling and humbling. They provided thoughtful, insightful comments that made this a better book. I am profoundly grateful to all of them. I am thankful and lucky to live in such an amazing community of smart, kind people.

ABOUT THE AUTHOR

Lee Wheeler

Reader. Writer. Dog Mom. Attorney.
Photog. Astronomy Nut.
Dream Believer.
Author of the fabulous debut novel *At Last*.

Lee started dreaming of being a writer when she was six. It took lots of years and a boring detour as an attorney, but now she's the author of the new book, *At Last*.

Lee is dog mom to Tanner the Lab, whose head is as big as a Maytag, Pollock the Borzoi, who sees ghosts around every corner and does not go bravely to meet them, and Ansel the Italian Greyhound, who is gloriously evil and smarter than she is. She writes with the dogs at her feet—that is when they aren't eating the woodwork, chewing the rugs, destroying their toys or digging massive holes in the yard. Lee spends her days in Pennsylvania. When she's not writing or playing with her dogs, she'll be behind a camera or a telescope.

Her best advice—never give up your dreams.

Made in the USA
Middletown, DE
16 February 2020